TIME OF LIES

Douglas Board

Published in 2017
by Lightning Books Ltd
Imprint of EyeStorm Media
312 Uxbridge Road
Rickmansworth
Hertfordshire
WD3 8YL

www.lightning-books.com

ISBN: 978-1-78563-034-7

Cover by Chris Shamwana
Typesetting and design by Clio Mitchell

British Library Cataloguing in Publication Data
A catalogue record for this book is available from the British Library.

Printed by CPI Group (UK) Ltd, Croydon CR0 4YY

To Jo Cox, MP
1974-2016
#moreincommon

The quotation opposite describes the test of an air-dropped hydrogen bomb at Semipalatinsk on 22 November 1955. Andrei Sakharov, *Memoirs* (New York: Knopf 1990) p. 191, quoted in Lorna Arnold, *Britain and the H-Bomb* (Basingstoke: Palgrave 2001) pp. 29-30.

The second quotation is from the poem *You Who Read No Calm* by Tom Merrill. Tom is a writer and Advisory Editor at The Hypertexts, an online literary outlet mainly but not exclusively devoted to publishing poetry.
http://www.thehypertexts.com/9-11%20Poetry.htm
Downloaded 15 November 2015 and reproduced with Tom's permission.

I saw a blinding yellow-white sphere swiftly expand, turn orange in a fraction of a second, then turn bright red and touch the horizon, flattening out at its base. Soon everything was obscured by rising dust which formed an enormous swirling, gray-blue cloud, its surface streaked with fiery crimson flashes. Between the cloud and the swirling dust grew a mushroom stem, even thicker than the one that had formed during the first thermonuclear test. Shock-waves criss-crossed the sky, emitting sporadic milky-white cones and adding to the mushroom image. I felt heat like that from an open furnace on my face – and this was in freezing weather, tens of miles from ground zero. The whole magical spectacle unfolded in complete silence. Several minutes passed, and then all of a sudden the shock wave was coming at us, approaching swiftly, flattening the feather-grass.

You, who read no calm reportings
Of alien, distant, dire events,
But shriek and keen as loves go down
Beyond all help, to violence;
Whose temple's walls, stormstruck and split
by sizzling bolts collapse around,
While mid the crash of chaos hope
Whirls in a death-spin to the ground;
You, who alone in deep distress
Cry out for help where there is none,
All you whom I shall never know:
I know a portion nonetheless
Of cruel trials you undergo.

PROLOGUE

Calm reportings

1

London, January 2019

My three-month holiday starts in Angela's office at twenty past three on Friday afternoon. It finishes at half eleven on Monday morning. You couldn't even call it a long weekend.

By twenty past three Tower Bridge has vanished in the sleet outside Angela's glass walls. I'm defying the weather with a lightweight gilet (Diesel but you won't see it in shops before March), jeans and suede deck shoes. A bald man returns my gaze from the mirror – five-foot-ten, thirteen-and-a-half stone, stocky but with a fair bit of muscle.

Do I look like I need a holiday? Have I ever had longer than a week? Smokeless flames smirk at the question from the designer campfire in the centre of the marble floor. Very executive bling – very pre-2018 meltdown.

Angela's not budging. 'Trust me, Bob. Come the summer you'll be overdosing on photo-ops – business leaders and new generation political leaders worldwide. The White House, for sure. In the autumn you'll start campaigning, and then you're flat out until May. When you win, you'll bust open that disappear-for-August political culture because you've got a country to save. The next three months will be your only break for the next three years.' She slips me two VIP tickets for next month's Atlanta Super Bowl. Okay, there are fifteen thousand better places to be than England's drippy, annoying take on winter.

Angela gives me a peck on the cheek and fixes a Shock News car. On the ride home I flick through my phone to see who's partying this weekend. I ponder my pick of three. Frankie's will be toptastic if he doesn't overdose on reggae. I might even stay over and catch Millwall.

The Millwall game finishes up lame-oh but it's good to have a sing. Don't tell anyone but I'm a bit rusty on the players' names, which won't do come the election. It was 2007 when half the squad came to my housewarming. On the upside, the party was well worth the bother.

Monday morning sees London still immersed in grey, like the bottom of a fish tank that hasn't been cleaned. I arrive at Odyssey at half ten. It's off Kensington Church Street, and the best venue by far for a Monday morning.

Yanni's taken the place back to the original three-storey Victorian schoolhouse. The room he calls 'the gym' I have to myself – full-size tables for snooker, table tennis and table football, and a single ten-pin bowling lane complete with pick-up machine. The bowling lane is called 'Capitalism': you knock all the 'workers' down by bowling at them with 'market forces', then 'the state' stands them up for another go. Yeah, Yanni is a bit of a nerd. For me politics just gets in the way of fixing stuff.

I've muted the two footy-sized TVs: on a Monday Yanni's addicted to Waste-of-money Central, aka the BBC. He has it on while he goes around minding the clean-up after the weekend. I'm drinking super-cold cider in a frosted glass while giving the snooker balls a work-out. The vacuum cleaner next door is part of the Monday morning vibe.

On screen seven semi-geriatric men in suits and two women file out from behind a wooden door with frosted glass windows. They sit at a curved table. For Chrissake, Yanni – BBC Parliament?! I check my Rolex – eleven twenty-three. Seven minutes till Odyssey starts serving chips.

Ten minutes later the nine stand up and file out. Now it's some squeaky clean thirty-two-year-old standing on the grass in Parliament Square. The caption says 'SUPREME COURT: NEW BREXIT JUDGEMENT'. I turn up the volume.

By half eleven I fucking need a weapon, so I smash the cue against the table, snapping it in two. Its jagged point is raw and splintered. A picture of a clock tower in a market square, four decorated classical columns on a square brick base, comes onto the screens. I hurl snooker balls at the screens, shattering the glass and scattering sparks. The loose end of a turquoise wire flickers with a flame as small as a child's birthday candle.

When Angela's on the phone I scream at her, 'Who the fuck do they think they are? Jesus, they think we're so stupid! My campaign starts now!'

2

London, January 2019 (2)

'So we've just heard the President of the Supreme Court read out the judgement. What does it mean, Kieran?'

'Well, Janet, it's a complete surprise. Everyone thought that the Court had shot its bolt two years ago. The Government got its ducks in a row and gave notice to leave the European Union a few months later.

'Today's case was brought by a three-truck haulage firm in Scotland, after Borisgate – the leak of five thousand emails exchanged between Brexit ministers in the run up to giving notice. Supported by crowd-funding as well as the Scottish government, the truckers got their case into the Inner House of the Court of Session – the highest civil court in Edinburgh. From there it came to London. The upshot is that by a five to four majority the Supreme Court have accepted a claim of "Wednesbury unreasonableness" and quashed the UK's notice to leave.'

'Quashed? What does that mean?'

'It means that our notice in 2017 was invalid. It doesn't count. Now the President of the Court did stress, this does not mean that the UK cannot leave. Indeed the Prime Minister is likely to give a fresh Article 50 notice later this week, as soon as the Government is confident that they have made their reasoning legally watertight.'

'Will we be staying in the EU another two years?'

'Probably not. If there is a fresh notice, formally the negotiations on exit terms would start again – but in practice all the pieces of paper with agreements written on them are still there. And none of the parties, the EU countries or the Commission or the European Parliament, will have changed their positions. For example, the IMF insisted on five transitional years in the European Economic Area as the price for helping us to bail out our banks last year – that won't have changed. So fresh negotiations could be a formality with the exit later this year as originally planned. This new judgement may be no more than an intense embarrassment for the Government.'

'Whatever the legal arguments, Kieran, isn't this judgement going to be seen by many people in this country as a gross interference with democracy? One hashtag going wild on Twitter is #judicialcoup. And what about the tiny majority, five to four?'

'Out of a panel of nine, a majority of one is eleven per cent, which is nearly three times the size of the leave majority in the referendum. And when you say "people in this country", remember Scotland voted remain. Three of the Law Lords noted that the Court was sitting as the Supreme Court of Scotland. Since we may still be leaving the EU on the same terms and the same date, talk of a judicial coup is a little excitable.'

'So what's the point of the judgement, Kieran?'

'Wednesbury is a market town in the Black Country – I think we're showing its clock tower behind me. Today it has no cinemas but in 1947 it had three, the Rialto, the Imperial Palace and the Gaumont. In 1947 the Court of Appeal had to decide whether the condition which the local authority had imposed as part of allowing Sunday screenings – essentially that children couldn't attend – was reasonable. The cinema owners said the condition wasn't reasonable. The court said it was. But the court laid down a principle that acts of officialdom could conceivably so fly in the face of reason and logic – in plain English, could be so stupid – that they would for that reason alone be null and void. The Supreme Court has just ruled, by five to four, that the way the Government went about deciding when to give notice was that stupid.'

PART ONE

Alien, distant, dire events

3

Helensburgh, Sunday 19 April 2020

Three of us are in Cairstine McGinnis's living room on Sunday afternoon with her 1920s tea service. Cairstine and her daughter look at each other across cold tea in bone china cups. My own gaze has escaped the double-glazing and dashed into the spring lawn. Once fondness bloomed there but now new things have pushed through. Splashes of purple and yellow from crocuses match the colours of two teenage members of a hockey team, climbing towards us. Helensburgh's streets slope down to the Firth of Clyde and Gare Loch in an American-style rectangular grid.

Photos fill the mantelpiece, frame clips holding tight to memories which Cairstine loses completely, like the Mary Quant admirer in a mini-skirt (herself, age twenty-nine). Cairstine's words come out spiky and tart, like gooseberries. 'That Kathy – you won't go leaving me like her!'

It's Kathy, her thirty-eight-year-old daughter, to whom Cairstine is speaking. Once Cairstine's mind had high caverns and cool vaults which stored the better part of Scottish civilisation, but the passageway to those spaces has collapsed. However, her tongue is as cutting as ever, like a cheesemonger's garrotte.

'Of course you'll not leave me,' Cairstine purrs, stroking

Kathy's arm. The skin on Cairstine's thin bones gleams like translucent silk. Something plastic and made in China falls loose from her pompadour; she brushes it back into place.

Kathy replies, 'Of course I won't leave you.' That's Kathy: keep calm and carry on smiling.

The twenty years I've known Cairstine are the twenty years Kathy and I have been together, since I graduated in 2000 at the peak of Cool Britannia. We married, and I moved into Kathy's flat in Putney, eight years later.

Kathy is the anchor of my life, but the Royal Navy hoists anchors. The top brass have decided to 'discover' her so we're not sure where we might be for the next couple of years – possibly Washington DC. In the meantime I try to pull my weight when she visits Cairstine. Helensburgh can be a tough gig for her to do alone. Often enough we'll walk down to the promenade where the bust of John Logie Baird, Helensburgh's celebrity, fixes the loch with a proprietorial gaze; if we feel like it we might stroll along to Rhu to see whether any submarines pass by.

Right now I'm staring as hard as I can at the crocuses, because Cairstine is about to make me explode into giggles. Kathy and I went to see Jimmy Keohane at the AlbaR last night, the club on North Frederick Street. After all, Glaswegian comedy is famous. The club was Kathy's pick, up-and-coming, so we overlooked its heart-on-its-sleeve Nationalist sympathies. Besides, Brexit and the collapse of English politics into a kindergarten had turned every comedian north of the border into a Nationalist. In London we missed the fuss about Jimmy's new material on dementia.

***

Setting off a hydrogen bomb is like telling a joke with a triple punch line – one which leaves hundreds of thousands of people irradiated, incinerated or turned into burning postage stamps by the blast wave.

Someone pulls a trigger – the first punch line. Inside a metal coffin two bits of stuff are hurled together by a conventional explosion. Harmless on their own, together they create the second punch line – an atomic explosion. That explosion hurls yet more stuff together to make a third kind of explosion, the kind you get inside a star: your own private star, coming now to where you now live. So Kathy pulled the trigger which sent us, harmless on our own, smashing into Jimmy Keohane; Jimmy sent us smashing into Cairstine; and then off we all go, twinkle, twinkle.

The AlbaR was like an upside-down gym. Benches, weight stacks and rowing machines hung at odd angles from bare ceilings and ventilating shafts. The place was heaving. Kathy had booked us into the eating area but the rest was standing-room only.

Until Jimmy came on, what we got was intravenous politics. True, we're in a General Election. Even in Scotland it's still a General Election. For the comedians, the politicians were like fish in a barrel.

Fair play, the governing parties – the two Tory parties and the Scot Nats – were getting crucified for the 2018 bank bail-outs. You have to hand it to the bankers, and by God as taxpayers have we done that with feeling. The Treasury had never really recovered from 2008, so when our banks fell over again we had to crawl to the IMF. This time the eighteen-year-olds have woken up to who's going to pay off the new debt (them), and how (unemployment). So even in a Nat club the Nat leader was getting a hosing, while the Frumpy Tories and the Future Tories were getting water-boarded. ('I see a few faces from last week. Now me nan brung me up to say sorry when I overstep the mark, and last week I did. I told a few jokes about the Tories and paedophilia. Well, I'm sorry. Tonight I'll stick with paedophilia.')

Then Jimmy Keohane came on. He was my height, five foot nine with a buzz cut. His humour was based on physical repetition. When he repeated a line, every hair in his eyebrows and every crease in his belly repeated what they had done four or five seconds before, exactly. His flesh moved like a freaky, computer-generated image. He kicked off with some gentle parody of marital arguments.

'You moved the spoon.' (He re-plays moving the spoon.)

'No way I moved the spoon.' (He re-plays not moving the spoon.)

'Are you fucking blind? Of course you moved the spoon. I blame your mother.'

We had no idea why we were corpsing, but we were. Then, before we knew it, Jimmy flipped subjects: he started dancing with dementia.

According to the biggest rumour ever, dementia is why the Queen withdrew to Balmoral in 2019, installing Charles as Prince Regent. Funny that, Jimmy said; we put the Queen away because she's started talking to plants when Charles has been at it for years. No, he argued, the Queen was just pretending to have dementia; the greed and idiocy of British politics had simply got too much for her. Who could blame her when Cameron had twice tossed the fate of the kingdom – *her* kingdom – to a referendum, like a coin?

And then Jimmy threw out the idea that is making me squirm in Cairstine's. What if the Queen was not the only senior citizen to have had a light-bulb moment? What if older people aren't half as stupid as we think? Maybe they've cottoned on that *pretending* to have dementia is a way to snatch back power and make everyone else's life utterly miserable. Besides, Jimmy claimed, how hard can dementia be to fake? What's more like dementia than forgetting the story you're making up?

With that, Jimmy brought us Roger and Johann, a gay couple, having tea with Roger's ma. Pretending to have dementia lets ma stick her beak ruthlessly into Roger and Johann's relationship, breaking it like a beady-eyed bird smashing an oyster against rocks. Just like what Cairstine was doing to Kathy right now.

4

Helensburgh, Sunday 19 April 2020 (2)

'Both of my girls were angels,' explains Cairstine, 'in their own way. But Kathy was very focussed on her career. I had to find my place in her order of things.' She beams a smile like a cracked dinner plate. 'She left me.'

'Ma, I'm here.'

'And where else would you be? It comes down to that man. I blame him.'

I assume she means me. The giggles will be unstoppable if I don't say something. Besides, I've flown four hundred miles to help Kathy play verbal tennis against a wonky ball-throwing machine: it's time to join my partner at the net. 'Usually it depends on the woman too,' I offer.

Cairstine turns to me. 'Oh, look at yourself giggling away, and thinking I don't know. No, you're not the man,' she explains dismissively. 'You're not Kathy's boss. He had designs on her. Trust a mother's instinct.' She looks back at Kathy, tilting her head to one side. 'Now Meghan was different. She was absolutely devoted to her ma. And she had a career as well. Of course she did.'

Is Kathy tired, or tired of being put down? Is she following dementia care advice? Whatever the reason, she puts a foot into the fantasy world of 'Meghan'. 'What career was that, ma?' she asks. 'Meghan's, I mean.'

Punishment is guaranteed, and it comes. 'Oh you're heartless! She had that terrible accident, didn't she? So she couldn't have a career.'

I laugh out loud – I can't help it.

Kathy throws me a look like a grenade. 'How could I know, Ma? There never was any Meghan.'

'That's wicked! Because Meghan would have –'

Cairstine's voice tails off. That's rare in this habitat.

'Because Meghan would have – ?' Kathy persists.

'Oh, she would have outshone Kathy,' Cairstine replied. 'I never said a word to Kathy, of course, but I knew. The way a mother does. Outshone her into a cinder.'

Hydrogen bomb test subjects standing miles away, with gloved hands clamped over their goggles and facing away from ground zero, have reported seeing everything turn blinding white. Kathy and I can confirm the accuracy of these reports. We finish our visit early, badly needing some recovery time.

**

Every year the local council slaps a fresh coat of dereliction on Helensburgh's swimming pool and fairground. We park alongside and walk along the seafront. By the time we pass the Ardencaple Hotel and Rhu Marina, Kathy has calmed down. She had drinking lessons (tequila slammers) in one and sailing lessons in the other. Both involved salt and experienced instructors. The Royal Navy was the obvious next step.

We walk tall out onto the spit, in Kathy's case from her service training, in my case from Pilates. Kathy's shorter but there's barely an inch in it. She walks purposefully, I'm closer to ambling. Let's say she got the runner's body and I got the forgetful jogger's.

Curly black hair tumbles down below my collar. I touch my crown. My locks are as come-hither as they were twenty years ago, maybe more so. Epidermal growth factor shampoo from Iceland is brilliant.

Kathy is in black stockings, a dark skirt and pastel blouse (that's the grown-up in-the-office side of Kathy), wrapped in a shawl. The shawl might as well have been designed by Tracey Emin; that's the Kathy who drank tequila slammers. Her chestnut hair is pinned in an office-friendly bun. Helensburgh trips have become work.

'Did she seem the same to you?' Kathy asks.

'The same old, I thought.'

'One day...' Kathy's eyes flick to mine. She was eighteen when I first saw the spark in her eyes. I still see it now.

'A care home won't be the end of the world,' I venture. 'Much as she'd like you to think it is. She might even enjoy it – discover some more long-lost siblings for you.'

'If you're not going to say anything more intelligent than that, don't bother saying anything at all.'

The loch itself is flat with a light grey counterpane of high cloud. Springtime is my favourite time of year to come. For instance, now it's gone tea-time and we've still three hours of daylight left, and no midges.

We walk out to the Rhu Narrows light, two hundred yards into Gare Loch on the end of a shingle spit. It's like standing beside a Belisha beacon on a traffic island, one-third of the way across one of London's clogged arterial roads – maybe the Cromwell Road near Earl's Court – but the Narrows is narrower. Three miles to the north, guarded by a stationary police boat and some undercover seagulls, is Faslane. In the event of a nuclear bust-up, this will be the first place in the British Isles to be vaporised, taking with it Glasgow and over a million people. The forests and heather of Loch Long and Loch Lomond would be ablaze.

Some of the seagulls eye us quizzically and call up reinforcements. A black police inflatable comes round Rosneath Point, darting about like a fly.

'Barry and Joan do a great job looking in on her,' I point out.

Kathy's worry lines report for duty. 'But their son has just bought that place near Granada. They'll be around less in the winters.'

I can tell she's thinking about the possible move to Washington. Kathy's boss is Patrick Smath. He pronounces it 'Smayth'. From what Kathy says, he's nice enough in a sorry-you-weren't-as-well-educated-as-I-was way. He's no Navy man but right up there, the most senior civil servant in the Ministry of Defence. For the last year Kathy has been working for him. If there is anything to Cairstine's mutterings about a man with designs on Kathy's career, that man is Patrick.

'He wants me to go to Washington, but spend some time with the war-gamers at Rhode Island first.'

'Don't you think war *games* says it all?'

'Zack, sometimes! I've told you … they're not games. They're about getting ready for the future. For goodness sake, think about the Russians, the terrorists, the hackers. No-one's playing by the old rules. If we don't practise, we lose. All our best people do this kind of stuff. Why Patrick thinks I'm one of them I don't get, but don't wind me up.'

I hold her close and bury my face in her shawl, in the smoothness of alpaca and bamboo. When my eyes open I'm facing Rosneath Point. Beyond the Firth of Clyde lies the Atlantic.

I catch my breath at a sight I've never seen before. A dark sword is being unsheathed at the water's edge. The sword slides into view between low, grey-green hills, yachts at play and a ferry boat. Its front is rounded but as alien and black as Kubrick's monoliths in *2001*. While the submarine turns towards us its length vanishes, but not for long: the god of destruction accompanied by eight armed boats and tugs heads our way. This is Shiva, with two periscopes and a sonar third eye. His trident can spit dozens of nuclear warheads more than 7,000 miles. He is coming in procession before us.

He passes us almost within arm's reach. The submarine is one-third again as wide as an athletics track, as long as an athletics oval. Fifteen-thousand tonnes drive through the water in silence. Wavelets touch Darth Vader's cloak before streaming in lines to lap obediently at our feet. The dorsal fin, the conning tower, rises five storeys above us. Diving planes protrude to port and starboard. The tail fin makes a defiant finger gesture out of the wake. We don't care to find out whether Shiva's bridesmaids will fire their heavy calibre machine-guns, so we don't wave.

And then he is past, handing back to us permission to speak while he punts his way up Gare Loch. Yes, one of the biggest insanities in human history has just passed close enough to touch. But see the other side of me, he now says. Watch me transporting underwater what you do not care to think about. I've been taking your fears to a safe place for decades. Thousands of sailors and engineers and physicists have worked hard at it. The least you might do is say thanks?

My mind takes flight in every direction. I seek refuge from large horrors in smaller ones, like Cairstine's invention of Meghan. What might any of us do to nourish survival, to exist, still to be noticed and talked about, as remembered grandeur fades? Is that how Cairstine thinks?

My questions about Cairstine could have been questions about Britain. Is Trident part of what we do to nourish survival, to exist, still to be noticed and (so we imagine) talked about in the world, as remembered grandeur fades?

Kathy is deflected neither by national dementia nor by nuclear annihilation. 'We need to turn back or we'll miss our flight.'

Two black guillemots descend to inspect a washed-up Morrisons supermarket bag. I take out my six-week-old vape pen. I used to smoke roll-ups but finding a tobacco-flavoured American juice has done the trick. I exhale a cloud.

'That was *Vanguard*,' says Kathy. 'She was the first Trident submarine – the first British one, I mean. Her first patrol was in 1994. From the garden I watched her put to sea.'

'So you were twelve and I was sixteen. Christmas number one?'

'East 17, you silly idiot – "Stay Another Day".'

My phone fetches the video. 'White parkas and Santa's dandruff!'

Kathy peers as we walk. 'Yeah. And we-can't-dance-so-we'll-sign-for-the-deaf-instead. Mind you, I was in love with Tony Mortimer.'

'Which was Tony?' I tease.

'Which one! Look at those eyebrows. The other guys were a bit scary for a twelve-year-old. Did I ever tell you your eyebrows look like his?'

'Only a million times – which doesn't make it true.'

***

At Glasgow airport there isn't anything better to do than get another reality dose from the national news.

It's been forever since the media went into full-on election mode. All the parties bar one are fucked. The Liberals haven't yet followed Lazarus out of their grave. Neither of the Labour parties are doing anything in Scotland; in England a lot of their supporters have gone Green. UKIP, the United Kingdom Independence Party, flaky at the best of times, turned out to have stronger competition – BG. More than one poll now has BG ahead of the whole pack, which makes me ill.

Television news has become living torture. Eight national 'parties' try to occupy the space previously squatted on incompetently by two or three, tying the broadcasters in knots with lawsuits. So the early evening news now occupies an hour, and the main nightly bulletin two. Change.org has a petition begging for the news to be replaced by the compulsory eating of toads.

The departure lounge has more than its share of election toads, in suits, on a Sunday evening. Tonight all of them are staring at their smartphones in a blissful daze. Apparently BG have fucked up.

The leader of the Britain's Great party is beaming at me from the screen across the lounge. Some people call it the Bob Grant party, or the Bermondsey Geezer party. Wearing black designer trackies with a red-and-white lion (standard BG campaign gear), Bob's thighs have squashed the turquoise telly sofa into submission. He's an inch taller than me and a stone and a half heavier. He's shaved his head since he was twelve. He claims the weight is all muscle, but I say it's congealed sweat off other people's backs. The screen has been muted but everyone in Britain knows his standard riff off by heart:

Britain's Great! 'Course we are. You want to know why? You need to be told? Then fuck off mate. Get out of my country. We don't want you.

I don't give a fuck if you were born here. Maybe you were born in the business class lounge at Heathrow. Maybe you're white as it goes, maybe latte or flippin' espresso – do I give a fuck? I've seen too many white arseholes born here, went to posh schools here, went to university here – you and I paid for them by the way – and they wouldn't know why Britain's great if you cut off their bollocks and shoved them where the sun don't shine. I say fuck off to the lot of them. This country's for people who know it's great.

You know the shit-bags I'm on about. You've seen them on the telly, they've been running our governments – this government, the one before that, and the one before that. Forget what the parties were called, it was always them with their cuff-links and suits-me-nicely pensions killing themselves laughing over the Third Way, the Big Society, climate change, the Northern Powerhouse and building grammar schools.

Because the words were just there to baffle us. They thought we were stupid enough to think the game was Scrabble. What the game really was, it was help yourself, mate, to my job, my home, my bank account, my country, just talk long words at me while you're doing it.

Call us stupid to fall for it so many times. But Britain's Great is doing the calling now and we're calling time. We reckon the mugs who pay the taxes are smart enough to decide the taxes. Cop this: since we're the only ones who do pay the taxes, that's just what we're going to do.

By the time the aircraft reaches the runway, I've pieced the story together: Bob Grant has attacked 'hardworking families'! The leading bunch of clowns farts in the nation's face! The airport connection wasn't up to streaming any video, but there's some live stuff of Bob that the Future Tories are so pant-wettingly happy about, they are pushing it from every hireable server onto every digital device in the British Isles.

I'm giddy, light-headed, happy beyond belief at the thought that BG's balloon is about to burst. Don't even think what this piece of off-white south-east London trash, someone who left school with a knife more times than he ever left with homework, might do with Britain's 160 hydrogen bombs if he got his sticky mitts on them. If I know my Bob, he'd set one off just to prove that he had the balls to do it.

In the early micro-seconds of a hydrogen bomb explosion – at Big Bang diddley squat, so to speak – there is the briefest of races. The first child of the explosion is a hole in the sky and an ascending chandelier of air-on-fire. But for a moment, the light from hell fluctuates as the second child of the explosion, a shock wave of exploding energy, overtakes the first.

There's another race which has been going on rather longer. Bob and I haven't spoken for more than twelve years. His shaved head is a bullet-proof reason for my curls. He is the second wave to my first. Born fourteen months after me, he overtook me a long, long time ago. Bob Grant is my younger brother, and I loathe him.

5

London, Monday 20 April 2020

From March until December Kathy's morning commute took her across the Thames on foot. She used the footbridge from Waterloo to Charing Cross. The upstream crossing gave her a view of the Houses of Parliament half a mile away. Her own workplace with the flags of the three armed services was closer still.

To be honest, the Ministry of Defence Main Building was a mausoleum. When Kathy had joined the Navy the idea that one day she would work here would have been ridiculous. Twice she had been runner-up for a fleet navigation prize, but navigation was about real things precisely observed; keeping her head above water in a stagnant sea of words was something else. She had expected to hate her present job, and some days she did; but choosing to walk to work in a way which put the Main Building's stone squatness in the centre of her view hinted differently.

As private secretary to Patrick Smath, Kathy's job was to make the permanent civilian head of the Ministry of Defence look good. 'Permanent' – he wasn't a here today, gone tomorrow politician. Smooth-faced graduates from Oxford and Cambridge lusted after roles like hers where reputations could be polished and noticed. They also told each other that Patrick liked a bit of uniformed skirt on the side.

At one level the job was that of a glorified PA and bag-carrier. She scanned the great man's in-box, dispatching anything which didn't need his attention and summarising what did. She was the hamburger-helper making Patrick go further. Kathy gave instructions to deliver what Patrick would want before he knew himself; he bounced ideas off her; and she wrote half of the 'personal' notes he sent to his political masters, his opposite numbers in other departments and the military top brass. If a shiny twenty-five-year-old graduate had got the job, they would have humble-bragged about it seven days a week.

But Kathy didn't humble-brag. What inspired her was working hard, having a respected role within a worthwhile team and doing something for her country.

On this Monday morning Kathy's river panorama was disturbed by a piece of democracy in action. Labour 4 You had moored a barge with a giant screen in front of the Houses of Parliament. The floating display worked its way through photographs of the party's forty-six Parliamentary candidates in their constituencies with a dynamic graphic of the party's strap-line: 'Britain 4.0'. Labour 4 You was relentlessly future-focused. 4.0 meant The-Third-Way-But-Better. Surveying the wreckage left by Corbyn, how selflessly Lord Mandelson had accepted the call of history to resign his peerage and stand for prime minister.

For Labour's larger rump, LKGB (Labour for a Kinder, Gentler Britain), the future was simply that part of the past which hadn't ossified yet. To them Britain 4.0 was the mark of Beelzebub, yet another sneer at the clause in the party's historic constitution on which Blair had smeared the faeces of 'the many, not the few'. Since hardly any voters remembered what clause four had been, Corbyn had attack dogs who pointed out that 4.0 predicted well Labour 4 You's likely number of seats in the new Parliament.

Electoral meltdown was the dish of the day being served

up in the dining rooms of all the older parties, including the United Kingdom Independence Party. UKIP's electricity had been stolen by BG and wired up to organisational discipline and youth appeal. What was left resembled a night out in a golf club for time-share salesmen.

***

Kathy's office block, the Kafka Central of British bureaucracy, was an eight-storey stone toaster with three pop-up slots: slightly larger slices of architectural toast towards the north (Horse Guards Avenue, where Kathy entered); slightly smaller towards the south. Here the main government drag was defended from the river and all other imaginable enemies by committees of the greatest sophistication. For example, if the Thames flooded, Whitehall would function unperturbed – it hoped – thanks to untiring ant-teams within this building such as WTF-WTF-WTF, whose report was now on Patrick's desk. The Ministry of Defence bred acronyms like a mangrove swamp.

In fact, the report was on Kathy's desk. She had to figure out whether any of the thirty thousand words (maps and tables not included) produced by WTF3 – the Whitehall Task Force Weather Threat Forecast sub-group on Wide Thames Flooding – deserved her master's attention.

Appropriately, the Main Building's construction had been delayed by two world wars. The anthill had arrived in the 1950s, built to designs already forty years old. Since then its journey in public esteem had been downwards.

Fifteen years ago modernisation had arrived. Private finance had eviscerated four miles of corridors and enclosed offices while leaving the squat façade intact. Blairism went beyond impregnating taxpayers with debt, it impregnated public servants with new minds. Now the destruction of Britain's enemies was planned by Kathy and her three thousand colleagues using the same pastel sofas, open-plan areas, Post-It notes and designer chairs as those on which Marks & Spencer planned Britain's lingerie.

Frankly, a lingerie team could have made better use of the pair of gargantuan stone breasts visible from Kathy's window. Two giant nudes, reclining on three-storey plinths, had been commissioned to watch the Ministry's entrance. Any good reason for this had been lost in the 1950s along with hat-wearing. The breasts now did what they could to repel those terrorists with strict dress codes.

Kathy's phone emitted two green flashes. She passed the message to Patrick. 'The deputy secretary of state wants us now, not this afternoon.'

Patrick Smath swung his legs off the desk. Lanky and energetic, Patrick had eyes the colour of aluminium, cirrus eyebrows and the hair of a celebrity scientist. 'I thought he was supposed to be at the dentist?'

'Indeed, sir.' The day she had asked Patrick how often he wanted to be 'sirred', the answer had come back in a flash. 'Sparingly. Unobtrusively. Attentively. Like ground pepper in a classy restaurant.'

Kathy followed Patrick into the ministerial zone, carrying four copies of the classified slide pack the minister wanted. After the first week she had settled on Navy 3A rig in the office: around politicians she felt more comfortable in a white shirt, black tie and lieutenant-commander's shoulder slides. In this building her rank was no great shakes but it reminded some politicians to give her the protections of the Geneva Convention.

Deputy Secretary of State for Defence Roger Hartington had a ministerial office with a desk, a meeting table and parallel sofas. 'Deputy secretary of state' was a self-invented fiction, but so what? None of his ministerial colleagues (his boss included) had felt contesting it would be worth the resulting personal gossip leaked to the media. Hartington was rumoured, not least by Hartington, to head the promotion list for Cabinet in the unlikely event that the Future Conservatives came top in the electoral slugfest.

On one sofa arm perched a bird with three ear-rings in his left ear, awaiting carrion – Hartington's special adviser.

'How was the dentist, Minister?' enquired Patrick. 'He left you able to speak?'

'Yes – I am sorry if that disappoints.' A self-satisfied chuckle escaped Hartington's blubbery lips. 'In fact I had to can the dentist – pressing matters, which is why we need to meet now. The security of our country calls. Besides, I find pain is much more blessed to give than to receive.'

The first ten minutes were taken up with a skirmish about the Polish defence minister. He wanted television cameras to cover his arrival to view Britannia's shiny new aircraft-carrier, the *Queen Elizabeth*. Of course Hartington had put him up to it. The real objective was election news coverage for Hartington himself welcoming the visitor on board the Royal Navy's flagship. BG were hammering the Future Tories on re-armament. Still, the Poles were reputed to be about to order three River class patrol boats which would be built on the Clyde.

The protagonists stared at each other for thirty seconds before Patrick acquiesced. 'I will authorise the visit, subject to the approval of the Cabinet Secretary. You and the Polish minister will have vetted, non-political scripts. Stick to them, or no broadcasting.'

'Good,' said Hartington. 'Now talk to me about drones. We keep hearing rumours that BG have got hundreds of the things.

You've been fobbing me off for weeks.'

The special adviser looked up. 'You've been obstructing the minister.'

'Bollocks! Far from obstructing, I asked my private secretary Kathy McGinnis to prepare the report personally. She has now done so.'

***

Kathy handed over her slides. There were two parts – first the story, then the numbers.

Drone policy was a mess and enforcement was worse. Enthusiasts could and did pepper the sky with hundreds of mechanical gnats, giving the middle finger to the Civil Aviation Authority's rules. Public bureaucracy had not ignored this insult – on the contrary, several drone-related versions of What The Fuck 3 had sprung into life. The costs and benefits of different drone policies had been quantified, business cases had been made, the 'drone community' and other stakeholders consulted and regulations drafted by the yard. These regulations could be deployed the minute someone actually took a decision on what was to be achieved (finessing her words was not Kathy's style). The special adviser scowled, but she thought Hartington smiled.

The draft regulations ranged from aero-device registration and the fitting of identification devices and lights to pilot licensing, insurance, public liability, taxes and recycling, as well as powers of interdiction in instances of aerial emergency. Fine legal words had been crafted by artisans; but they were also words prepared in just one country. While Brexit meant Britain no longer needed to wait for Europe, drone costs could not come down until different countries had got their act together. In other words, drones were an entirely typical international policy snafu – situation normal, all fucked up.

Two forces had the potential to break this logjam, Kathy noted, although neither had yet done so. A tragic accident involving a commercial airliner; despite some enthusiastic attempts this had not yet happened. Or the ravenous desire of a handful of global companies with cash-heavy balance sheets and recurrent technological wet dreams. Who would be the first and biggest to have drones delivering to your garden, collecting from your balcony, watching your home in Spain or your kids walking home from school…or perhaps your partner leaving the office…

The net result: the British authorities hadn't a clue about 'nerd drones' – one-offs bought off the shelf at Maplins by males who would have been better employed inserting their rechargeable batteries into vacuum cleaners. Manufacturers' records suggested that there could be tens of thousands of them, but most had an endurance of 20 minutes or less. One study suggested fewer than eight per cent remained flyable six months after purchase.

However, intelligence about commercial fleets was another matter. With drone law in such a mess, companies and other large organisations were terrified of legal risks. Fewer than fifty drones flown by large organisations were licensed to enter built up areas.

Hartington's spine had been straightening as Kathy spoke. Now, at last, to the heart of the matter. By definition, this figure included any BG drones. Kathy pointed out that none of the claimed sightings of BG drones had survived close investigation. It suited BG to spew futuristic techno-babble about flying black triangles with silent electrostatic propulsion, solar cell longevity and extended dwell times. But frankly? BG's drones had as much evidential backup as the rest of BG's claims, which was none. The proliferation of black triangles with sides one metre long in the background of individual YouTube clips was pure games-playing piss.

The minister was delighted to hear it. Even before she had finished, Kathy could see his attack dog turning his mind to how this assessment could be leaked to the media – which was why she had hand-delivered her slides in hard copy only, and now stood to take the copies back. Patrick beamed.

Kathy thought her work was done but Hartington had something unexpected up his sleeve. 'I'd like to detain Lieutenant-Commander McGinnis on a personal matter,' he explained, showing the other two the door. The adviser's eyes narrowed. Patrick's did the opposite. Kathy's cheeks went pale and stiffened like a starched shirt.

6

London, Monday 20 April 2020 (2)

Kathy promised Hartington not to say anything but she spilled the beans straight away to Patrick when Terence drove them to the Athenaeum – the first time Patrick had taken Kathy to his club. Embarrassingly for the Cabinet-ready Future Tory, Hartington's sixteen-year-old by his first wife had joined BG's youth wing – the Vigilance.

'Now it makes sense,' said Patrick. Hartington had wanted to talk to Kathy because she knew about drones.

Hartington had shown Kathy a photo-booth shot of his son. His hair was gelled but off the collar. His sweater was immediately recognisable, the black crew neck with a red and white lion at the top of each arm. Out of shot Andrew would have been wearing a red belt, black jeans and black trainers or boots. The Vigilance accepted members from fifteen.

Every high street now featured a former charity shop with blacked-out windows, computer screens and a couple of older members on 'guard duty'. The movement had been extraordinarily successful, reaching 50,000 members, mostly, but not entirely, young men, in less than nine months. The pull was earning pocket money learning to remote fly drones in practice sites in Nevada. Unlimited square miles of nowhere to crash in and dawn arriving just after lunch, British time, made the Vigilance an adolescent paradise.

Hartington's ex had become worried. 'Andrew has spent most weekends with the Vigilance over the past six months,' Hartington explained. 'He's been promoted to lead a section. They're training for a big event. That's what made his mother get in touch. She'd prefer it if Andrew was outdoors more, and she doesn't see much of his friends. But they're safe, they're under supervision, they don't have wild parties. The thing is, Andrew's started cutting school. You're in charge of the country, my ex says. What are the Vigilance really doing?'

'What did you tell him?' Patrick asked.

'That it's got bugger all to do with daylight hours. It just looks like square miles of nowhere because that's cheap as chips for the geeks to make on computer screens. It's not flying, just gaming, but BG have thrown a really clever wrap around it. Their blacked-out stores are the old internet cafés done up differently.'

'It's a smart wrap.'

There was silence for a minute. Kathy changed the subject. 'At least you're shot of the lawyers.'

'Amen and hallelujah.' Patrick had been going through a divorce. He had spared Kathy the details, but for three months legal telephone conferences had sprouted in his diary like tumours – blink and there was another. He always emerged from them in a foul mood.

Terence dropped them ten minutes' walk from Buckingham Palace and St James's Park, beneath the gold statue of Athena. 'Taking her to celebrate the decree absolute,' was the gossip shared between those envious of Kathy's job. That thought never entered Kathy's mind. Her job was to focus on what was occupying Patrick's mind, which was as clear as a supertanker bearing down on a dinghy in the middle of the Channel: deep alarm about the General Election. And if he was snogging anyone, Kathy imagined that she would be some kind of film starlet with a sideline in rocket science. If she existed, Patrick had been smart enough to keep her name out of the media as well as out of his official diary.

The Athenaeum was like an ornamental pond full of Establishment carp: a meticulously regulated environment for breeding the British ruling class. Kathy had no clue what to expect, beyond something posh. Perhaps a pageboy would rush forward. That was her experience of the luxury hotel near her workplace – the Corinthia. The Corinthia and the Athenaeum sounded like peas in a pod.

Despite admitting women members since 2002, to enter the club's swing doors with confidence required something which Kathy did not possess. She had not gone to any of the relevant schools, unlike Patrick who was a Jesus man (Jesus was his Cambridge college). In these schools the keys to an elevated kind of Britishness hung on racks – racks which had had names on them for centuries. If you attended one of these establishments, becoming either famous or grateful was obligatory. Both was nice.

Inside there was no rushing forward; there was no rushing at all. Members crossed the marble floor of the pillared hall to hang their own coats and those of their guests. In most places Kathy felt secure in her 'middleness' – not old, but not a pipsqueak; not beautiful, but equally not ugly; no clever-clogs but far from stupid. Yet in the Athenaeum ordinariness felt risky. Her naval uniform remained her trusty shield, but had she missed a small ladder in her tights? Might gauche averageness leak out and stain the red ochre mosaic?

She chose minor variations on what Patrick chose – vodka instead of gin with tonic in the bar, creamed parsnips instead of potatoes with the roast beef in the dining room – but by the time they went for coffee in the library, her tongue had loosened. The Athenaeum was a cocoon of little rules, a bird's nest made by weaving together peculiarities. Here the point of everything, Kathy argued, was to be unlike everywhere else. Phones were not allowed. Working was not allowed. The member, not the waiter, wrote the food order on a pad. The menu had no prices. Coffee was taken in the library. On the grand staircase, presiding over the whole show, was an oddly-numbered clock.

'It's as if you can't do things by common sense any more,' she complained. 'It makes me feel like I'm six years old again.'

'You're sounding like an ungrateful politician,' Patrick laughed. 'Everything is a conspiracy. The unwritten constitution. The Civil Service. The BBC. The tall policemen. Trust me, the whole world is a web of cock-up, not conspiracy.' He shared some stories about the Pentagon which made Kathy's jaw drop.

In fact, Kathy's name had come up less than a week ago in conversation with Patrick's American opposite number. Hearing about herself like this was an excruciating out-of-body experience, like being called for a photo shoot for Vogue; Kathy was sure that at any minute Patrick would realise that he had confused her with someone else. But without missing a beat Patrick followed up with a solicitous enquiry about Cairstine. When Kathy gave her honest and pained response Patrick half-closed his eyes in sympathy, mentioning someone in his own family and giving her right hand the briefest of supportive touches.

Since the library was the place for coffee, this was where they were sitting. Patrick's attention was flattering but Kathy was the tiniest of the pawns on the chessboard on which he was playing. She would never be able to play the games Patrick played so effortlessly. At least, she assumed not; nor was she sure of wanting to be the kind of person who could.

'The theory that we civil servants are in charge is patently not true. I've never known politics to be in such a mess. It's not just one party, it's all of them. If it had been down to you and I, we'd never have allowed it. Look at this!'

He gestured towards the evening paper. The headline announced the election pledge unveiled by Labour 4 You on the barge: BEYOND 24/7 – THE NEW STANDARD FOR PUBLIC SERVICES: 36/9.

Kathy picked the paper up. 'Thirty-six national targets backed up by nine principles of public life.'

'It's bonkers.' Patrick waved his hands in horror, the political scientist confronted by the refusal of the democratic experiment to obey the laws of logic. 'One party promises but doesn't deliver a 24/7 NHS, so the next party has to not-deliver something better. I bet focus groups said 36/9 sounded better than 24/7.'

Thirty-six divided by nine was four while twenty-four divided by seven was three point … The whole thing was beyond daft.

Patrick stood up and thumped the back of a Chesterfield sofa. The behinds of countless scientists, mandarins and bishops had polished the red leather to a slippery sheen. 'The game's changed, and we're not ready for it. *We*, the Civil Service. We're still doing the same old, same old. We're preparing briefings for eight possible new governments because we always have, and every page I turn makes me feel we're missing the point. We analyse speeches and manifestos as if they were propositions in geometry, but look at what Brexit turned out to mean. It was a dance craze – the game was show up and make moves. The moves were right if everyone else in the club danced with you.'

'The other problem with manifestos is rabbits out of hats,' Kathy mused. 'Stuff that never was in the manifesto, or is opposite to the manifesto. Like May and grammar schools or Osborne and his budgets.'

Patrick nodded. 'Or Gordon Brown giving up control of interest rates.'

'Instead of briefing, what about some war-gaming?' Kathy ventured. Within the Ministry Patrick was the arch-evangelist for gaming surprise scenarios when preparing to fight an enemy. She realised that politicians were not supposed to be the enemy, but on the other hand they certainly weren't friends.

The light in Patrick's eyes went up a hundred watts. 'You know ... why not? Democratic war-gaming. Kathy, you've done it. The data boys can crunch the social media and the wild cards in other countries as well, Trump, Le Pen, Beppe Grillo, AfD. The Scandinavians too. What a shame: we started reading their crime novels and they started reading our rightwing blogs. And call RADA or Equity and find some people who can play our next prime minister. Confidentially, of course; not a whiff to the media.'

'You want someone to play Bob Grant?'

'He's first on the list – the least house-trained and he might win.'

Kathy joined Patrick by the window, looking out on Pall Mall. 'Do you really think so?' Kathy asked. 'Even after Brexit and Trump, it seems impossible: no-one in BG has done anything in government before. They've never asked a question in Parliament, let alone answered one. If you were a passenger in a jet, you wouldn't elect a pilot who'd never heard of flaps.'

'Voters aren't seeing it like that. For them it's more like the regular pilots keep crashing the plane, so let's bin the lot of them.'

'But now Bob has attacked hard-working families ...'

'And has he gone down in the polls, or up? He could announce the strangulation of the first-born and his numbers might still go up. It's scary. But we'll deal with it. It's our job.' *We* the Civil

Service. *We* Patrick and Kathy.

The Jaguar XF was waiting in Carlton House Terrace so Kathy accepted a lift to Waterloo. Terence had spent the last two hours giving the car a hand polish. Such was the place of nostalgia in this part of London that the car's shimmering roof reflected the glow of a gas street lamp. Was there also a hovering black triangle? Kathy's head snapped back but she saw nothing. It was just her imagination working 36/9.

7

London, Tuesday 21 April 2020

I'm sitting in my studio working on estate agent jokes – that's the back bedroom at 102A Walsingham Road, Putney. The sash is up, my head is down and the chilled beats of 'I Smoke Two Joints' (the Sublime version) loiter briefly above the pages of today's *Guardian*. Squalls are promised for the evening.

This after-dinner gig is on Saturday – fifteen minutes, £200 cash in hand and dinner – for some Putney estate agents. Traditionally Saturday is estate agents' busiest day in the office. My agent Troy booked me for it six months ago. He remembered my three ridiculously successful months of telesales for a Chelsea developer, calling numbers in Moscow and Hong Kong and Dubai in a Royal Shakespeare Company voice. My success was pure luck: the three months came after the Brexit plunge in the pound and before the 2018 crisis. Still, Troy sold me into the gig on a ticket of an actor's lessons on closing the deal, plus no travelling expenses.

Six months ago the fact that my calls were deal-opening not deal-closing seemed like high pedantry, and the gig went clean out of my head until I turned over the double page for April in my diary. (When you're as busy as I am, two pages to a month is fine.) Shit! I've gorged on sales videos on YouTube and can bluff my way through seven minutes of lessons, max, but that leaves me half-dressed. Seeing Jimmy Keohane made me think, there's a painless second half – just get them laughing.

Where we live, the terraced houses in the low 100s in Walsingham Road 'benefit', in estate agent speak, from back gardens. They benefit even more from compactness. The three bedrooms are small and you can forget *en suite*. Looking at our own handkerchief of green, you could roll it up and store it in a drawer overnight.

I can see into the garden of 106. That's the end-of-terrace grassed dead zone. It's trimmed monthly and repels birds, cats and foxes ultrasonically. It sold for £1.4 million just before the crash. An absentee Singaporean dentist bought it for its one-hundred-foot garden. He should have counted his apostrophes carefully – it's a smoker's garden, one hundred inches. Estate agents and apostrophes – two declines in civilisation for the price of one. Starting from scratch I've got two pages of laughs just out of estate agents and size.

The owner of 106 has never been to the property. We know that because 104 which adjoins is owned by our neighbour, Alan Tinker. Our place, 102A, is the ground and first floor maisonette on the other side. 102B is the studio flat above us, let by a digital company for short-stay executives. Alan, a retired banker, is constantly about like a friendly owl, reassuring rather than prying: more neighbourhood clock than neighbourhood watch. He chats to the lady who visits 106 once a month to do the necessary and run a mower over the garden. She's never met the owner.

In his jocular way Alan blames the 2018 financial crisis on the sale of 106 – global financial markets seized up two weeks after the sale, *et après ça, le déluge*. 106 is no penthouse, nor even a city centre love nest, so Alan reasons that it was bought by someone *ordinary*. Alan uses the word 'ordinary' a lot: ordinary tomatoes, an ordinary production of *Othello*, that sort of thing. Anyway, a market in which someone ordinary couldn't be arsed to see or rent out a £1.4 million property investment was a market heading for trouble. The ensuing horrendous financial meltdown stopped Alan's winter pilgrimages to Cape Town ('a very ordinary B&B in Sea Point but the location is charming') and obliged him to invest most of his pension in 104. There are two spare bedrooms so his children can visit – one bedroom for each marriage.

I get the *Guardian* on paper despite the price. Having a security blanket that flips between portrait and landscape just doesn't work for me. Today's main editorial is a Tracy Island masterwork of pointless passion and lucidity: the two Labour parties should recognise a national emergency, merge and invite Thunderbird 4 – sorry, Polly Toynbee – to be leader. It's scary how hope has been sucked out of our national life, and it's getting hard to breathe. I've never found it more important to read about how the world should be, not just how it is.

I'm about to put my hand back to the humorous plough when I half-imagine Alan calling my name from the front of the house. When I hear 'Zack!' a second time, I grab my vaper and head downstairs.

Alan is standing in front of 104, facing an incongruous pair: a stocky forty-year-old in a shiny double-breasted suit, and a fifteen-year-old schoolgirl in an outfit from *The Prime of Miss Jean Brodie*. The man obviously needs directions back to the cruise ship where he mangles songs for pensioners. The schoolgirl is holding a clipboard. The give-aways are the giant rosettes: a red and white lion clawing a double ribbon in black and blue. Why is Alan wasting his time talking to canvassers from any of the parties, let alone BG?

'Sorry to bother you, Zack, but it seemed the simplest way to show them that 102 isn't empty.'

'Why would it be empty?' I ask the canvassers.

'We're checking, Mr…' The crooner peers over the schoolgirl's shoulder. 'McGinnis? 102A?'

'Parris.' I assume they are looking at a copy of the electoral roll.

'Of course. Delighted to meet you, Mr Parris. Ed Williams, your local BG councillor.'

I ignored the proffered hand. 'You might be local in Wandsworth but we've no BG councillors here. Anyway, no-one in my house will be voting BG at the election, and my friend here is too smart for your clap-trap' – Alan nods vigorously – 'so feel free to move along and stop spoiling his day.'

His assistant exhibits her braces. 'We're not canvassing for votes. Please vote for whoever you want.'

'I shall. We call it democracy. I expect they'll cover it in your classes soon, unless someone abolishes it first.'

'I hope not!' she exclaims. 'I'm not old enough to vote yet. What we're doing is for after the election, when we're in power. Have you heard about BG's Empty Homes Survey? So, 102A isn't empty, but what about 102B?' The clipboard is a tablet; she switches hands and it flips from portrait to landscape – ugh. 'There's no-one at 102B on the electoral roll.'

'Where's your authority to carry out this survey? You're not the government yet, you know.'

Ed gets back in charge. 'We've identified that 106 is empty. Mr Tinker confirms that.'

Alan nods sheepishly. 'I didn't realise… I was a bit slow.'

'Alan, it's not your fault. Blame these two. So, your licence?'

'There's no licence needed to stand up for British homes for British citizens. We're going to pick protected areas where only British citizens will be allowed to buy residential property.

Tories, Labour, they both sold Britain to foreigners, when we have had a housing crisis for three decades. But we're calling time on all that.'

'You won't dare. House prices would collapse. You'd destroy everyone's savings!' Alan starts to shake.

Ed gives him a funny look; maybe before cruise ships he worked in prisons. 'That sounds like banker-talk to me. You weren't a banker by any chance? Alan Tinker – make a note to check, Jeanette.'

'We hate bankers,' chirps Jeanette as she works the tablet. A gust of wind flattens her skirt.

The whiff of banker whets Ed's appetite. 'Do you know what they have in banker heaven, Mr Tinker? In Switzerland? They have strict laws on foreigners buying property. What's sauce for the goose… You're not an estate agent by any chance, Mr Parris? We hate estate agents almost as much as bankers. Selling our country to foreigners.' I get the eye scan which he just gave Alan, plus I'm wearing an at-home cotton polyester jumper from which the smell of weed never washes out. 'No, long-haired lazy arse, more like. Get yourself a job. You should be ashamed of yourself, living off Miss McGinnis. Or Mr McGinnis.'

I spit on the pavement and hit Ed's left shoe, a scuffed salesman's special.

***

It was a wet ten-past-seven when Kathy exited Putney station. She judged it a close call whether she would make it to 102A before the gusts threw her umbrella around like a shuttlecock. Zack had texted to say that Alan was joining them for supper; could she pick up a bottle of red on her way home? Given Alan's views on ordinary, Kathy would normally have headed to Waitrose to pick up, perhaps, a Montepulciano d'Abruzzo. However, the extra fifteen minutes' walk would have been not so much tempting the weather god as sticking her hand down its trousers. Instead, the Rear Admiral was en route. How much harm could any pub do to an unopened bottle of Chilean Merlot?

She pushed past the signs saying 'no football colours' and 'Every Tuesday: double burger and extra chips for £5.99' to enter a surprisingly clean, brightly-lit pub. The special offer was doing a brisk trade at numbered tables. Kathy kept her raincoat buttoned and her uniform to herself. The assistant manager, announced by his name badge and barely in his twenties, was helpful, cheery and well-organised. When she passed on the Tuesday offer, he didn't miss a beat in pointing out that Wednesday was curry night. He even went down into the cellar to bring up a case of Merlot, instead of pretending that the crimson blend on the shelf behind him was all they had in stock.

Kathy's eye roamed lightly over the Rear Admiral's slice of London: two pensioner couples, two middle-aged couples with four young children and two babies, a group of older men who might have been there all afternoon and two groups in their late teens – girls in awkward shoes and cheap jewellery, and mainly white young men with flat-top haircuts and the occasional tattoo. All the tables sagged under pint glasses and plastic ketchup bottles. Kathy's glance didn't linger. In any case the tableau dissolved in a roar thanks to the wide-screen television.

The heavens burst when she was barely three minutes from home. Fighting the wind with her umbrella saved her top half, but from the knees down she was dripping. The door of 102, and then the interior door to 102A, led to the aroma of Zack's home-made lasagne. Zack had perfected a recipe with four cheeses, aubergine and dried porcini mushrooms which fixed most problems temporarily. Neither the two of them nor Alan were vegetarians: the recipe was simply better without meat. Creating tasty cheap meals was something an actor could take pride in, and Zack did. Alan kissed Kathy on both cheeks and Zack gave her a hug. Once she had changed out of her wet clothes, they told her about the BG survey.

'I get confused,' mused Alan. 'They were surveying empty homes – or they said they were – but their policy is about foreign ownership.'

Zack shook his head. 'That's no more confused than any other party's policies. We've got total mental chaos going on. What about 36/9, for heaven's sake?' He whistled a version of *The X-Files* theme tune.

Kathy offered a memory. 'BG said something two months ago about taking over empty homes, but it wasn't clear they meant it.'

Alan's confusion worsened. 'Are they on the left or on the right? They want to slash benefits but take over empty homes. They want to spend more on defence and they attack business – well, financial services. They're against immigration but for black people. What's the game?'

'Game' reminded Kathy of her conversations with Patrick. He hadn't been joking about war-gaming the election. She had been on the phone all day getting that to start next week; not that she could share confidential Civil Service information with Alan. She might with Zack later. Instead she said, 'Their game is changing the game.'

'Except the game is still getting elected.'

Zack got animated. 'Sure, but look at their visit this morning. They didn't do traditional canvassing. Instead they acted as if they didn't need to; as if they were going to win.'

'And will that work?' Alan demanded.

'Who knows, but it's a strategy – BG's strategy is different. Look at what Bob Grant said about hard-working families. He was very clever. The other parties thought he had attacked a sacred cow and rubbed their hands with glee. But Bob out-manoeuvred them. He said what everyone knows but, until him, no-one had said: that 'hard-working families' was a gimmick made up by politicians who didn't know a real hard-working family from a hole in the ground. The more the Future Tories shouted, the more Bob pointed out how many wives they'd had, how many homes they had, which schools their kids went to, how many of them didn't have proper jobs… What are the polls saying; he's gone up?'

Kathy nodded. 'He has. Including among former Conservative voters.'

'BG are buying the election with money,' Alan opined. 'Not advertising, but the Vigilance – which is paying to get youngsters and the unemployed off the streets. Buying votes, even. Where's the money coming from?'

'Bob's worth at least £20 million,' said Zack. 'A refill, Alan? We'll sit down in five minutes.'

Alan shook his head vigorously. 'I tell you something, BG's got other money, that's for certain. I dealt with people who were worth £20 million. Hell, I hoped to become one myself. Now, an ordinary guy looks at someone worth £20 million, and thinks he's got all that to spend. But the guy with £20 million is thinking, I can't afford to slip below £17 million, maybe £15 million worst case. BG is spending way beyond what Bob's got. All those computers, and they pay allowances until you're twenty-one, and wages after that if you become an organiser. That's how they blew UKIP out of the water – big money and serious organisation.'

Alan paused as hailstones rattled the windows. 'Did you ever think one day Bob was going to be famous?'

'Of course not. No-one in Bermondsey grows up to be famous. I mean, except Michael Barrymore.'

Kathy got up from the sofa. She had been watching Zack's mood, listening to his laughter. Most of all she watched how fast he was sinking the red wine – tonight he was going gently. She was happy about that for its own sake and because it hinted that the day's writing had gone well. That augured well for the surprise she would pitch him after dinner. Why not jump at the chance to play Bob behind closed doors? Why not get paid to take the piss out of his brother? What Patrick wanted most was to shock his civil servants out of sleepwalking into a BG government, if that was the election result. But she knew that she mustn't misplay it. If Zack thought it was a gig she'd wangled as a favour, based on his resemblance rather than his acting, forget it.

8

London, Wednesday 22 April 2020

The jokes have been coming too easily: on Wednesday morning it's time for writer's block. After the storm the sky is grey with patches of blue. High clouds whip past like bank robbers. I wake up with a headache so bad that fixing it will be a codeine job. The gig is Saturday night. I finished yesterday in a good place, but I need to keep going. Friday and Saturday I need to chill out, tie bow-ties and rehearse.

Normally I leave codeine out unless I'm in a show: today will be an exception. Since mostly I'm not on stage, I call that sensible self-medication. When I am performing, I *seriously* need not to fuck up, even if it's discussing the finer points of car insurance with a dog. In my line of work you don't get to play Rosencrantz, let alone Hamlet, if you can't talk car insurance with a dog. *What's Hot in St Albans and Harpenden* liked my Rosencrantz for three weeks last year.

I call Troy. For all his faults, surprisingly often he is helpful. I'm hoping it will be that way this morning, and I'm in luck. I jump in an Uber to find the thirty-year-old wearing a polka dot neckerchief in the 'sun lounge' of a Kensington hotel. It's a quarter to eleven in the morning but two large glasses of white Rioja are already on the table (there's an 'On me, Zack, on me,' as I arrive). I know it's going to appear as a deduction for expenses the minute I have any earnings to deduct the expenses from, but still it's a nice gesture.

Allegedly white Rioja never gives Troy a headache, so I explain that he can share mine. Troy skims my script for Saturday, his eyes accelerating towards the last page like a bishop who has stumbled into a tranny bar. I take a discreet, I-don't-drink-in-the-morning-but-I'm-being-sociable mouthful. 'Not bad, Zack, not bad. So you've decided to play the second half for laughs. Fine, but it can't all be cock sizes and you need an ending – like in a firework display, some fuck-off thing that says, this is THE END; APPLAUD!'

'Agreed. I'm hoping you can give me some inspiration.'

'Hope away. It's free.'

Troy pulls out his smartphone. 'Example. You thought about doing an estate agents rap?'

A what?

'So here you go – an online lyrics generator. Put in 'estate agents' and get some lyrics for free. Bang. Done it already.' He hands the phone over, and I scroll down.

Goin' for the grips every day 'til the grave
Neither did real estate but still put you in your place
Acres separate my estate from neighbors
So log out and soak your lyrical papers
I'm letting all my niggas grab a plate
That's right I know you don't do real estate.

My head swims a bit. I read the lines a few times. 'I'm not sure that works for me,' I say uncertainly.

Troy shrugs and pours himself another glass. 'It might work for them – they're twenty-year-olds mostly. And they'll be off their faces on the white stuff. You could read them *Railway*

Tickets of Tasmania and they'll crease up.' He points at my glass. 'Drink up, if you want the creative juices to flow. I don't fancy doing all the heavy lifting.'

Twenty minutes later we've cracked it: famous locations from Shakespeare's plays re-done in estate agent speak. 'Dunsinane. Unique opportunity to acquire eleventh century hill ramparts with outstanding opportunities for bloodshed and modernisation. Dynamic forest views.' After scribbling like mad I thank Tony profusely and hurry home to get some new material down while I'm on a roll. A number 14 bus takes me most of the way, followed by a ten-minute walk. The codeine has kicked in, I'm feeling a lot lighter. I stop at the corner where 106 is.

A fire engine is parked alongside. Its lights are flashing but hoses are being coiled up. The smell of soot and wet sacking is strong but a cartoonist would caption the scene 'after', not 'before'. Mud from a water-logged miniature garden spills into the street. In 106 itself, the glass in the patio doors has shattered but I can't see any external damage upstairs. Someone has painted in tar-black letters on the end-of-terrace wall 'BRITISH HOMES NOT EMPTY HOMES.'

Alan, is he all right? I expect to see the neighbourhood clock on the pavement but he's not there. I wander into the road and don't see a car with two people inside turning towards me. The car accelerates but I slip on wet mud and fall backwards towards the pavement. I have time to notice that the sky has turned a clear eggshell blue, like a children's colouring book, with a smudge of black smoke climbing towards it like Jack's beanstalk. What I don't have time to do is get out of the car's way.

9

London, Thursday 23 April 2020

When I wake up, Kathy is standing beside me holding my hand. I have an intravenous drip in my arm. A tall thin man, clever and in a suit, stands next to her. I assume he's the surgeon admiring his handiwork.

'How are you feeling?' Kathy asks. She pops an extra pillow behind my back.

Damage control reports come in to my brain. The ones from distant territories like the feet take a while. 'All right,' I say warily. 'Light-headed. A bit thirsty.'

Kathy pours water from the bedside jug. 'You were so lucky. It was a really vicious blow to the back of your head, and a lot of blood, but that's all it was. They've run tests overnight and they'll let you out this afternoon or first thing tomorrow; I'll come back to take you home.'

I wait for the surgeon to utter his medical babble, but he just smiles and exudes intelligence. 'No operation, then?' I ask.

Kathy replies no. They had to shave my head to do their examinations; they wanted to be sure they weren't missing anything which could cause problems later, but it all came up fine.

She sees that I'm still staring at the man in the suit. 'This is Patrick Smath,' says Kathy brightly. 'My boss at the MOD. He wanted to come by and say hello.'

'Hello Zack,' he says. 'Call me Patrick.' So not a surgeon, just the same cutting mind and upmarket bedside manner. These are not the most auspicious circumstances in which to meet the man who may divert the next year or two of our lives to the other side of the Atlantic.

'Patrick – Zack Parris. I've heard a lot about you from Kathy. Although nothing classified, of course.'

'The only thing which would be classified is how much of my job is done by Kathy. With luck I'll get my knighthood before anybody notices. My car was bringing both of us this way so of course I wanted to pop in. I'm only sorry not to be the bearer of chocolates.' Kathy has told me many times how Patrick can be graciousness personified, if he wants to be. 'So you and Bob are brothers.'

'After a fashion.' I start fingering my scalp. The back of my head is still bandaged. I can't see the skin – there is no mirror in the room – but it feels bony and bumpy, I can tell it's going to be prison camp white. 'I changed my name, and we don't talk about each other.'

Kathy takes my hand and puts it back by my side.

'Bob hasn't mentioned a brother in any of his interviews.'

'It's mutual, but I've given fewer interviews. Bob thinks I'm a waste of space. He thinks all actors are. It seems we're nearly as bad as bankers.'

'Fascinating,' says Patrick. 'Of course, what I would most like to have brought you is an arrest.'

'I'm sure it was an accident,' I say. 'I slipped on some mud.'

Patrick shakes his head. 'I didn't mean that, although I'm sure the police have taken the driver's statement. I meant the petrol bomb into 106. I can promise you we're onto this like a ton of bricks – police leave cancelled, the works. A group of us in the centre of government, including the Home Secretary, receives daily reports on the investigations. We're utterly determined to nip this kind of vile attack in the bud.'

'What was it?'

'Very amateur, thank goodness. A plastic bottle with some petrol and a timer. It seems a good part of the petrol evaporated during the night before the timer went off. Having no curtains or carpets in the living room helped. But if the fire service had been delayed, if there had been a stiff breeze up Walsingham Road...'

'Is Alan OK?' I ask Kathy.

'He's fine. He was calming the Bangladeshi family in 100 when you turned up. He's got a bottle of prosecco on ice for us this evening.'

'Good old Alan.' Fuck, what about the gig? I'm guessing that my head will still be bandaged tomorrow. I return to Patrick. 'It was BG, I assume?'

'We're putting all BG and Vigilance organisers in south-west London through the wringer – including the guy who came round doing the survey. But I'll be honest, it's mainly deterrence. Unless we get a forensic break we're unlikely to see an arrest. Putting an extra watch on your street, that sort of thing? We're certainly doing that.'

Patrick's phone bleeps. He grimaces at Kathy. He moves to leave, taking Kathy with him. 'Bollocks. Will you excuse us? More politicians have escaped from the kindergarten. It's tempting to say the sooner the election's over, the better. But we'd better all be careful what we wish for.

'Oh, you might be wondering about the private room.' Patrick gestures around. I haven't thought about it, but of course he's right – it's not an NHS ward. 'The MOD will take care of it. It'll help keep any media away. Your neighbour Alan is catching most of that, and doing well, from what I've seen – a statesmanlike example to our masters. If they let you out in time, maybe you'll join our role-play briefing tomorrow afternoon?'

Kathy's shown me how Patrick is a master manipulator, but I can still enjoy a class act when I see it – here's a private room, come do our role-play.

They go and I fend off a Filipina nurse who keeps saying, 'You Prime Minister, you sign book for me'. I text Kathy to bring a large hat when she comes back.

I turn to contemplate Saturday's gig. Not only have I lost a day and a half since leaving Troy, but I'm stuck for the next few hours with no notes and no internet, just wall-to-wall election garbage on the television. I trade a promise to sign my brother's best-seller, *Getting Britain Back*, for some paper and a pen. The book's ghost-written, obviously. I should think the last proper sentence Bob wrote was when he was sixteen. He entered a competition for one of the first PlayStations.

I beg the wide-screen television for inspiration. A ghost-writer would suit me too. I realise that's pretty cheeky for someone who has just escaped cranial fracture, brain surgery and arson, and pinch myself.

***

By lunchtime the real doctor, Anjuna Joshan, confirms that I'll be released after breakfast on Friday – she wants me in one more night to be certain. I'm disappointed but realise that I am still in shock from the accident, and carry on surfing the TV for pigswill ('Future Tories pledge flat income tax') and comment on pigswill ('They think this is a game-changer but we'll have to see').

To prop my eyelids open I watch *Short Sharp Shock*, Angela

Deil's Thursday afternoon show. As the polls shift towards BG, trust Shock News to be there, leading where the wind blows. I met Angela only the once, twelve years ago, but some things about people don't change.

On screen, Angela has gained rather than lost vim. A short skirt shows off the thigh work-out devised by her personal trainer (all the rage after Trump brought them into the White House to tone up the eye candy). Her stilettos are a perfect colour match to her hair. Both radiate the colour and tang of Valencia oranges. Whether nature or nurture are owed the thanks, age shall not weary her curls, nor the years condemn.

The camera loves her. In return her body language makes clear that breaking out of the corporate suite to do her own show on a Thursday afternoon is just so much fun. Her target isn't numbers but evening news editors and drive-time show hosts hungry for stories with a bit of fire in the belly and pre-TGIF sparkle. Angela's speciality is news-oriented cocktails, putting guests into the blender and shaking them up before scooping crushed ice over their battered reputations.

The cocktail-in-progress is a Stupid General. The recipe starts with a plump, retired grandee of the army who is living in a bygone era and ends with a rout.

'It's a question of whose finger can be trusted on the nuclear trigger,' Angela summarises.

'Exactly. Our nuclear deterrent is in the direct charge of the Prime Minister. There is a video link from No 10 to the control bunker, from which the signal is sent to one of our Vanguard submarines which is on patrol somewhere in the ocean, ready to fire, at all times. One submarine's missiles could annihilate tens of millions of people.'

'And Bob Grant can't be trusted.'

'That's not just my view, but the view of a number of serving officers at the highest levels across the armed services. It's a national concern. The time comes when one of us has to speak out. The British public needs to know.'

'If Bob Grant was elected prime minister and gave the order to fire, would those officers obey? Or would we have a coup?'

'We absolutely obey lawful orders.'

'A duly elected prime minister sounds very lawful to me. Or does someone like you suspend democracy when it happens not to be convenient? Because what BG's saying is that there's a group in society, a ruling class if you will, which fixes things regardless. Forget what the ordinary voter thinks. It sounds like you're part of that ruling class.'

'That's rubbish, if I may say so. I personally have served governments elected from three different parties. The loyalty of the British armed forces has never been questioned.'

'What BG's saying is, those old parties are really all part of the same game, and BG's different. By coming out and expressing concern like this about BG but not about the other parties, aren't you proving their point?'

'It is different to have a leader of a party, an unknown quantity – frankly both the leader and the party are unknown quantities – saying that he would have no hesitation in nuking the Kremlin on a first strike basis. Unprovoked. That's unheard of, and exceedingly dangerous.'

Angela Deil leans forward. 'Is it mad? Is that what you're saying?'

The general is oozing bathtubs of sweat. Angela probably told the studio engineer to set the general's spotlights to rotisserie.

'Because, General Goring, you've got to go one way or the other. Either we've got a dangerous madman on the loose, who should be locked up rather than running for Downing Street – bear in mind that according to the latest polls, you'll need to lock up about twenty-eight per cent of our viewers as well – or Bob Grant's view, that Putin has been running rings around us for years and Bob's calling time, is a valid opinion. Even if it's not your personal opinion. Even if that opinion is a criticism of those like yourself at the top of the defence greasy pole. Besides which, running onto the pitch in the middle of an election in your red general tabs to tackle Bob, and Bob alone, is pretty questionable.'

The general comes to the boil. 'How dare you!'

'How dare I? Let me turn that around and ask, how dare you? Well, would you dare pull the nuclear trigger? Would you retaliate? Imagine Manchester's wiped out by a nuclear bomb smuggled to terrorists by Russian commandos on a holiday trip to the Coronation Street studios. Forget being a general, be the prime minister. Do you wipe out the Kremlin in return?'

'If I may say, Ms Deil, you don't know anything you're talking about. That's a ridiculous scenario.'

'And I may say, and I do say – do you retaliate? Why don't we find out right now? What would you do if I hit you?' Angela and the general are both standing up, inches apart. Suddenly she draws her hand back and slaps him across the face, reddening his left cheek.

Goring's eyeballs swivel. He gasps for sanity but, not being the sharpest tool in the toolbox, he finds none. Does he strike back at a woman, the CEO of one of the country's principal media, on television? In a discussion programme? How incredible. I hate everything about this election because rotten and stinking as it is, still I cannot look away. Reality is changing and I am sea-sick. Rules which used to work don't anymore.

Goring grabs Angela by the shoulders. Will he punch? Three seconds of gasping and glaring feel like twenty before he barks, 'You'll be hearing from my lawyers,' and storms off the set. Angela resumes her seat and smiles at the camera. 'Well, it

Alien, distant, dire events

seems you don't retaliate, you talk to your lawyers. How very civilised. But here's the short sharp point: Trident is an utterly pointless weapon unless our enemies think we would use it. I suspect our enemies think Bob Grant would use it. After a short break, I ask a leading economist: will house prices be a financial game-changer in this election? Or on 8 May will we find that we're back to the same-old, same-old?'

10

London, Thursday 23 April 2020 (2)

Patrick cradled his forehead while Kathy killed the television in his private meeting room. 'If only they'd asked me' – he meant the chiefs of the armed services – 'I'd have told them. With so many retired generals to choose from, why go back to the Triassic period? General Goring up against Angela Deil!'

'They did ask,' Kathy reminded him. 'You did tell them. And Goring was a disaster. The gossip [the information shared among her private secretary colleagues] is that all the generals at pasture expected to be kebabbed, so they let Goring volunteer. Senior officer retires with pistol, all that.'

'If the senior officer had retired with his pistol he'd have caused a lot less trouble. Look, Kathy, these role-plays next week – we've really got to up our game across Whitehall – dramatically.'

'Now I can tell Zack who some of the other actors will be and promise him a script, I'm sure he'll say yes.'

'Say this from me: his country needs him. I need the shit scared out of people in this building who think BG isn't going to happen, or that if it does that it'll be back to business as usual. Of course we'll pay – premium for short notice – preparation time – you name it.'

'His concern was that you might expect him to write the material, but you've put that to rest. Before the pavement had a go, what was doing his head in was a fifteen-minute gig he's got at an estate agents' dinner on Saturday.'

Patrick looked up. 'Saturday?'

'Yes, why?'

'You've got a date Saturday night. With me and the Cabinet Secretary.'

'Shima Patterson?'

'Exactly. BG are lining up for their biggest rally so far. It's on Bob's home turf, at the reprieved Millwall stadium, but with rock star technology and live link-ups around the country. I've persuaded Shima that we need to be there *incognito*. We need to feel this beast in its lair, on its home ground. I'm sick to death of reading briefings and op-eds written by people who know less than we do. We need to know what we're up against.' Patrick paused. 'Hmm, replace that with "what we're up for".'

Kathy pondered why her boss and the Cabinet Secretary would want to spend Saturday night at Millwall with her – as opposed to plain-clothes police protection, for example? With Patrick, the answers were always multiple. On this occasion she guessed that he wanted an ally, that he had a hunch about how Shima would react to a woman, and that unveiling Bob's sister-in-law would be an ace up his sleeve.

He was dangling in front of her an amazing career opportunity: hours up close with the most powerful civilian in Britain. Was she up to it? Was she up *for* it? What Kathy wanted to say was, 'Me, really? Are you sure?' but she'd learned. Any of her opposite numbers on the private secretary network would snatch the offer out of her hands given half a chance. So she played the game. Was it what she wanted? Of course it was, and yet at the same time she was unsure. 'Shall we go in my car? We'll be less conspicuous.'

'That's a great idea. But how will Zack feel that you're not there? There's a limit to how stupid I want to look, begging him to do his bit for the country and pissing him off at the same time.' Through the glass door Patrick could see a blue-jumpered officer with Royal Air Force shoulder boards arrive at his desk.

Kathy laughed. 'If I can tell him what I'll be doing he'll think it's a hoot: two of the cleverest people in the country going to Millwall to pick holes in his brother. It's a trip to Cairstine which I'll be missing, not his gig. My whole line with him is, it's estate agents, it's not a major performance. I can't say Cairstine will miss me, but I'll have to cancel a flight to Glasgow.'

Patrick held the meeting room door open for Kathy. 'Then we've got a deal. I owe you a flight up to Helensburgh.' His gaze swivelled to the new arrival. 'Wing Commander, how can I help?'

'I thought you'd want to know right away: finally we've got one of the BG drones. Of course we haven't formally traced it to BG, but it's obvious – a jet-black triangle, one metre sides, about two and a half kilos in weight.'

Both Patrick's and Kathy's faces lit up. 'That's great news. Where did it come from?' Patrick asked.

'The Metropolitan Police have just brought it in. Several members of the public saw it come down on open ground in Southwark Park. Its batteries must have failed. Fortunately no-one was hit.'

'You've dispatched it to Farnborough?'

'A car is on its way now.'

'Good. I'm afraid you'll need to spoil the lab boys' weekend – I want the analysts crawling over it all night and all weekend if need be.'

'I doubt you'll be spoiling their weekend. You might be helping a few marriages instead. If the thing is half as interesting as BG want us to believe, they'd be over it all weekend anyway. Now they can say it's an order. I'll speak to the team right away.'

Kathy went to check her voicemail as the RAF officer withdrew. Finding an actual BG drone so soon after completing her report was exciting. 'That could be really interesting.'

'At this stage balsa wood and rubber bands would be interesting, unless of course it's a plant. Why Southwark Park? Is there a park in Southwark?'

'It's close to Millwall,' Kathy hazarded. 'I can't think of anything else near there. Oh, listen – something from voicemail. Angela Deil would like to speak to you.'

Patrick dropped into his chair and popped his feet up on the desk. 'Fancy that. She probably wants me to say whether it's constitutional for retired officers to make fools of themselves during elections.'

'Zack and I met her once, a long time ago. It was at a party Bob was giving: she was with him.'

'What did you think?'

'Smart. Always on the look-out. I remember thinking, I wonder what she's on the look-out for.'

'A future prime minister, perhaps.'

Kathy laughed. 'Well, she'd have had to have been clairvoyant to have spotted Bob then. It was more than twelve years ago. Bob invited us round to his house-warming. Afterwards Zack gave Angela a new name, which I couldn't possibly tell you. Like the Ice Maiden, but worse.'

'Canine?'

'Worse.'

Patrick winked. 'It must have been some party.'

'It was. In fact, it was the last time Bob and Zack spoke.'

11

Eton, September 2007

'I blame John Betjeman's friendly bombs,' Zack opined. The area around Slough station had been rebuilt with English Modern Town Centre Lego – the special edition including a faux Zaha Hadid bus terminus. A supermarket stuck its supersized car-park behind into their faces.

Betjeman's bombs had spared the station so that Britain could keep an independent strategic reserve of Victorian ironmongery. Once-white garden-fence trimmings fringed the station's roofs, reminding Kathy of Cairstine's crown of lamb with paper frills. Cairstine had put out the family silver and excelled at it three weeks before.

Opposite the taxi rank posters introduced the country to its prime minister, his government ten weeks old. 'Not flash, just Gordon' looked downwards and to his left, his hands buttoning his suit, crumpled hair failing to protect a furrowed brow.

Over crown of lamb Cairstine had toasted a Scots prime minister at last – proper Scots, someone she had even met at the University of Edinburgh. Kathy had been no less chipper. Barely one month into the job Gordon had announced two new aircraft carriers, biggest-bollocks-ever ones. The Navy was intensely proud, even as they dubbed the two ships *Unaffordable* and *Unserviceable*. They would be launched in Scotland, at Rosyth.

Lunch in a British garden can be glorious, with sunshine and on occasion without wasps, verbal or otherwise. Last month in Helensburgh had been exactly that. The lamb was accompanied by new potatoes and a salad from the garden. The finale had been McGinnis bread pudding with berries, cream and whisky. Zack had just landed his first leading role, not West End but on the way. Kathy had just finished her first year as a lieutenant. Doors were opening and they had decided to get married in 2008. Zack would be thirty and Kathy twenty-six.

So when a phone call came out of the blue to the newly-betrothed to say some new doors were opening for Bob as well – a house-warming for a renovation which had been nine months in labour – Kathy was surprised how little she had to twist Zack's arm to accept. 'You've changed in the past five years, I'm sure he has too,' she had pointed out. Later Zack had gone into a predictable tizz about the impossibility of buying a present for a brother who had sold his business for a reputed £20 million. In her usual way, Kathy had sorted it.

Fifteen minutes after reaching Slough they arrived at a stone-fronted house in a twisty lane. The taxi dropped them in front of a garish façade bathed in lights like a specimen in a display case. More lights were set into flagstones bordering the drive. The floodlit front door was ajar.

'What a disgrace!' An elegant woman dressed for cocktails at Cannes stormed out, accompanied by an intensely embarrassed fifteen-year-old in white tie and tails.

It was Kathy's turn to panic. A phone call was all very well but printed invitations had their uses, such as specifying dress code. But when she looked inside the house, she saw varying assortments of track suits, shorts and flip-flops, with skirts cut so skimpily about the hips that anything from Ibiza to Ibrox appeared acceptable.

A group camped inside the front door cheered as a darkened, chauffeur-driven sedan pulled up. Three men in their twenties and matching blue suits, barely worn, bounced up the steps.

'Footballers. There'll be a few of those,' Zack said. 'Millwall, obviously. One of those might be Gary Alexander, their new hope?'

From the first reception room Kathy and Zack could see at least two others, similarly-sized, and a large garden. Each was noisily occupied by different gangs. Teams of designers with different concepts (Versailles, oriental fusion and something from Mars) appeared to have competed in the different spaces to create the most expensive effect. Some of the gangs were in business suits, some were in smart casual but most were in the sports and supermarket attire which had greeted them at the door. Zack was nervous; it had been five years since he and Bob had bumped into each other at King's Cross. 'Remember your temper,' Kathy whispered.

'*My* temper?' Zack's shoulders snapped back, ready to be provoked.

'Bob's is worse, but you're proving my point.'

'*Far* worse.'

'It's not a competition.'

'Wotcha, Jack? How come we don't see you down the Den no more?' Zack was embraced in a beery hug by a stocky middle-aged man in a suit two sizes too small. 'This your bird? You gonna introduce us?'

Zack introduced Kathy, leaving the schoolmate whose name he could not remember to introduce himself as Steve. Zack explained that the two of them had just got engaged, but intended to live in Putney which wouldn't help getting to the Den. Steve's business, concrete mixing, was turning over nicely.

'The boys will be dead chuffed to see you. And the missus.

God, it must be ten years at least. And keep your eyes peeled for John Berylson. The Yank. He's just put a ton of dosh into Millwall.'

'An American's bought the club?' Kathy asked. Millwall's Lions ('No-one likes us, we don't care') were ferociously south-east London.

'We don't care, if he sorts the place out. Would you believe six fucking managers in two fucking years!' Steve was on an important mission to get a round of drinks at the bar but made Zack promise to find them in the 'Chinky' room. 'Karaoke's gonna be starting in half an hour.'

'Let's head into the garden, let me get myself a roll-up,' Zack said.

'You don't have to go outside,' Kathy pointed out, gesturing at the wide array of used ashtrays. 'But it will be quieter. We don't need to stay too long once you've met Bob.'

'You're right. I didn't think that they would be that drunk by five in the afternoon, but I forgot.'

In the garden Dr Nassia Sotiris spotted Zack and introduced herself. 'Forgive me, but Bob mentioned his brother might be coming? You resemble him so much, Jack. Apart from the hair. Even the eyebrows are similar, although Bob's are slightly flatter.'

Sotiris was dressed like a professor of something very clever who happened to be employed by Vogue. Kathy caught the way Bob's name rolled off her tongue. She couldn't help wondering if other intimate parts of Bob might have rolled off there as well.

'I'm Zack.'

Sotiris touched Zack's arm. 'Zack, Zack. My mistake.'

Kathy intervened, her alarm bells ringing. 'Do you know about the house? What a lovely garden.'

'Absolutely,' Sotiris gushed. 'Bob didn't buy this place until he could also get the strip of land, down there. Do you see?

Beyond the trees.' She pointed to the foot of the garden. 'There are the famous playing fields of Eton. Or at least some of them, Agars Plough. There are quite a lot elsewhere as well. But then there are quite a lot of boys, over one thousand three hundred Did you see one of them earlier in his school uniform? I'm one of the beaks. Sorry, masters. We're committed to helping all our students discover their passions.'

'That was a school uniform?' Kathy exclaimed. 'I thought it was three months' wages.'

Muscles clamped Zack from behind. 'Would you believe it, bro? I live next to a school where they help you discover your passions. Where Jack and I went, if you discovered your passions, they fucking put you inside. True or not, bro? Millwall. Girls. Music. Es. Good you could make it. And you must be Kathy.' The breath which pressed against Kathy's cheek was hot, neat alcohol.

12

Eton, September 2007 (2)

'Hello Bob,' I say, as Bob gives Kathy an appraising look and a kiss. He's got an inch on me in height but his paunch spoils the effect. His head is still shaven. I see the small tattoo behind his left ear but no more earring.

'I've heard so much about you,' Kathy says.

'Well, forget it all, especially anything about knife fights. I'll show you the scar later.' Bob winks. 'All this is a new start. I've sold up the business, all the lard is coming off' – he slaps his belly – 'and Nassia is going to educate me, aren't you? Fix me up proper…' – he seems to be stopping there, but then adds – '…ly.'

I don't need to be Brain of Britain to work out what Nassia Sotiris is doing with Bob – £20 million means you don't have to use aftershave, although he could do with a generous spray right now – but what's Bob doing playing school with a doctor? The last he told me, he couldn't stand wankers who bothered with college and that. Wankers like me.

Memories come back as I watch Bob sussing Kathy out, almost by sniffing her. I say to Sotiris, 'What's your subject?'

'Sociology.'

'Is there much call for it in a boys' school?'

'A lot!'

Surprise me. Eton is a testosterone fondue – boys only,

between the ages of thirteen and eighteen. I wonder how many have crushes on Nassia Sotiris? 'Thirteen hundred boys sounds like a state school. Isn't Eton supposed to be exclusive?'

'It is exclusive. All the boys live in houses of about fifty, so the educational experience is very personal. We need the size in order to offer an exceptional choice in activities as well as studies.'

Bob is man-handled towards one of the reception rooms by an atomic-powered redhead. She contrives to be both deeply apologetic and imperious at the same time – a journalist who has spotted a big-wig Bob should meet. 'Hi, I'm Angela. No offence guys?... Are you really his brother?...Ohmigod, I'll bring Bob back right now. Like, before right now.'

Kathy joins my conversation with Nassia. She wants to know about my name. 'I was born Jack Grant, but I changed to Zack Parris,' I explain. 'I'm an actor. Bob and I don't really approve of each other. To him being an actor is a complete waste of space, whereas to me being a dangerous selfish ignorant twat trumps that by a mile.'

'How long have you been at Eton, Dr Sotiris?' Kathy's sonar is pinging like mad.

'Please – Nassia. Four years.'

'Well, it's been very nice to meet you. Zack, why don't we get some food?'

'Great idea. Well, Nassia, I wish you luck with my brother. He's a tough one.' It's an exit line but for some reason my hormones have different plans. I add, 'So, what kind of sociology should I call you up about – do people call you up about?'

One-legged she slips a stockinged foot free of her left shoe, extracting a business card perfumed with talcum powder and her contact details. She holds my gaze throughout. 'I specialise in the sociology of precocity. How and when individuals in different classes and social settings discover that they have unusual talents – star quality, if you will – and how that social setting reacts, positively or negatively. You know the expression 'cutting down tall poppies'? So Eton is a greenhouse for tall poppies, having provided nineteen of your prime ministers. The school is part of my research, as well as my teaching. And Bob is also a tall poppy, coming from a background more or less opposite. He is exceptionally talented – as both of you are as well, that goes without saying. One day it would be interesting to interview you, Zack, to see how things were for you growing up.'

Kathy's reply is firm. 'No exceptional talent in my case, Dr Sotiris. I count myself lucky to be a lieutenant in the Royal Navy. If I go places, it won't be because of exceptional pixie dust: I'll go because the Navy sends me. I'm starving, Zack, and I've seen carvery sandwiches.'

***

We come out of the food tent with freshly-roasted-turkey sandwiches, complete with sage stuffing and cranberry sauce. Kathy attacks hers with gusto. The buffet also offers chip butties on *ciabatta* or supermarket white, with fresh tomato *salsa* or Heinz, and a daunting display of langoustines dressed with caviar. We didn't join in the banter in the buffet queue.

'I thought there'd be a pool.'

'Bob's learned his lesson from Barrymore, right? That's why there's no pool.' Earlier in the week, Barrymore had been told there would be no charges.

'The lesson is don't be a fucking poof.'

'Too right. Bob ain't no poof.'

When we're free from the tent we roll our eyes. 'Don't forget we need to give Bob his present.' Kathy tapped her bag.

'You're right. Let's do that and leave, shall we? I'm glad I came to show my face, but it's all a bit weird. Not to mention unpleasant.'

Through bits of turkey Kathy mumbles, 'Yes. We'll finish our sandwiches and go hunting.'

'You'll not go talking with your mouth full, aye, not like that Kathy.' I exaggerate Cairstine's inflections.

When we find Bob it is with his mouth full – full of vodka, lying on the floor of the kitchen. Above him on the breakfast bar is an ice sculpture sitting on a refrigerated base, owned (according to a bright red label) by *Shock News*. In the crowded kitchen the red-head is presiding, counting to twenty in a *crescendo*. A backing chorus makes up in enthusiasm for any unfamiliarity with the larger numbers. The counting matches the emptying of a glass of colourless liquid into a hole in the forehead of the ice sculpture, a life-size nude. The nude lies on her back pouting at the ceiling. Her lower parts show signs of global warming: the left foot has melted up to the ankle, while the right leg has been amputated at the knee. Behind her a regiment of Stolichnaya empties parades on the breakfast bar.

The vodka, now chilled, bubbles up from the nude's navel and carves its own channel across her belly to cascade from between her legs into Bob's open mouth.

I know Kathy has seen stuff in the Navy, even taken part a couple of times (she told me once about an apple-bobbing contest, but it wasn't water in the bowl). But the mum storming off with her boy suddenly looks like the height of restraint.

From his earthworm perspective Bob sees the two of us and winks.

'Sixteen... seventeen...'

Fortunately a lot of the vodka lands on the floor. The glacial erosion in the pubic region had become estuarine, so the colourless liquid falls in a wide, torn sheet.

'Nineteen…' A camera flashes.

'Twenty!'

Bob springs up to hooting, high fives and a kiss from Angel. He looks around triumphantly.

'What a cunt,' I say, loud enough so only Kathy can hear.

***

We still have to get shot of Bob's present, so when he has been wiped down with a Shock News towel and stumbles towards us with an iced tea, I point towards the garden's most reclusive corner.

'Try it,' he says. 'It clears your head like fuck,' he adds, shaking his like a hairless dog.

'No thanks bro,' I respond. 'I've got a life.'

'You're winding me up – you got a life? All credit to you Kathy, Jack never had one before. Tell him to be careful with it.'

'You might want to be careful yourself,' she says, trying to be light-hearted as she hands me her bag. I take out two thin rectangles, about seven inches by five, and hand Bob the first. Kathy has wrapped it to make a nation of shopkeepers proud.

'You know that picture we thought was lost? The one Aunt Jessie took, of ma and the two of us in Southwark Park for the fireworks.'

Bob's alcoholic fog is pierced. He takes the present and looks up.

I continue, 'I was clearing junk to move into Kathy's and found it. We've made you a copy and framed it.'

Bob clutches it to his chest, before stumbling again. 'Sweet, bro. I appreciate it.' He laughs and ribs me. 'Shame you're in it, but I guess you can't have everything.' The photograph hovers precariously in his grip.

The second rectangle is an unwrapped paperback, but a fraction of the normal thickness. 'I don't know that I would call this a present, but I hope you might want to have it anyway.'

Bob studies the title, *Copenhagen*. 'You think I should go?' he asks.

I shake my head. 'It's a play. By Michael Frayn. Look.' I riffle the pages so he can see them laid out as a script, not prose. 'Two physicists, Niels Bohr and Werner Heisenberg, meet in 1941 during the war to discuss making the atom bomb. You're interested in the Second World War, Churchill and all that.'

Kathy makes a supporting run. 'Niels Bohr will be Zack's first leading role! A really big role opening in January in Birmingham. Zack hopes you might want to keep a copy of the play as a souvenir.'

Bob laughs. 'It's about Germans making the atom bomb? But they don't, do they? Is Churchill in it?'

I shake my head.

Bob holds out his hand. 'Sorry Jack, the vodka – congratulations. Well done mate. Your first leading role.'

'Thanks Bob.' I gesture at the house, the garden and the guests. 'You got yourself a leading role some time ago. Congratulations too.'

'Cheers.' Bob sways, fingering the book before jabbing it in my chest. Suddenly his face is all smiles. 'All those times we argued? I said acting was pretending, and you said it wasn't.' Bob turns to Kathy and rolls up his left sleeve. He shows her the three inch scar near his shoulder which I know well. 'I used to say to Jack, that's not pretending. But I get it now. You are in this play, and this play isn't about pretending, it's about what shit really happened when these egg-heads meet and change the course of the war.'

My brow wrinkles. 'Nobody actually knows what did happen when the two scientists met. Nobody alive. We have a few letters.'

Bob holds the script up between two fingers. 'Got it. That's why it's so thin. Not a lot of words, nobody knows what happened.' He claps me on the shoulder. 'I thought for a moment you got ripped off there, bro.'

Kathy senses she is in a good position and shoots for goal. 'In fact, the play is more than two hours! Two hours, three characters. It will be a fantastic break for Zack.'

The gnat which originally had Bob's attention span wants it back. 'It's all cool with me. Just as long as it's not a load of bollocks in fancy made-up words.'

I stare at Bob. I've no clue whether I'm getting through or pissing in the wind, but I'm giving him what I've got. 'The play is about giving things another go. Frayn calls it doing "another draft". If you read it, think about you and me, brother. When something's difficult in a relationship, that's all we have – giving it another go.'

Kathy holds my hand, and reaches out for Bob's. He stays out of reach. I fire my last shots. 'OK, there is an alternative. The alternative is we *don't* do "another draft". We decide we already know. I already know what you're like. You already know what I'm like. We stop. We stop now.'

Bob pitches forward. Glass tinkles as he drops the photograph and the script and throws up over them, before collapsing face down. Kathy steps forward, the decisive first aider. He's got a pulse, I want to tell her; he just hasn't got a mind. She's going to clear his airway – rather her than me. 'Call an ambulance,' she says.

Now that's a plan. At the very least I can embarrass the scumbag in front of all his guests by calling the ambulance from the house. Oh, I'm not hoping for his death – just something a bit salutary.

Fuck it, by the time the ambulance comes, Bob's fine. Some ice from the sculpture helps his headache. Angela is nowhere to be seen.

Bob's not even mildly embarrassed; he doesn't know what embarrassment is. We exchange pretences: he pretends to be sorry for throwing up over the photograph and the book, and I pretend it's no bother.

On the train home Kathy and I have half a compartment to ourselves. 'Tell me again about the knife fight,' she says, her head nestling against my shoulder. 'You didn't have knife fights, did you?'

No, I tell her; then I tell her the story once more. More exactly, I tell her the only part of the story which I've told anyone. I was seventeen and doing a Saturday shift re-stocking shelves in the supermarket, so I didn't see anything myself. Bob was sixteen, the other boy, Tel, was fifteen. They were from the same estate, but there was a gang from a neighbouring estate. Friends, enemies, bravado, knives. It got out of control. Bob and the other boy got stabbed, the fifteen-year-old very seriously. Bob made it to hospital, the youngster didn't and died. It was a shocking and very personal educational experience, although not quite the same as Eton.

A copy of the *Daily Mail* lying on the next seat says Britain will be swamped after European chiefs bring in an extra 20 million migrants from Asia and Africa. Another story says a Hollywood actress has spent £226,000 on plastic surgery but still can't get a role. Demi, I feel your pain.

Two weeks later confirmation came through about my role, and I start the happiest time in my life – planning our wedding and a successful career. The happiness lasts until December when the theatre is gutted in a fire. There are insurance problems, the director of the production is also a director of the theatre and he has to sort them out – so no production. I'm as gutted as the theatre. Time for another draft. Fortunately they do them in pubs.

13

In the morning the *Shock News* front page is an over-chubby general impersonating an enraged lobster beneath the headline: WHO DEFENDS BRITAIN – THIS MAN OR BG? Patrick is so keen for me to attend this afternoon's role-play briefing he's given Kathy the morning off to play nurse. The man has barely met me but he reads me to a T.

Kathy brings a hand-woven Panama. After I've used the private shower (twice the size of our bathroom at home) we head for a costume shop near Covent Garden. A plus from normally having the right hair for an ELO tribute band turns out to be that getting an emergency wig is easy. Serve me right for poking fun at Cairstine's pompadour: the curls scratch like hell but do the job.

Kathy drops me at a nondescript office building across from Waterloo station. I make my way up to the seventh floor with Jeremy Corbyn. Although we are not 'in costume' I can see why the MOD wanted to do the meeting somewhere discreet. They have achieved that: the conference room they've hired shares the floor with a private clinic. There's a steady traffic of all shapes of men to the gents, returning with urine samples. I wonder if any of them are estate agents.

In the conference room six of us sign pages of mumbo-jumbo

on secrecy before being handed individual folders – three or four closely typed pages of scenario description plus a similar amount of 'script' suggesting how we open the role-play next week. A frisky thirty-five-year-old with nerd glasses explains that each of us will have our own half day role-play with civil servants (in my case, military as well). The group will come in having swotted up and analysed our parties' manifestos and speeches, but otherwise blind. The first hour will be an extremely lively meeting in which each of us lays out a scenario with demands and instructions. In the second hour the civil servants will then have thirty minutes on their own to formulate a plan, returning for half an hour to attempt to persuade us to agree; a cycle which will repeat in the third hour. All the discussions will be filmed and observed by psychologists, who will analyse what went well and what went badly. Finally, we'll chip in our own take on what pissed us off or won us around.

Around the room there are giggles and smirks. The thirty-five-year-old frowns severely. Boris Johnson shows me his first page – bring back hanging, auction it as a reality TV franchise compèred by yours truly. The group breaks up to get into role.

The BG scenario makes my blood runs cold. China has massacred fifteen civil rights protesters in front of the Legislative Council building in Hong Kong and declared martial law. Several business leaders as well as a vocal part of the Hong Kong public have invoked British protection under the Sino-British Declaration of 1984. The Premier warns that any interference in China's internal affairs will result in daily blackouts in Britain's China-owned electricity supply 'until they see the light'.

As Prime Minister Bob, I want electricity bosses fired and the Navy's flagship *Queen Elizabeth* sent to the scene. The carrier is barely ready for operations, with only six short take-off and vertical landing fighters deployable; I will demand adding a force from the Vigilance with drones. The Navy will insist that it has no ability to protect its flagship within easy reach of thousands of Chinese aircraft, shore-based missiles and stealth submarines: I will accuse them of cowardice. Widespread power cuts could bring the Government down. The loss of the *Queen Elizabeth* could trigger nuclear war. Will I be persuaded by my staff, or just double down?

Behind the scenario is Bob's photo and a psychological profile. I'm intrigued that they have managed to predict his temper – he's been very careful to keep that out of public view. The psychologists think that beneath the bluster, Bob is nicer than Trump but more unpredictable. I think he's fooled them on the nice bit. I read the scenario a second time. When I look around, the room has got ten degrees colder.

From Waterloo it's an easy train journey home. I tell Kathy that the scenarios scare the shit out of me. She reminds me of the way I took the piss out of war-gaming at Helensburgh. I tell her she did a great casting job: the physical resemblances were secondary and variable, but by the questions we had when we finished reading, it was obvious that we would all deliver. The thirty-five-year-old even had to stop and think a few times.

We both have big days tomorrow. Kathy goes to bed early while I finish the joint left over from Wednesday; I'm more excited than I thought about having a walk-on part in a national drama, and I need to wind down. Nuclear war puts estate agents into perspective. When I am under the covers I place my hand on the small of Kathy's back and feel her rise and fall.

She and I have been talking about whether, if we end up in Washington for two years, that might be the time to have a baby – I can be at home while she does a bit of the evening 'power career' thing. Not having friends around won't matter too much. Also we'll be back in this country before kindergarten

– the thought of an American accent in the nest freaks both of us out. Of course if my career was taking off … The truth is, as an actor I'm an aircraft who will never do more than taxi along the tarmac.

Might I still get a lucky break? But my mind traps that thought and turns it around like Lionel Messi. Not getting killed when I fell off the pavement was my lucky break.

14

London, Saturday 25 April 2020

For its biggest rally yet, BG made the obvious choice – Millwall's Den. Rigged out rock concert style with cable, suspended speakers and giant screens, the location reeked of symbolism. Home of the Millwall Lions. The part of south-east London where Bob Grant had grown up and where he was BG's parliamentary candidate. The docks and the vanished dockers, slaughtered since the 1950s by containers, cheaper labour, a shrinking and weightless globe followed by an exploding and wait-less web. The forces which took their livelihoods were so huge that the names Britons attached to them, like Thatcher or the unions, were no more than initials carved into the world's park benches – puny attempts to say that sometime, somebody had been here.

The stadium was a 20,000-capacity Meccano rectangle opened in 1993 to replace one nearby. It was sneered at from vertiginous heights by all the 'statement buildings' within eyeshot, especially the Shard and the financial skyscrapers at Canary Wharf across the river, all less than five minutes away by helicopter. Towering capitalism looked down at Southwark and Bermondsey, its neighbour once criss-crossed by a historic web of small industry but now overwhelmingly residential, and pondered briefly how it could squash some more life out of it.

The stadium's main claim to fame was that humans still congregated there. If a goal was scored the crowd could be heard in the supermarket car park a mile away. They could be heard notwithstanding the traffic and the trains, or the jets powdering their noses in the sky before gliding down to Heathrow twenty-five miles to the west, or the myriad beats of private music. Not to mention the unceasing rhythm of chat – 'He was like, and I was like ... No, really?' – by which south-east London counted down the minutes to death.

Millwall's song – 'No-one likes us, we don't care' – would have suited Thatcher and the unions as well as BG. But tonight it was 'Britain's Great! End of!' chanted by a capacity crowd which greeted Kathy, Patrick and Shima Patterson as they exited from the recently-added New Bermondsey overground station.

The police advice had been to forget about cars but to remember plastic Union Jacks, a sea of which surrounded them. As well as the obligatory one of those, Kathy had opted for a sweatshirt, jeans and trainers. Patrick had gone 'snap' but with an extra zero on the price of each item, including the Union Jack, while Shima had stuck with a crumpled beige version of her Whitehall uniform of a jacket and trousers. Together with her stockiness, Shima's dress sense had easily earned her the nickname 'Angela Merkel'.

Shima wasn't carrying a flag. She was wearing dark glasses. Both actions risked drawing the attention she wished to avoid. None of them was carrying personal phones, cameras, papers or identification; Kathy had a pay-as-you-go Nokia which tracked their position and would let her speed dial through to their invisible tail.

The crowd was so mixed that the main risk of being 'outed' was failing to shout and jump and wave their arms. Kathy reckoned that most of this would fall to her, so she threw herself at it with gusto. Looking at the fervour around them, Kathy wondered when it had taken root – minutes, days or years ago? No one around them looked like a plain clothes officer, which was as it should be.

The crowd had been stoked by a disastrous news story for both sets of Tories which Shock News had broken during the afternoon. Street-corner conversations had been captured at January's World Economic Forum in Davos between bankers and Conservative ministers and special advisers, some on long-distance mikes, some on video followed by lip-reading. Nothing was longer than a few minutes, but together they sealed a damning impression. Politicians and bankers alike were frightened of the renewed global crisis, the trillions of public cash used once more to float the finance system off the rocks, and the ever-stronger populists. But however well or poorly those talking knew each other as individuals, the fragments of conversation made clear that these were 'mates' in a club for whom there would always be space in the lifeboats.

Kathy led the three of them round to the turnstiles for the West Stand. Patrick had secured a corporate box. Inside they could hear one warm-up speaker after another lambasting the sitting duck target. The Financial Secretary to the Treasury had resigned at mid-afternoon, but the era when a resignation meant anything had gone. It seemed that the country was not having it – not any more. The Archbishop of Westminster threatened excommunication of any Catholics found to be embroiled in 'egregious conspiracies against the poor'.

The six-seat box was tucked away in a corner. It was more than enough to give the three interlopers some privacy to talk. In fact, the set-up was perfect. They would see anything happening on the podium on the giant screen while absorbing the overwhelming sense of occasion – Mexican waves, the floor shaken by stamping feet, the lot. A tureen of ice with bottled lagers, wine, water and soft drinks sat next to sausage rolls, prawn mayonnaise sandwiches and vegetarian samosas – a refreshment package included with the box. Kathy had to pinch herself at the company she was keeping.

'Did you go this year?' Shima asked Patrick. 'To Davos.' He shook his head. 'I went for two days with the Prime Minister,' she continued. 'I can't imagine how they got those recordings – we were all searched within an inch of our lives. But it can hardly be a coincidence that they've released the recordings now.'

'A special rally on BG's home ground ten days before the election, with Canary Wharf skyscrapers in the background,' added Patrick. 'BG make the established parties – if we can still call them that – look like Sunday afternoon amateurs.'

'I can't see how today's news is going to do anything other than increase BG's lead.'

'Agreed.'

'Has the post-mortem on the drone shown anything?'

Kathy's ears pricked up. 'Nothing formal yet, but I talked to the lab at Farnborough a couple of hours ago. They're horrendously guarded about the propulsion system, but that's because they're slobbering all over it from a science point of view. You're talking something faster and with vastly more endurance than the helicopter drones we know – from silent hovering to eighty-five mph for, they think, ten hours non-stop, while only weighing a few kilos. Propulsion apart, it was nothing special – guidance, battery and a modest payload, in this case a digital camera. Probably half the kids in the stadium have something as good in their phone.'

'So, on balance is that good news or bad?'

'I'm betting on two outcomes, Shima, and my gut doesn't like either of them. The propulsion system clearly isn't some kitchen-scientist job. Possibly a decade of work and hundreds of millions of dollars have probably gone into it.'

'Which means BG is in bed with a very large corporate with a strategic interest in drone services, or a nation-state. The Russians, branching out from the hacking they did in the US election. The US itself. China. Possibly Korea or Japan,' Shima mused.

'Or Israel. In either case the relationship is undisclosed by BG. Frankly, the whole thing has to be deeply covert if it's a nation-state, given how BG bang on about Great little Britain.' Patrick gave his flag a wave and gestured out of the window. 'They'd go ape-shit if it was a foreign power. Anyway, a corporate is my first bet. My second is the device isn't a prototype, and it's not bespoke. That drone wasn't just produced; it was mass-produced. Mass as in, even bigger than the Vigilance.'

Kathy spoke up. 'But the regulators counted fewer than fifty drones in corporate hands allowed to fly in built-up areas.'

Patrick grinned. 'I guess we'll watch this space.'

'For that purpose, I use these.' Shima fished some opera-glasses out of her jacket pocket and trained them on the rows of seats, many still empty, within the VIP cordon. 'I'll shout if I see anything red-headed.'

When Shima got bored she handed the glasses to Kathy and launched into an intense discussion with Patrick about coalition scenarios. Until this morning a tie-up between BG and one of the Conservative parties had seemed the most plausible, but the Davos leak had blown that out of the water. Other scenarios fared no better, coming apart faster than gimmicks out of a Christmas cracker. Yet past elections in Britain had hammered home that a party like BG might lead the polls comfortably, but fail to win the national vote. Or it could lead the national vote but get few members elected to the House of Commons.

Even in Britain's impoverished Navy, Kathy had kept watch with something more than opera glasses, but soon she got the hang of them. She spotted a few faces which she recognised, most obviously Annabel Wale, BG's chief of organisation. Her platinum blonde short-back-and-sides and high cheekbones had come up often in Kathy's research into BG and drones, because Wale headed up the Vigilance. Barely in her twenties, Wale was the BG wunderkind who had re-invented political engagement for young people in the way Zuckerberg had re-invented college yearbooks.

Sitting next to Wale was a face which at first Kathy struggled to place. She racked her memory for where. Eventually she hunted on the right shelf in her mental library. It was Nassia Sotiris, the beak from Eton at Bob's party. Kathy counted the deposits of age which twelve years had left on Nassia's skin: none.

***

The giant screens re-circulated the day's *Shock News* – headlines, tweets and interviews: TORIES, BANKERS, OUTRAGE AT DAVOS. An aerial shot of the snow-covered eyrie – brief, since Davos itself looked too much like a public housing project to sustain Hollywood levels of excitement. So swiftly onto close-ups of Swiss private banks – SWITZERLAND: WHERE THEY KEEP YOUR MONEY – inter-cut with aerial close-ups of Davos's famous and not-so-famous visitors 'saving the world economy', or hobnobbing and sucking up according to taste. Few facts were presented, to save the audience the inconvenience of knowing anything during their rush to outrage.

Abruptly the screens filled with an orange waterfall of hair and the stadium filled with a roar. Up the ramp towards the stage a cameraman jogged behind Angela Deil. Wearing a singer's skin-coloured radio mike, she milked the setting like the pro every personally-trained inch of her was.

'Hello Bermondsey!' Another roar. To the camera, 'How's she cutting, Liverpool? Newcastle – are you ready to *political* party? The time is coming to make Britain Great again.' The predictable chant starts up.

'The time is coming to choose a prime minister who is one of us. Who shares our dreams. Who will make us proud. A prime minister who can be proud of having built a brilliant international business from nothing – from no GCSEs, no help from the taxpayer, no help, of course, from any bankers' – the last point wasn't actually true but that didn't matter – 'from a workshop under a railway arch right here in Bermondsey!' The footballing section of the crowd essayed 'Come on you Lions!'. 'He has also organised the most imaginative and the most *needed* political party in our country's history!'

The applause, unforced, continued for at least a minute – a standing ovation yet the event had barely started.

Kathy was glad to be in a private box. Shima looked at the crowd, dismayed. Patrick looked like someone who had just landed a hole in one. 'I was right. We had to be here.'

Angela waved for silence. She didn't get it, but she got enough leeway to drop her volume some decibels. 'And I – and *Shock News* – and all of us – need to say a big thank you to BG especially today. Because it was the Vigilance who flew the drones at Davos' – an explosion from the crowd and on Patrick's face – 'and who released those vital truths which we all needed to hear.' The explosion turned into cheering. 'On that score, a shout-out to Aidan Hall in Newcastle. We call him "Batman" – he led the Vigilance team who flew the drones at night and parked them on the roofs of buildings, ready to watch out for us during the day.'

Bob was just visible now at the back of the stage, half-shadowed.

Without turning her gaze from the crowd, Angela gestured backwards and shoved the decibels as far into the red zone as they would go. 'Ladies and gentlemen, please thank – and welcome – our next prime minister – Bob Grant.'

In the sky the passenger jets sinking towards the west tugged the sun lower, behind the roof of the west stand. When the floodlights came on, the shadows inside the stadium sprang to attention.

15

London, Saturday 25 April 2020 (2)

Three minutes after the planes tug the sun lower at Millwall, I watch them sink past the floor-to-ceiling glass of the banqueting suite at the Crowne Plaza Battersea. I've never seen so much cocaine; it must have been delivered by Jewson's in a sack. I ask the waiter who takes me to the top table to change my side plate; someone has snorted off it.

For me the excitability of the banter isn't so much a shit sandwich as a shit Battenberg cake. Brown stuff: only the chairman who did the invitation has the slightest interest in thoughts on 'closing the deal'. White stuff: my bald look makes everyone slap me on the back and tell me Bob Grant jokes. Brown stuff: I simply don't have the balls to get up and impersonate my brother. Shaking vertebrae in my spine tells me it's not going to happen. White stuff: they'd probably laugh themselves silly if I read them *The Cat in the Hat* (sadly my copy is at home).

In a blinding flash during cauliflower soup I'm rescued by a divine courier from the Muse agency. I can play Bob's brother: not me but Spike, a sibling I make up. Someone who grew up with Bob and knows him backwards. Someone whom Bob has never mentioned, and within a minute of Spike opening his mouth we will know why. That's easy. It's what I can do: make-believe, play-acting. Spike has the licence to kill which Zack missed out on. In dinner jacket and black tie, I'm even dressed for the part.

So when the uneaten chicken in a Malay sauce has been cleared away, I kick off with a guaranteed winner with this audience – the BG plan to slam the brakes on foreigners owning British homes. The fire-bomb and the BG 'canvassers' makes the issue local. But what Spike can tell them which Tom and Dick can't is what kind of council flat Bob grew up in, and how he 'went to Eton'. They know Bob's dad was half-Egyptian, but not how he fucked up his first shag.

Once I get to the vodka dripping from the ice maiden I've got them completely. (I leave Angela out of it – I still have some survival instincts.) Fists on one table start pounding out 'BG – end of!'. I worry that I'm about to be attacked, but in a split second realise that it's a sarcastic reversal of Bob's slogan. I'm being cheered on.

The next bit accelerates into a blur.

I remember going for #HateBankers, since today's news has been wall-to-wall Davos. Estate agents are next, I point out – dung beetles living off bankers' droppings *and* selling our homes to foreigners and exploitative buy-to-let landlords.

I finish by explaining that really I'm an actor. I didn't get cosmetic surgery for this gig, but because looking like Bob might be the only way to stay safe under a BG government. I throw in a couple of tips: how to get your head shaved free on the NHS, and don't forget ten minutes in the tanning lounge.

What a shame Bob's not here to see. Milord is on stage right now with his own big number to do. Sure, not everyone has to fall for him – tonight shows that. But his audience is 200 times mine. And something comes home in the mini-cab with me besides a thank-you bottle of bubbly: an unexpected and uncomfortable thought. Suppose he gets to Downing Street:

maybe I could do a wildly successful satirical show? Something with vox pop fizz, like *The Revolution Will Be Televised*. I could be the prime minister's alter ego, popping up at front doors or in supermarket queues, taking the piss out of his policies.

Even as a boy, a happy Bob was a Bob with everyone else brought down to his level, or six inches lower. I'd fought that all my life. Satire would still be fighting him. But would it be enough? Who joked about the huge amount that cabaret did in the 1930s to arrest the rise of Hitler and prevent the Second World War? Peter Cook, I'm thinking. If Bob gets his way, do I ride his coat-tails? For fuck's sake, I don't want that choice.

***

The spotlight moved and Kathy saw Bob in the flesh for the first time since Eton. She was glued to the opera-glasses. Pictures in the media rarely gave a sense of build. Bob's legs were stockier than Zack's, less shaped, but he had worked off some of his paunch. Even Bob's eyebrows had been plucked, making them a touch closer to her teenage heart-throb in East 17 and a bit less like country hedgerows. Kathy was surprised to notice that Bob had raised heels. Zack was five foot nine, Bob an inch taller, not a height which particularly needed extra inches.

But movement left no chance of confusing the two brothers. Bob was always moving, a panther in his own domain, exploiting a thirty-by-ninety-foot stage with a two-hundred-foot catwalk leading at head height into the packed stadium. Kathy remembered Zack occupying space – as Julius Caesar, for example, in the summer festival in Mont-Saint-Michel. But what a difference: Julius Caesar took measured paces, with gestures rehearsed and words scripted. If the brothers were in two cages with the audience outside, in Zack's case neither performer nor audience would touch the bars, whereas on that Saturday evening in the Den the cage bars melted.

The stage and catwalk turned into tiles of light beneath Bob's feet. Light and dark resolved themselves into British Pathé newsreel of the coronation review of over 300 ships of the Royal Navy, off Spithead in 1953. Kathy knew today's count was fewer than seventy. The Russian navy had 200, building back towards a Soviet fleet of 600. Granted, one missile from a Vanguard submarine could throw more firepower further than the entire 1953 fleet. But one, maybe two, torpedoes could sink Britain's entire at-sea ballistic capability in a minute.

Bob ambled down the catwalk into the crowd, followed by a camera-man. 'Less than a mile from here, five hundred years ago, Henry VIII built a dockyard. At Deptford. That dockyard, here in South London, gave birth to the world's greatest navy.'

Bob stopped, far enough down the catwalk to stand under open sky, clear of the stadium's roof. He looked around, a shaven-headed forty-one-year-old publican beaming at his twenty thousand Saturday evening regulars. Wearing grey chinos and a red polo shirt with a discreet white lion, he moved as if to wipe some tables. Instead he intended to wipe the floor with old-style politics. The screens closed in on Bob's brow, his eyes narrowing as he looked directly at the camera. 'Starting tonight, near Deptford, we will give birth to a new country. Safer streets, stronger borders, new jobs, new hope. Starting tonight.'

He broke back into a conversational tone. 'At BG, we treat you with respect. We don't talk like politicians do. When they say "tonight", you know they don't even mean at the election in ten days' time. They mean maybe three years after that *if they win, if they can be bothered, and if you're damn lucky*.'

Another change of verbal gear, his right finger underlining in the air the first word of the sentence. 'Tonight – tonight –

tonight! – you'll see a new force for Britain. Experience a new energy for Britain. Admire a new ambition for Britain. Our country great once more. Let me tell you how.'

For forty minutes with no autocue, Bob Grant ranged over the economy, the constitution, defence, foreign policy, health, education and welfare. He served up a substantial first course – a new class of citizenship for Britons born in this country to British-born parents or parents serving in the armed services and police. For them priority housing, no NHS waiting lists and the first two years of university or vocational education free. For these 'lionhearts' there would be a special gold lapel badge, and a prison sentence for its misuse. Patrick and Shima shook their heads.

Then he invited his audience to eat their fill from a buffet of existing BG promises. An end to National Insurance contributions and the House of Lords. The United Kingdom protected – no playing dice with the country, like the Conservatives. Welfare payments to stop after nine months. Local communities to zone British-only home ownership areas. Six Dreadnought submarines to replace four Vanguards carrying Britain's nuclear deterrent. A one-hundred-ship Royal Navy. Five hundred additional aircraft, including drones, for the Royal Air Force. Leaving the EEA right away; saying boo to the IMF.

Bob had two courses to go. The third was bankers. Their greed was shameless. They had put their fists into the taxpayer's pocket *once more* without so much as a 'sorry' after the first time. The other parties had made laws which meant no banker or ex-banker was likely to have to cancel their second skiing holiday, let alone go to jail. While the Future Tories caught at Davos were particularly shocking, all the other parties had been too corrupt or scared to do anything.

When Bob broke his pause to yell, 'Until now!' the crowd

boiled over. BG had acted at Davos, Bob explained, and unlike any other party, BG would act in government. From day one, anyone who had ever earned more than £75,000 in one year from a bank would have to wear a regulation-size 'B' sewn onto their outer clothing, or go to jail. He said it three times so that it sank in. The crowd danced deliriously while stewards threw yellow eight-by-four-inch Bs into the air and onto the stage.

Kathy's head swam: the whole event was unfolding in some parallel universe. She could not imagine any of this happening. Patrick looked wan. Shima had petrified into a gargoyle.

The finale – strong borders, controlled immigration, safe streets, BG's heartland staples, familiarly disturbing or reassuring according to taste. But what was going to be new?

Bob called Annabel Wale up onto the stage. Naturally she was in Vigilance uniform, with a red and white lion just below each shoulder. Her black crew neck sweater and red belt had a designer cut, as did her figure-hugging black jeans and boots with gladiator straps, but she paid full homage to the uniform worn by two thousand youngsters stewarding in the stadium. The youngsters in the crowd went wild for their idol.

Watching the two together, Kathy grasped the purpose of the raised heels; without them, Wale would have been slightly taller. This rally had been orchestrated to the inch.

'The Vigilance guards our greatness and protects our hopes,' barked Bob, adopting a fiercer tone. 'That greatness and those hopes don't belong to BG but to the whole country!'

The crowd roared back the Britain's Great refrain. 'The role of the Vigilance is stepping up. It will take time to build up our armed forces as we have promised. But I pledge that from tonight the Vigilance will be there in support, a powerful extra force, at the service of the whole country. The Vigilance has been training, and is ready, for this larger role. From tonight it will have a system of ranks, and a special uniform for officers. Tonight, let me introduce to you, General Annabel Wale!'

Bob wrapped around Wale's shoulders a scarlet knee-length cape, clasped on her left side with five gold chevrons. On her right side was blazoned the inevitable white lion, a foot high. She waved to the crowd and then the stadium plunged into darkness. The green exit lights were the first to become visible, before Bob and Annabel were bathed on stage by three spots in red, white and blue.

'Welcome to Britain's fourth force!' Bob declared. Four roving searchlights stabbed up into the night sky from the corners of the pitch.

'Giving their own time, the Vigilance's volunteers have learned a skill which will be as definitive of the twenty-first century as driving a car was in the last.' Bob pointed upwards.

Out of the dark they came, first one, then six, then a dozen, then more, black triangles flying in slow formation. Searchlights intersected the hovering triangles.

Patrick grabbed the opera-glasses. 'Clever,' he said. 'The night and the lights make it easy to give an impression of hundreds. But there might only be –' he paused, '– thirty?'

So Patrick was as surprised as everyone else at what came next. The searchlights went out and lights on the drones themselves came on. Eventually Kathy counted two hundred triangles overflying the stadium, hovering in formation for a minute to fill the sky with a giant 'BG'. They flew off while the stadium lights gradually returned.

As faces and bodies in the crowd took shape once more, it would have been possible to imagine that nothing had changed. But, Kathy realised, everything had changed. The people who thought they were in power, weren't. Even a lowly lieutenant-commander might have just put paid to her career by making a complete hash of her report. Eyeing Kathy, Shima Patterson might have been about to say something along those lines but a fierce shake of Patrick's head cut her off.

Wale spoke. 'Tonight, as Bob promised, BG has given you proof. The Vigilance is ready *tonight*. Thanks to the Vigilance, Britain has stronger borders, safer streets, challenging activities for young people and investment in their skills *from tonight*. Because we pledge to work, not for BG but for a Greater Britain, *from tonight*.'

Under Bob a bar stool had materialised. The friendly publican had returned in giant close-up. 'Friends, our future is close enough to touch. In ten days, let's call time. Time on politicians who stole our children's chances. Time on foreigners who exploited this nation's trust. Time on experts who sneer at what ordinary people can do. In ten days let's not just touch that future, but through the ballot box grasp it and make it ours. And never, never carelessly give it up.'

Kathy checked her watch: fevered yells of 'Bob! Bob! Bob', applause, girlish shrieks, high fives and stamping feet reverberated round the stadium for seven minutes.

Patrick's head was in his hands. Shima glowered, rigid with rage or fear.

Two confident knocks at the door of their box snapped them out of their traumas. A Vigilance officer – what else was there to call him? – entered. In his early twenties, he was the proud wearer of a smile and a one-chevron cape. 'How has the evening been for you, ladies, sir? Up to your expectations?'

Kathy clutched at a straw: the glorious new Britain would still include customer service-speak.

'I'd have to say it exceeded them,' Patrick said disconsolately.

'Delighted to hear that.' The young officer turned to Shima and extended his hand. 'Welcome to BG, Dame Patterson.'

Shima stiffened, ignoring the hand and the gaffe. So much for *incognito*. Amplified throughout the stadium came a drum roll. The officer turned didactic. 'Please stand and face the flag for the national anthem. All of you, please.'

The larceny of her country's symbols outraged Kathy. 'As an officer in the Royal Navy, I certainly stand for the national anthem. But this is a private box and this isn't an official or royal occasion –'

But Shima stood and turned, so they all did. The Queen remained alive, so the country still petitioned God to save her. As twenty thousand voices sang, Bob and Annabel hauled an enormous Union Jack up from the stage to the rigging above. It was a Marines-on-Iwo-Jima visual epigram: the nation's honour raised high, thanks to sacrifice, courage and leadership. The picture occupied the whole front page of the next day's *Sunday Shock*: no words were needed. See page three for a cut-out-and-use 'B'.

Never before had the words of the national anthem stuck in Shima's throat like barbed wire. Every two months she journeyed to Balmoral to pay her respects and to offer a fragile figure a short account of the world. If anyone was losing their mind, it wasn't Her Majesty. Next time Shima would take a spade: the Queen liked to rehearse meticulously. It was time to dig a grave, in order to practise turning in it.

PART TWO

Loves go down

16

London, Friday 1 May 2020

Genius will out – my booking for one role-play turns into three, rising from nine participants on Wednesday to fourteen today. Each half-day in the offices next to the clinic in Waterloo leaves everyone shattered. The civil servants and military slink off like guilty survivors of a bomb blast. They throw envious glances at patients giving urine samples. The anxious patients are bemused. On Wednesday and Thursday I take two extremely well-deserved joints out of their case and sit down with a bottle of wine for an hour in the darkened briefing room.

That's not happening today, however; halfway through the show Patrick arrives with a smiley Chinese man with meticulous hair and a loud suit. They stay to the end. Fuck me, the Chinese observing a role-play about a mad Englishman and the South China Sea? Fortunately that is above my pay grade.

Today's role-play is my last, thank God. Kathy said to vary the aspects of Bob which I play up; the MOD may keep outsiders' noses out of its secrets, but internally the gossip machine is fast. Today owed as much to Bruno Ganz as to Bob Grant: there were shades of *Downfall* and Hitler's bunker as I stabbed fourteen breastbones with my finger.

'What a finale!' applauds Patrick as the blast victims file out. 'You've done an outstanding job.'

'I don't know about that, but thanks for the extra bookings. I took them as a vote of confidence.'

'They were. Sadly they were also a reflection of BG's polling. Still, that's next week's challenge. In the meantime please meet Brigadier General Chuck Leung of the United States Air Force. He has experience of exactly what we need from the Pentagon. Chuck, Zack Parris.'

'Surely a pleasure to meet you, Zack. We've got much in common.'

'Really?'

'Up to 2017 I ran Armed Forces Entertainment. Call it the biggest creative studio and booking agency you've never heard of. You're a fine actor, sir.'

I blink. Patrick puts a reassuring hand on my arm. 'You're gasping for a drink, which is on me, but in ten minutes. I've promised Chuck an experience which not many tourists can take: a London commuter pub on the Friday before a holiday weekend. But take a few minutes, Chuck, to share with Zack the superb insight you'll be giving our people next week.'

It takes Patrick all of the minutes and several false starts to connect Chuck's laptop to the room's projector ('see what I'm like without Kathy?' he apologises). While he struggles, Chuck tells his story.

'When Trump was elected in 2016, we were caught with our pants down, none more so than our military. A new President brings in his own civilian advisers – thousands of them. But the senior military stay the senior military. So Armed Forces Entertainment pulled this training video together in secret within two weeks of the election. We had no idea how a Trump presidency would turn out, but we had to shake the generals out of business-as-usual, and we didn't have you to role-play. So the way this video was used, we explained to the generals that it shows Trump about to make a key appointment to his Cabinet. When the video finished, they had to come up with arguments to dissuade him from making that appointment. So the same but different to what you've been doing.'

'Did it work?'

'It was a good phase one – we got attention, and we got focus on how various business-as-usual arguments and techniques might well crash and burn. The video wasn't a solution, but it created a hunger for solutions. Solutions was phase two, and three, and four. That's why since 2017 I've headed up a new department, OSP – the Office of Strategic Perspectives.'

'So my sending guys back to their desks shell-shocked is phase one. You're phase two.'

'Well, next week Patrick's asked me to share in confidence a few of our wins.'

'Wins like?'

Chuck turns to Patrick, who is trying to connect cables under the conference table. 'Go ahead, Chuck,' he calls out. 'Zack's a good 'un. He's one of us.'

'Well, with Trump, clearly you play to his massively superior intelligence. So we headed him off Iran, for example, by persuading him that the country doesn't actually exist. The whole Iran problem is made up, a strategic ruse by the Chinese, just like climate change. We backed it up with data, classified satellite pictures and stuff and then said, join the dots. How many months did Clinton and Kerry waste on a country whose existence, in point of fact, has never been scientifically established? Who do you know who has been to Iran, Mr President? And how did they know that where they were *was* Iran? A brilliant mind – he got it straight away.'

'Shit,' I say.

Chuck shrugs. 'It took eighteen months before we hit paydirt – abolishing monogamy. We produced shed-loads of computer simulation to show that monogamy was this whole outdated thing which was particularly hurting the efficiency of the military, not least our commander-in-chief. Imagine, we said, if your rank and file soldiers were as motivated as the Mormons? And think how much more effective you could be if you could have a Second Lady, and a Third Lady? I mean, the time saved on lawyers and alimony, for one. Not to mention Utah. As you know it became his signature issue. He was so grateful to us that afterwards, he kind of just did what we asked.'

'Done it!' exclaims Patrick.

The video lights up the far wall of the room. A security classification – SECRET: FOR TRAINING PURPOSES ONLY – is followed by an aerial shot of the White House and the opening flourishes of *Hail to the Chief.* Through a window in the Presidential quarters we zoom into a bathroom the size of Texas. In the middle is a jacuzzi with the Presidential seal. The camera approaches a Donald Trump-lookalike from over the shoulder of the woman he's in the jacuzzi with. Both are naked.

'You used digital?' I ask.

Chuck nods and then laughs. 'Look-alike actors and then digital. Or maybe we hacked into Trump Tower – take your pick.'

The Donald says he's about to appoint his Secretary of the Interior. The camera swivels to show a smiling woman with a striking resemblance to his daughter. Her breasts displace a generous quantity of soap bubbles. 'As President, I only appoint the most qualified individuals to my Cabinet. Ivanka Trump is by far the most qualified person for this role. First of all, like her exterior, her interior is fantastic. Plus, she has experience in business and design.'

The camera zooms in on the woman's face. 'All my career, I have totally stuck to classic, fundamental principles of business and design. And the most fundamental principle I have learned is, you can never have too much white space.'

'Drinks, everybody?' says Patrick with a grin.

17

London, Thursday 7 May 2020

Kathy opened the front door of 102A to cannabis and the sound of Zack talking too loudly on FaceTime. Zack had left the studio door open and not noticed.

In the last week she had seen him stoned more often than she cared for. A vape liquid from the States brought back by an actor-friend hadn't helped. It was stronger than he was used to, she was sure. The smell, an inch left in the bottle of Sauvignon on the kitchen table and what day it was sounded a big alarm in her head. Alan was expecting them next door in under an hour.

The final week's polls had been unrelieved gloom. All had given BG a lead of between four and eight percentage points, and now it was election day. Kathy had come from the train station via the parish church of British democracy, the polling station. Rosetted supporters (one per party) had waited outside, the ten-minute polite queue had shuffled forward, her name had been found and read out, and finally she had made her mark with a pencil last sharpened and chewed in the 1930s. Like thirty million others she had placed her voting paper into a black padlocked box. The boxes and their counting at 10pm were jealously guarded by democracy's Vicars of Dibley, the returning officers, but in truth that night all the boxes belonged to Pandora.

Zack came down the stairs and into the kitchen. Kathy poured the last of the wine down the sink. 'Did you vote?' she asked, an edge in her voice.

'Sure. This morning.'

'I hope so.'

'Are you saying I wouldn't be arsed to vote against my brother? Come on.'

'We're due next door in forty minutes and you need a shower.'

'I had one this morning.'

'You need another now.'

'But it's only Alan. Lighten up! Eat, drink and be merry, for tomorrow we die.'

Kathy skewered Zack with her gaze while opening the pedal bin with her foot. 'It's not *only* Alan, it's also me. I hope that's the only bottle of wine you've put away.'

'Of course it is.' Then Zack crumpled slightly. 'I'm sorry, Kathy, it's been really rough today. I don't know. You know those role-plays? At the time I thought Patrick wanted to shock his people, and I had a bloody good laugh playing mine. But war in the South China Sea could be happening tomorrow.'

Zack put his arms around Kathy from behind and gave her a peck on the neck. She didn't resist but neither did she melt. 'Yes, I had a good day. Thanks for asking,' she said.

'Oh come on. You've just walked in the door.' Zack opened his mouth again but thought better of it. He went to shower.

In the ten minutes before she could do the same Kathy browsed her social media. It was lamentation squared, interrupted by the occasional obscene hilarity. In a new first for the mother of parliaments, a candidate had been thrown out from a polling station for indecent exposure. There were zillions of pictures on Instagram.

'Look at this,' one of her friends had written. 'Sick!!!' Someone had set up BG2021, a channel streaming mash-ups imagining future life under BG. The link took her to one which was off the scale in terms of likes and abuse, called 'the Final End Of'. A packed Holocaust wagon-train slowed to a halt inside a camp: 'End Of' appeared on the screen. Some sicko had added a perky TV ad melody from 1978: 'Cook... cook... cook... cookability; that's the beauty of gas.' The original British Gas logo now read Britain's Great. Kathy hit the off button.

While she showered herself, Zack made himself a coffee. Then he sat on the end of the bed as she towelled herself dry and sprayed on some Coco Mademoiselle.

'I think we should take Cairstine to another specialist,' Zack suggested. 'I did some looking today and found one in Edinburgh who specialises in analysing speech patterns. Otherwise she might end up holding back your career.'

'I'm not going there. Look, Zack – it would mean taking two days off work. Even if you were offering' – she looked at him briefly and switched on the hair-drier' – Cairstine would scream blue murder. In the end, what earthly difference does it make what nonsense she comes out with? Even if another specialist found something, the best we could expect would be another set of pills. She's on six different ones as it is.

'Besides, she's not the only one who's hurting my career. You think you're helping but you're not. We have to figure out what we want, for us as well as Cairstine. You're not doing the listening which would help. Washington for two years isn't some expenses-paid Mark Warner couples holiday, it's about who would I become. Who would we become. Topics I don't fancy discussing with a cannabis plant. Did Troy hear back from the BBC?'

Zack winced. 'The Beeb don't want to do a satirical show about Bob. Read that how you want.'

Kathy pulled on her stockings. 'Maybe what they think is, there aren't going to be satirical shows under a BG government.'

***

Alan's original suggestion had been, 'We'll huddle round a fire and fend off the hailstones of democracy with *raclette*.'

Learning a French board game had sounded an excellent way to pass the heavy hours of election night, but *raclette* turned out to be a melted stinky cheese called, by some, angels' socks. Served with warm new potatoes, cold cuts and salad and a bottle or three of Roero Arneis, Alan promised that the result would be delicious. Throwing scalding malodorous goo down one's throat sounded disgusting to Kathy but could fit the election experience perfectly.

In fact, the food was moreish and fattening as hell. For 'cold cuts' read a shoulder of Iberico ham held in a purpose-built wooden and metal bracket. Zack was handed the carving knife (Kathy stepped in) while Alan did tricks with cheese using – well, Kathy could only describe it as an electric doner kebab machine for the upper middle classes. The resulting mixture of salt, fat, aroma and alcohol was the equivalent of opening your living room door to find the four horsemen of the gastronomic apocalypse in an orgy. Kathy's taste buds joined the party.

On television, Britain was giving birth to a new government. Like birth contractions, meaningful facts came painfully slowly this early in the evening. Distraction was being provided by a brunette in a green trouser suit standing outside some prison walls, topped with barbed wire. Except it wasn't a prison.

'We'll cross now to Oonagh who's standing not ten miles from somewhere many of our viewers will have been – Loch Lomond. Tell us, Oonagh, what are you doing there?'

'Indeed, I'm standing outside Her Majesty's Naval Base Clyde – also known as Faslane, the base for our submarine fleet. Because in the next few hours – in fact sometime between five and six thirty tomorrow morning, according to our experts – that's right, we expect to have a new prime minister. And a few hours later, once they have been received by the Prince Regent to take up office, to kiss hands as it's traditionally called, that individual will take control of our nuclear deterrent – of eight Trident missiles carrying up to forty hydrogen bombs lying somewhere in the ocean on board a Vanguard submarine. But there's one respect, Robert, in which the current prime minister will remain in charge – probably for several weeks.'

'Really?'

'Absolutely. Our deterrent submarines are on patrol for three months at a time. Each captain carries a sealed letter written by the prime minister telling him what to do if he – or of course she – finds one day that he can't get any communication from the United Kingdom – if he finds one day that Westminster, and perhaps the whole country, has been wiped out. It's one of the first things a new prime minister has to do. Many who have been in that position say that writing those four letters to the submarine captains – many of them have done it by hand – brings home more than anything else the awesome responsibilities which they have taken on.'

'The power to kill hundreds and thousands of people, on behalf of all of us.'

'Exactly. But it could be up to three months before the first Vanguard patrol sails from Faslane, behind me, carrying the new prime minister's wishes – because nobody knows where the one at sea right now is. And for the sake of the deterrent, it has to stay that way. So the existing prime minister's instructions will remain in force for that time.'

'Oonagh, thank you very much. I think we'll all be crossing our fingers that none of those letters need to be opened anytime soon. And now back to those shoppers in Bristol, who are telling Tyson which frozen foods they think our politicians resemble. He's been getting some pretty interesting answers.'

***

As the evening wore on, the stone-faced expressions of the spokespeople for the mainstream parties spoke for themselves. They declined to comment or speculate until the polls closed at 10pm. BG, on the other hand, was squealing with excitement.

At 9pm the cameras were waiting as the BG-striped helicopter skirted the Canary Wharf skyscrapers to touch down beside riverside warehouses on the Isle of Dogs. The Vanguard helipad faced across the river towards Millwall. Reporters clustered around Bob like flies on a rotting peach.

'Bob, Michelle Deeks, your candidate in Houghton and Sunderland South, has been asked to leave a polling station after stripping off. Have you anything to say?'

Bob Grant turned towards the camera, gravitas phasers set to stun. 'Anyone who wants to get their tits out for Britain tonight is all right by me. Tonight, the only tits out that matter are the ones we need to throw out of Downing Street.'

'End of,' murmured Zack in a ghostly wheeze of vapour. 'There's a Richard Deshaye movie we could watch on Sky.' For both Zack and Kathy, Deshaye was the epitome of brilliant acting, although it pained Zack to be the same age.

Kathy wasn't having it. 'Zack, why don't you take a nap? I can wake you up for the results. What will happen matters. As citizens we need to be there, and awake.'

Unsurprisingly Alan's theory was that prime ministers had

become too ordinary. 'Look back at Churchill, Attlee, Thatcher, even Wilson for God's sake – they were giants compared to this lot. Someone started putting our leaders in the wash without reading the care label. Major, Blair, Brown, Cameron – they've shrunk smaller each time. OK, May took us back to Brown, but that was only one notch. I'll fetch another bottle.'

'Zack needs to stick to water for a bit, and I'll do the same.'

'Not to worry,' Alan chirped. 'It'll be there when we need it later.'

***

Need it they did. Last time round, a national exit poll had been prepared during election day by five experts locked in a room, digesting reports from 140 polling stations on how 20,000 voters said they had voted. At 10pm on 7 May 2015 it had smashed an axe into Britain's electoral mould with an accurate prediction of a narrow Conservative majority, de-stabilising the Labour Party and taking apart the Liberal Democrats.

This time round at 10pm the experts finished the job they had started five years earlier. They declared that BG was on course for 294 seats in a 600-seat House of Commons. The splintering of the other parties and the vitriolic relations between them meant that BG would form the government easily. No other party was predicted to get into three figures.

'For God's sake, wake up!' Kathy shouted at Zack. She was on the edge of tears.

Alan had popped into the bedroom. He came out like a fashion model on a catwalk, wearing a pewter-coloured Ralph Lauren V-neck. Onto the left breast he had stitched a yellow B, eight inches by four inches.

'What are you doing?' said Kathy as the dam burst and the

tears came. 'They haven't passed any laws yet.'

Alan took her in his arms. Zack was beached on the second sofa, lying on his back with one arm on the floor. His snores sent puffs of cheese and garlic into the air, like distressed smoke signals transmitted by a tribe of Native American gastronomes. Prevailing conditions prevented the tribe from receiving any messages back.

18

London, Friday 8 May 2020

The following morning the seventy-seventh prime minister of the United Kingdom of Great Britain and Northern Ireland went to kiss hands. To the deep annoyance of the Prince Regent, Bob insisted upon turning up at twenty past seven in the morning. After all, builders up and down the country were at work then – why not the Prime Minister? Bob arrived at Buckingham Palace with two bacon rolls in a paper bag. The Prince Regent refused his, scarcely able to credit that he had to speak to do so. Bob nonchalantly munched both, leaving a light dusting of crumbs on the carpet. Within thirty minutes two staffs had briefed Bacongate to the media with opposite spins.

Kathy and Patrick were at their desks by eight. The gravity of the occasion had prompted Kathy to add her Royal Navy tricorn hat to the white shirt with shoulder slides, dark tie and trousers. Patrick's suit was his most formal dark herring-bone, his tie white with thin red and black diagonal stripes – faintly BG but in fact an official college tie (his college had eight). At some point the call would come for Patrick to enrol the new prime minister into the country's nuclear secrets.

The MOD's meeting rooms were swept nightly for bugs. When Kathy arrived, Patrick led her into one and came to the point. 'I want him. Zack. He's our ace in the hole.'

'Meaning what, sir?'

'I've been thinking about those role-plays. We pay him some money, he grows his hair back, he keeps quiet. No media shows, no stand-up comedy, no blogging – in other words no attention, no following, online or anywhere else.' Patrick crinkled his nose. 'Well, he's used to that. We pay him handsomely for six months – all Official Secrets Act of course, no kiss and tell. Maybe some kind of low-profile fellowship at RADA. After six months he would be a free man. His country might never need him. But if we did need him, he would be there.'

'To impersonate his brother? Doing what? Making a broadcast to the country? Attempting to get the Cabinet to agree the opposite of what they all believe?'

'It might not be anything like that. We might ask him to talk to Bob...'

'...Not if you wanted Bob to listen.'

'All right, maybe Zack gives us something on Bob from when they were kids, gives us some kind of hold to stop his brother destroying civilisation as we know it. Frankly, as you can see, I've no idea what we'll need. Everything's crazy now and we need aces up sleeves. I haven't been able to put the whole picture together. But I need you to ask Zack. In fact, I want you to sell it to him as your idea.'

'Why?'

'You know how to press his buttons. Is it patriotism? Is it sticking it to Bob? Is it saving the world? Is it the chance of an audience?'

'I won't do it, and it won't work,' Kathy replied. 'Bob becoming prime minister is probably a disaster for the country, maybe for the world, but we don't know. But what I do know is, this is Zack's last chance at a big break. Some kind of show taking the piss out of his brother. He was on such a roll after that estate agents' dinner. But since then he's got depressed again.'

'He's got years of career ahead of him.'

'No, he's got years of failure ahead of him. Say what you like – believe me I've tried – that's what he feels. He's forty-two. It won't be long before I find I've got a depressive alcoholic on my hands. Maybe I've got one already. It's not funny.'

Kathy looked Patrick between the eyes. 'I'm sorry, sir, but I'm not going to tell Zack to hide away when he needs the big time, and for the first time in his life it really could happen. Although apparently the BBC don't want him...' Kathy looked up curiously. 'I don't suppose you had anything to do with that?'

Patrick shook his head. 'As you know, the BBC don't give a monkey's what the MOD thinks.'

'OK. I can't let Zack walk away from his moment in favour of some 'maybe' which isn't even a plan. Even if it is a bit of cash.'

The aluminium glint in Patrick's eyes didn't flicker for a second. 'So make me a plan. A fuck-off plan.' He opened the meeting room door and gestured towards Kathy's desk. 'Take the morning to go think. Mornings-after the great democratic orgasm, I've seen so many of them. They're quiet. Number Ten will be trying to put together the Cabinet. Then there are all the junior ministerial posts and the whips; BG have never done it before, it'll take forever. I'll bet the nuclear briefing will be cancelled; that happened to me last time. So take a walk. Try the Cabinet War Rooms: we might be needing them again soon. Or the spa at the Corinthia – my ex said it was very luxurious. Put it on my expenses. Do what works. Bring me a plan.'

Kathy was silent.

'You think you can't do it, but I know you can.'

Kathy didn't believe him. Her brain cells were in chaos. Still, taking a walk felt like a good idea.

***

Kathy crossed Whitehall. A triangular drone loitered like a crow above the Banqueting House. She strode past the scarlet tunic, gleaming cuirass and helmeted white plume of the mounted guard at Horse Guards Parade. In two minutes she found herself in the fifty acres of St James's Park. It was too early in the day and in the year for the park to turn into a sweaty, packed, crumpled rug for locals and tourists to doze, partly stripped, in the sun. For now the park was showing itself in another guise, a magical handkerchief of green lying between Whitehall and Buckingham Palace.

Historically the park was an anticipation of a Disney theme park. Monarchs from Henry VIII onwards had treated the scrap of land visible from their windows like a playpen for landscaping. There was a story that in the 1600s the park had been home to camels and crocodiles. Now, the exotic beasts had been elected to office.

It took Kathy six or seven minutes to reach the Blue Bridge, guided by a daylight moon. The bridge straddled a storybook lake. From the bridge Kathy looked eastwards, back towards Horse Guards. Beyond sat the MOD three-slice toaster flying the flags of the Armed Services. The Foreign and Commonwealth Office, framed by the London Eye, rode the horizon like a duchess framed by a tiara. Nestled in the duchess's skirts was Downing Street.

For a while the machinery of British government was going to resemble a Siamese twin, with Patrick Smath exemplifying one type of head and Bob Grant the other. In her bones Kathy felt that only one could win. Which would it be?

Patrick saw in Kathy 'potential'. To Kathy, both what he saw and why he saw it remained mysteries. How far might she rise?

To his level – obviously not. So how far? Who could say? At any rate, far enough to find herself well beyond the system of possibility which she had envisaged for her life. Spending a couple of years in Washington DC was simply the outward sign of this – if anyone at school had predicted her mixing with a former black President at Kalorama cocktail parties, she'd have told them they were barking. It wasn't the going abroad which frightened her (after all, she had joined the Navy), nor leaving Cairstine for a while – as long as it was just a while. Whether Cairstine liked it or not, she would need supported housing, even though her physical health was still good.

Some of Kathy's concerns had to do with Patrick's role and motivations. He was a game player par excellence. She had no doubt that his perception of her potential was sincere, but was it exaggerated? Would he care if he lifted her sights too high? Did he care about her, really? She skipped over the possibility that being newly divorced, might he care too much and in the wrong way.

Her biggest concern about a high-flying career was the kind of person she would become. Someone who would learn (by having to pretend that she already did it) to think about the realm of top jobs as her career habitat, her natural savannah. Someone with limited chances of return to her system of original possibilities, what she had dreamt of as a child. That system might consist of a handful of undistinguished planets circling what Alan would definitely call a very 'ordinary' sun, but it was her home.

With Zack, in Kathy's mind the issues were clear-cut. Kathy didn't doubt that Zack cared deeply for her, and for people more generally. He would have no difficulty moving to Washington to support her career, and a change of scene might banish creeping disappointment for a summer. Maybe they would have a baby. Yet although Washington clocks were five hours behind London, they ticked at the same rate. Returning to London aged forty-five and no further ahead would be a recipe for re-doubled scariness. In Kathy's mind's eye, Zack was accomplishing nothing beyond burning up his forties one day at a time. 2020 could be, and had to be, a breakthrough year for him. Somehow his relationship with Bob would be part of it.

West of the bridge sat Buckingham Palace where the new order of things in Britain had been inaugurated less than two hours earlier. The Prince Regent's standard was flying. Had the Queen withdrawn from public life because she could no longer tolerate its odious idiocy? Had dementia had taken her, as it was taking Cairstine? Could whole countries forget themselves, lose the plot and start spouting nonsense?

A greylag goose wandered across the bridge on foot with the self-satisfaction of a sergeant major. Oddly for a royal park within sight of the Palace, the railings on the bridge were almost identical to the ones in the council estate she had known as a child – tatty light blue. Bathed in the perpetual collision with the Atlantic, the Scottish railings had rusted more.

By the time Kathy had stared at the Palace for several minutes, to her surprise she realised that she had the germ of a plan. She stood there unmoving for a further fifteen minutes before she acknowledged that it was more than a germ. She would return with the plan Patrick wanted.

More than that, Kathy decided, she would return the compliment he had paid her. If he wanted to go ahead with the plan, she would explain, he would need to think it through properly – it involved detail which was far beyond her, and which she didn't want or need to know. Crucially, she decided to insist, Patrick would need to present the idea to Zack as his own.

19

London, Tuesday 12 May 2020

A quarter to eleven, day five of the BG government. In fifteen minutes I go LiveChat to the whole country from the Green Drawing Room. Angela's just tweeted that it will be the biggest live audience for any British prime minister since VE-Day. I make her right. Officially we're publishing a 'White Paper' called 'Housing: Our National Priority', but as far as I'm concerned, at noon we're putting on the web the first British priority homes areas – national in dark blue and local in light (Vigilance members will get the info via an added-features app).

From noon today only Britons will be able to buy homes in the dark blue zones. From next January, only Britons will be able to own homes there. In the light blue zones local authorities will be able to decide whether to copy. And clap your eyes on this – we mean only Britons who have paid proper income tax for the last three years.

The buzz of making things better just like that for everyone you grew up with is ... it's totally amazing. One hundred per cent. In the next twenty-four hours, this government will deliver more affordable homes for Brits in places we want to live than any government in my lifetime. You don't believe me, I get it. We're sick of politicians' lies, and you're thinking – who's to say I'm any different? I say, stick around and see for yourself.

Thirteen minutes to go and some muppet has hired a truck from Pinewood Studios to turn Downing Street into Santa's grotto. Snowflakes in May. I mean, really? With global warming?

'The dickhead who fixed that,' I bellow at Bill, gesturing out the window. 'Cut his nuts off!' Bill's a bird, she's the youngest of my private secretaries. Friday I found out I have four private secretaries. Quick as a flash I said, 'OK you're all called Bill. Economies of scale.' LOL.

Turns out it's for real, a freak snowstorm. After my LiveChat the front page of the *Evening Standard* screams 'Hell freezes over' and underneath: 'Economists predict 45 per cent London house price fall in twenty-four hours.'

Calm yourself dearie – forty-five per cent is the fall for foreigners or companies because you've got to sell. Makes sense for that to be the *Standard*'s headline; it's owned by a foreigner, right? For Brits like you or me, we're talking fifteen per cent. Price-wise we reckon your gaff will be back where it was back in about 2018, that's all. OK, we're talking the pits of 2018, when the bankers and debt crisis had us all by the goolies. Still, we're dealing with the bankers, right?

Bill is reminding me of my appointments this afternoon. What makes her so goddamn sexy is Pilates. I asked her, she told me, and all my staff are going to do it. (What's the point of being prime minister if you can't get all your staff to do Pilates?) Just look how she hangs it all together, slinking past the desk like a pole-dancer's python.

Bill's not just the youngest of the Bills but the best – by a distance. She got her degree from the same place Jack went (the University of the Elephant and Castle to you and me)... Same place, different bloody outcome. No prizes for guessing where the other Bills went.

Just this morning it turns out the young Bill and I were both fans of *Borgen*. 'The first series came out in my final year, 2010,' she says. 'All of us studying politics watched it. And then Helle Thorning-Schmidt became prime minister of Denmark for real.'

'I watched it because 2010 had been my first General Election. Back then, politically I was a waste of space – UKIP, would you believe.'

'The third series was a bit off.'

'Too right. Fortunately, by then Angela and I had started to build a twenty-first century party. The first thing we said was it had to be really popular with youngsters. Did you vote for us?'

Bill laughs. 'You know I'm a civil servant, I can't answer that. But I can wink.' She winks. I love it.

Already people ask me what were my first words when I got through the door of Number Ten. I tell them straight: 'Was any of this tat Churchill's?'

Of course, none's the answer. And we wonder why we went downhill? Now we've got one of his desks up from Chartwell and put it in the Cabinet ante-room, roped off like in a museum.

At the weekend we wrapped a banner around Big Ben saying 'under new management'. The Union Jack fluttering in a blue sky above the clock face, and underneath that the banner – would you believe the video of that was the hottest thing on the internet on Saturday? That's the internet *like in the whole world*, right?

Britain's Great! End of! Fancy a pint? This kicking arse is thirsty work.

***

You sit yourself right there, get a good view of the action. No, you're not in the way at all. Meet my mate Zaf, Zafir Khan. Zaf likes standing, so we're sorted. What do you reckon: we're three minutes out of 'government land' and into this pub – hand pumps and glass, brass and wood, the whole lot polished up like a tart's wedding ring. Zaf runs his finger over the tables, no marks or anything.

'What my mother calls "proper English",' he says.

His finger pauses on some unexpected dust. Fair enough, with the occasional thuds from the ceiling. Upstairs Shock News are installing broadcasting gear like you would not believe.

So this Whitehall boozer, the Red Lion, claims to have been the local for every prime minister until Ted Heath. After that, with the IRA and what not, the later ones bottled it. No doubt they started necking supermarket special offer packs instead like the rest of us (not). Anyway, a pub called 'The Red Lion' couldn't have been more perfect for BG, yes? Annabel came up with the plan.

Here on the ground floor we have LiveChat cameras. They look slightly larger than the ones every pub has for security. When they're broadcasting a tiny light flashes. Microphones are in the brass chandeliers. It's all part of doing Prime Minister's Questions our new way.

I explain the deal to Zaf. Every Wednesday we'll run a raffle for half a dozen MPs to ask questions. No special deal for the Leader of the Opposition – some traditions have to die, and anyway, the rabble still can't agree who it should be. Right now we've got four of them claiming the job. What a shambles! Still, it means we can crack on while the old parties protest to Mr Speaker about car parking.

Wednesday lunchtime the MPs from the raffle will be here in this pub. We'll fill it with punters no problem – picked, obviously, but ordinary Brits from all over the country. The tickets for the first Wednesday sold out in three minutes. I'll arrive, get a round in, show the MPs who's boss and then get on to the real questions. Trust BG – a prime minister you can have a drink with *and he'll buy his round*. Punch and Judy in the House of Commons – end of!

'I love it, boss.' Twenty-five years as a London cabbie have hardly touched Zaf's Brummie accent. He takes a gulp of lime and soda.

Zafir Khan MP, Secretary of State for Transport. When I told him, you could not believe his face. Together we've just made the three-minute stroll across Whitehall in the afternoon sunshine.

We bowed when we passed the Cenotaph. Actually, no-one planned that; it's just something I started yesterday. Then Angela said it would be really good if all Cabinet Ministers did the same. So we get out and stand side by side with our drivers whenever we're passing in our cars. It buggers up Whitehall traffic but what the fuck? It's a great message, because it never crossed the mind of the ruling class to do it.

'How's the Department of Transport coping with a boss who has actually worked in transport?' I ask Zafir. 'One who's done the knowledge, in fact.'

'Well, Uber are wetting themselves.' We both giggle. 'To be honest, boss, I haven't found the civil servants as bad as you said.'

'They've made you a private prayer room, facing Mecca?'

'Lambeth Palace, actually. But how did you know?'

'Don't let me down, Zaf.' I tap my nose. 'You're slacking. Those box sets of *Yes, Minister* didn't go round the Cabinet at the weekend because I wanted to shorten everyone's Christmas shopping list.'

'Yeah right, boss. I'll definitely watch them next weekend – that's a promise. Anyway, thanks for seeing me today. That was really helpful – all the departments have got the picture. We'll announce our drones policy in four weeks.'

'Our backers will cut us some slack, but slack's not a word I want anyone in my government hanging around with.'

Zaf and I hug and he waves goodbye.

***

I've finished the Japanese craft lager, a very nice drop, but a pint of Pride will be the better image for my next appointment – Patrick Smath. Here, he's on LinkedIn. Cambridge. Eton as well. Happy days!

Amazingly, all that pricey education wasn't completely wasted. I check Patrick out as he comes through the Red Lion's door. The LinkedIn studio shot looks like it was taken yesterday, which means he's started looking for his next job. Smart guy.

'You must be Pat.' It never hurts to land the first blow. Demonstrating my knowledge of the British constitution – we pay him to do what I want – I make him get two pints of Pride and some pork scratchings. 'I think your office had a bit of a brain failure, Pat? I was never asking you to brief me on the nuclear deterrent in a pub. We'll walk over to my gaff after just the one. But I like to get the measure of a man over a pint. Best way, I reckon. And best to do it before any shit hits the fan.'

Pat eyes the foaming head on the hand-pulled ale. He has the lips of a man bracing to drink washing-up liquid. Still, you have to do these things to collect a knighthood. He lets some words out. 'When that happens, Prime Minister, let me guess – you'll be the shit and I'll be the fan?'

I grin. I do like a bit of class – always have.

***

The black door inscribed 'First Lord of the Treasury' is already opening as Pat and I pass under the wrought-iron lamp. The door and the lamp on its arched supports date from the 1770s, when the original house was near enough one hundred years old. On the door this afternoon is Aude from Nigeria, a walrus with a wrinkled nose of kindness and don't-mess-with-me fangs. She called me 'Bob' from the off, so I've taken to her. She sniffs my breath.

'Oh my, Bob, and did the Good Lord remind you to settle your tab? I'll not be going into no record books as the first doorkeeper at Number Ten dealing with bailiffs.'

'It's all sweet, Aude. Pat paid. Remember, I'm counting on you to get me that chair with neither of us getting nicked.' I'm talking about the black leather Chippendale beside us in the entrance hall: it's a hooded number and retro, perfect for my man-cave at home, with sixteen surround-sound speakers recessed into the coving.

'You do it like I told you, Bob, and we'll both be fine. Paint up your van as Bermondsey Furniture Restoration. Don't be embarrassed, I can help you with spelling. In the morning I'll pin a note on Mr Chippendale saying he's due a clean and then I'll be at my hairdresser's all afternoon, having a facial and manicure. You reverse up and finish the job. Trouble is, you politicians are all talk and no action.'

At the top of the grand staircase I pinch myself. In the last hour a photograph has been installed, knocking all the other inhabitants of the house down one peg. Bowing to tradition the photo is black and white, but shows a shaven-headed man considerably younger than most of the others, wearing a golf shirt with the top two buttons undone. Cameron in 2010 looks as youthful as me but more Starbucks caramel *frappuccino*. Me, I'm more *latte macchiato* with no sugar.

The White Drawing Room is the best room for windows and light. It's being fixed up as my office. 'Sorry about the tip,' I say to Pat, who mutters something about Rome not being built in a day. Two embroidered sofas went yesterday, leaving their cousin arm chairs – yuck. They'll be gone the minute my white leather ones arrive from the Eton house. My glass desk and lucky white Herman Miller Sayl deluxe are in, of course, and one corner has a couple of rubber gym mats. Gym mats on deep pile carpet is pretty crap, and at the moment I've only got stuff for bench presses and squats, but we're getting there. Wishy-washy landscapes were banished from the walls on Saturday. I swivel round in the Sayl while Pat sorts himself out on an armchair.

A clock on the mantelpiece announces tea in Downton Abbey – another piece of crap which hasn't died yet. An old Bill (LOL) is lurking in the doorway – Annabel would like some time with me in half an hour. I nod and signal him to leave us on our own. If Pat can't tell me how to destroy the world in less than half an hour, he's not the man I think he is.

20

London, Tuesday 12 May 2020 (2)

'This is the first of four briefings on our nuclear deterrent, Prime Minister. All the briefings are secret and personal to you – for your eyes and ears only. The first two normally take place on day one or day two of a new government.' Pat pauses.

I tell Pat not to overdo the pointed silences, he might prick himself.

'Prime Minister: be flippant if you wish, but these briefings address the circumstances in which you might order more people to die than have been killed in all wars to date. And our shared responsibilities to our North Atlantic Treaty partners in deploying a force of this magnitude. Call me old-fashioned but so far I haven't spotted the subject's funny side.'

Pat stands up and looks out into Downing Street from the other side of his armchair. I'm engrossed. This man's intelligence is ornate, painstaking, beautiful if you like that kind of thing – like the armchair's embroidery. Any use to me? We'll see. Pat's right hand smooths the crease in his trousers and then balls slightly, as if he is going to fight. I've been spotting give-aways like that since I was six. Well I had to, to make dad bugger off eventually (Jack didn't do nothing, of course; just got a book on substance abuse out of the library). Now the fingers of his left hand are extended like finely tuned violin bows on the armchair's top.

So, he's going to try to play me? Good luck to him, he'll need it. Recently out of a relationship I see – a whiter shade of pale circles his wedding finger.

'Today's briefing is concerned with the authority which you alone in this country hold...' – again a pause – '...to order the firing of our submarine-based inter-continental ballistic missiles. That is so long as you lawfully remain prime minister. As a safeguard, the authority of the Chief of the Defence Staff is also required.

'In the next few days you need to choose two of your colleagues as your nuclear deputies. These are the individuals, normally Cabinet Ministers, to whom you entrust your authority in the event that you are incapacitated or communication with you becomes impossible. When you have made your choice, the Cabinet Secretary and I will arrange for them to be briefed.

'Today I am also explaining to you the four identical letters which your predecessors since Harold Wilson have written, and which you now need to write, giving instructions of last resort to the commanders of our *Vanguard* submarines. These letters are only opened in the event that any of those commanders, deployed on patrol, determines that communication with the government of the United Kingdom has ceased and will not be recoverable – for example following a devastating nuclear attack on this country.

'Your second briefing will be conducted by your private office. They will show you the video link from this building to the submarine command centre and the procedure for an authorised launch order. You will practise this drill every six months.

'Thirdly, the Chief of the Defence Staff will brief you on the destructive power of different targeting options – for example using different warheads or scatter patterns, or a ground-burst versus an air-burst. He will also cover the schedules of targets held ready to be loaded in the event of a period of heightened threat. More schedules can be prepared if you judge it necessary.

'All the information I have described has the highest national security classification. Except that there is a final piece of the jigsaw, called ACERBIC, which has a higher classification still. That will be for you and I to go through at some point in the next few weeks, in a room in the MOD Main Building set aside for the purpose.'

ACERBIC? News to me. 'So my forerunners and yours have been playing footsy in a bunker in the MOD since Harold Wilson. Very cosy.'

Pat relaxes his guard a millimetre. 'ACERBIC has only existed since John Major. You could say he invented it.'

I don't usually fidget, but I am swivelling to and fro in my Sayl. After Pat's effortless superiority, I make it time to get the organ-grinder and the monkey back into their places.

My hands are palms upward. They move in circles. There are forty-two muscles in the human face, and all mine are gym-toned. I strike an awestruck note. 'All this incredible power. What do the Yanks call it? Shock and awe. Has it worked all these years, would you say Pat? Kept things on the rails? Running smoothly?'

Pat can stand taller and he does (Pilates, I wonder). 'The selfless men and women who make the deterrent work have done an outstanding job. Trident, and Polaris before it, have kept the peace. And your manifesto backs the Dreadnought programme.'

'Expands it to six boats, in fact.'

'That's right.'

'But when I said shock and awe, Pat, I wasn't thinking about fission and fusion. I was thinking about your briefing. Every new prime minister comes along, and from day one in Number Ten – well, in my case, day five – a mandarin like you swanks around, scares the shit out of us and ties us up in secrets so we can't move. So things keep running smoothly, which means the way *you* want them to. So is that why we have a nuclear deterrent – to keep democracy safe in the hands of experts? Experts like you?'

'With the greatest respect...' Pat stops, seeing the next punch coming.

'*Yes, Minister*. Great series. Perfect for Boxing Day afternoons with a glass of Scotch, wouldn't you say? But maybe you're more of a port man.'

Try the civil servants' emergency brace position, why not? Everyone should practise it occasionally. 'Our role is simply to advise, Prime Minister. To put such expertise as we have at the country's service.'

'At the country's service, Pat? Or at my service?'

He doesn't miss a beat. 'At your *lawful* service, Prime Minister.'

It's ridiculous but something bugs me about the fact that he's taller than me. I stand up anyway. At the same moment Annabel Wale and the sound of laughing crash through the door, followed by a hapless, oldest Bill and three of Annabel's girl-friends from college in Essex.

'Deputy Prime Minister,' says Pat, slightly off-balance. A good moment to strike, and I don't intend to lose it. General Wale is of course Deputy Prime Minister and Secretary of State for Defence, with responsibility for all four of our armed (well, within twelve months the Vigilance will be armed) services.

'I heard you were here, Patrick,' Annabel replies. 'But actually I'm just showing the girls around. Bob, join us when you can?'

I nod and tell Bill to get cracking on a couple of buckets of Prosecco. No, Bill, not bottles, buckets – ice buckets, more than one, with more than one bottle in them... Yes, in the living room of my flat upstairs. Give me strength.

The interlopers withdraw. I return to Pat. 'So, be of some lawful service, then. If you can. Show me your expertise. Tell me something about the letters of last resort which I can't find out in some book by Peter Hennessy. I'll give you a clue. I've read three books by the prof. He's top man when it comes to books on Britain's government.'

Pat rises to the challenge. He says with one hand on the door: 'Decide whether to target Coulport, or leave it to the Americans. You know, national pride, that sort of thing? The kind of shit decision that's right up your street, Prime Minister, as far as I can work out.'

***

When Pat's gone I look at the Ordnance Survey map for Loch Lomond and Inveraray which another Bill has laid out on my glass desk. Gare Loch is a thumb of water pressed hard against the witch's finger of Loch Long. The Royal Naval Armaments Depot Coulport sits on the finger, barely two miles as the crow flies from Faslane on the thumb.

However the crow's path is of no use either to warheads trucked in road convoys from Berkshire to Coulport's mountain bunkers, or to Faslane's submarines, which need to U-turn in the Firth of Clyde before docking at Coulport to be armed. Ever since the Yanks first invented the atomic bomb, barring the occasional Cold War spy, they have kept their nuclear secrets to themselves. From Faslane our submarines travel to Kings Bay, Georgia to pick up and return our Tridents. A bit like a time-share, we own a share in the missile pool, not any missile in particular. But our warheads – up to twelve on each Trident, each with its own target – have to be Limey design and Limey manufacture, and they live at Coulport.

And so to the puzzle which Patrick left me to work out. The puzzle wouldn't have troubled Harold Wilson in 1968. Then, if any of his letters had been opened, Britain would have been lying under a Soviet nuclear cloud, spiralling perhaps out of an incident in Cuba, Czechoslovakia or perhaps behind the Iron Curtain in Moscow. Obviously not just London but Coulport and Faslane were on the Soviet list to incinerate within the first minutes – end of.

But today Britain might be beheaded, politically and militarily, by a catastrophic attack on London which leaves Coulport untouched. Maybe untargeted, because the terrorists don't need to bother – for them London is plenty. Or perhaps Coulport is targeted for conventional attack, aiming to nick the warheads. And so – Pat's point about the Yanks – how long before the United States takes preventive action? Churchill would be their role model – we struck the French fleet after the fall of France: Mers-el-Kébir and Dakar, before finally they did the decent thing and scuttled themselves at Toulon. Do we do the decent thing and drop Loch Long into hell ourselves, or do we let the Yanks do it to us?

'Bob!' exclaims Annabel from the open door, Prosecco in hand. She's in a pink shirt dress and bare feet.

Don't even go there. I'll give you a clue: she's got a partner. A partner who looks like Nassia Sotiris's daughter.

I say, 'Five minutes, honest,' and the Deputy Prime Minister retreats to shrieks of laughter. The Bills have prepared a list of 314 individuals who have phoned to speak to me since the election (the first thing they seized was my old mobile, 'for security'. I didn't argue once young Bill explained how easily it could get me assassinated). I rifle through the list to S and there is Professor Nassia Sotiris and her number in Oxford. She called Saturday morning to offer her congratulations. The

Downing Street switchboard connects me to the number but it goes through to voicemail.

**

It's half midnight and I'm doing papers in bed when Nassia calls back. At this time of year, the chances are she's been marking exam papers.

'Bob! I can't believe the switchboard put me through.'

'I told you, anytime up to half one. Don't you know, I'm the Prime Minister now? I get to lie in bed doing my red boxes till at least half one.'

'Every night?'

'I reckon. For the foreseeable, anyway. So midnight's a great time to call, now the switchboard know who you are.'

'And you are in bed?'

'Deffo.'

'And you're wearing?'

'Deffo.' After a few seconds we both chuckle.

'Well, many congratulations! You've made it to Number Ten.'

'One Etonian beat me to it. They got one prime minister and one near-miss.'

'Forget that – yours is a historic achievement. Enjoy it.'

'Thank you. Come to dinner and enjoy it with me.'

'Anyone you have dinner with is news. I'm not sure I want that.'

'What's the problem? Neither of us are married.'

'The news is a cess-pit. You're so close to the guys at Shock News, you don't see it.'

I laugh. 'Oh *the guys* at Shock News? You mean Angela. You're jealous.'

'Jealousy's not something I do; you know that. Except I am

jealous of my sleep. However, besides congratulating you, I wanted to make sure that you haven't forgotten my Christmas present.'

'We're going to announce our policy tomorrow. We want Guinness World Records to certify it as the fastest fulfilment ever of a political promise.' Nassia's present was a promise that if I got elected, I'd fix for European academics to stay in Britain. Don't just fix it for me, she said; remember how Britain benefitted from all the scientists who fled from the Nazis. Which reminds me of that weird play of my brother's – I forget what it was called, but Nassia got me to read it. I'll tell you about it some time.

We air-kiss and finish the call. The adrenaline of the last fortnight refuses to die down, so I'm knackered but can't sleep. I think of my predecessors watching from the main staircase and wonder which of them slept in this bed. None, probably; I seem to remember the furniture in the flat is private. Probably Annabel organised my bed, in the same way she organises everything else.

The last two papers I read are the Treasury's latest private numbers on the 2018 bank bail-outs (Jesus wept! We so need to fix those bankers), and an analysis of the likely European response to us breaking the rules of the single market – our nationality rules on housing, for starters. Seems the EU are looking to hit us hard and fast – faster than legal proceedings and fines. Bringing trade to a halt would hurt them as much as us, so what else can they throw? Hippolyte Ducros, the President of the European Commission, has tweeted that Europe can be 'as creative as the UK is insolent'. Bring it on!

Level with me: you can feel it surging through you, can't you? The buzz of change?

21

London, Wednesday 13 May 2020

Deputy Prime Minister Annabel Wale announced today that Britons living in the EU who wish to remain in those countries should register on the Fair Immigration website in the next thirty days. EU citizens living in the UK who wish to remain here should do the same.

General Wale said, 'BG will negotiate vigorously and confidently on behalf of Britons who want to remain in Europe. Here's the deal: for every Briton accepted by the EU, we will accept one EU citizen in Britain.'

Rules published on the Fair Immigration website state that to qualify, Britons must be up-to-date with their UK taxes. If more EU citizens want to live in the United Kingdom than Britons wish to live in Europe, points will be used to allocate places, with preference given to business owners who generate employment; surgeons, doctors and anaesthetists; and individuals with scarce skills or advanced technical or academic qualifications. Currently 3 million EU citizens are estimated to live in the UK and 1.2 million Britons in the EU.

22

Gare Loch, Tuesday 19 May 2020

Cairstine stood on the spit, brought by her neighbours Barry and Joan. Kathy waved from the submarine, so Patrick followed suit. Cairstine was partly obscured by half a dozen serious walkers. Patrick and Kathy were easily close enough to see the red, white and red of Austria stitched into their knapsacks. But Cairstine's wig was exposed rather than obscured. To judge by appearances it was receiving a testing from the brisk south-westerly breeze which it hadn't received before.

From the shingle strip, Kathy and Patrick were obvious: Kathy in her officer's tricorn and jacket with sleeve lace (two and a half gold bands and a whorl), Patrick in a pin-striped suit and a John le Carré tan raincoat. Both wore slim-line inflatable life-vests. They were standing on *Vengeance*'s hull just behind the main fin. Further astern two ratings finished making the boat ready to vanish for two months. Before then a helicopter would winch them off.

Before cast off, from his breast pocket Patrick had produced a slightly crumpled, stiff hand-written envelope for *Vengeance*'s commander and executive officer. They had watched while the commander had locked the letter in his personal safe. Then Patrick had presented gold pins to members of the crew who were starting their twenty-first nuclear deterrent patrol. They had spent four, perhaps five, years of their lives waking and sleeping in a steel tube; an underwater tube shared with the end of the world.

'What's four years?' one of the crew had replied. 'I've spent that long waiting for Microsoft to download frigging updates.'

When they were topside Kathy commented that Bob's letter of last resort had looked a little crumpled.

'I'm afraid so. My last resort was to use a hair-dryer on it. Unfortunately my spaniel took too close an interest in Bob's plans to guide us into the after-life.'

'You didn't replace it with a letter of your own?'

'I might have been tempted,' Patrick allowed. 'Just for a minute.'

Patrick and Kathy were riding more than ten feet above the waves, but standing on a hull with curved sides and no handrails was disorienting. They were head and shoulders above the little sailboats and motorised bath toys in Rhu Marina. *Vengeance*'s conning tower rose three storeys above them, her masts and periscopes higher still. Beneath their feet was a mini-city, population one hundred and thirty-seven. Gannets performed a diving display off the port bow.

Gare Loch receded behind their flotilla of guard boats. To Kathy the sea on which, and beside which, she had grown up was a comforting blanket. Today the blanket was pewter and bronze, zipped together by *Vengeance*'s white wake. Sixteen black circles, like an eight-by-two blister pack of lozenges, stared up at her from the submarine's hull. The diameter of each circle was longer than Kathy herself. Pop one lozenge for a giant headache.

The Prime Minister could take the decision to 'pop one' anywhere in the world. The authorisation would need forty minutes to get from the bowels of the building in which Kathy worked to *Vengeance* at an unknown location. Fifteen minutes later one of the covers at which Kathy was staring would open underwater, expelling a sixty-ton missile in an amniotic cloud of steam and gas. The missile's motor would ignite when it had cleared the watery deep. For thirty minutes the missile would arc through space, steering by the stars before chucking its warheads at targets 4,000 miles from the launch point. At which point stand by for a really giant headache.

Turning west, *Vengeance* passed the ranks of seagulls perched on the capsized hull of the *Captayannis*. The wreck had sat half-sunk in the Clyde estuary like a broken paving stone since 1974. In that time the miners had been defeated, peace had been negotiated in Ireland and the British economy had been blown to pieces four times – once a decade, like clockwork.

The south-westerly wind had nudged the channel between Largs and Bute into a gentle swell. Fine salt spray picked up by a gust struck Kathy on the cheek like a fencer drawing blood. When she had been a young girl, Kathy had spent hours on the seafront at Helensburgh, sniffing the air, dreaming that if she tried hard enough the Gulf Stream would bring her the smell of peat from Ireland, or juniper pollen and hot springs from the Azores. One day West FM had reported a deposit of sand from the Sahara.

At the other end of the Gulf Stream, close to the northern tip of Florida, sat Kings Bay, the American base to which British ballistic submarines travelled to exchange and service their missiles. Kathy had once spent a weekend with a university friend camping and cycling in the local parks: they got close enough to the wild horses on Cumberland Island's beaches to imagine brushing down their coats of chestnut and pebble. If events put her and Zack on the other side of the Atlantic, she would take him to Cumberland Island. Kathy sniffed the air again, straining for the least hint of horse-breath or saw palmetto. But what was in the wind today was the smell of betrayal.

Patrick's lips faced empty sea and receding grey-green hills: he had no intention of anyone other than Kathy reading them. 'For a couple of nights I didn't sleep well, but now I'm fine. Something somebody said to me helped. I want to pass it on, in case you've been getting the same heebie-jeebies.'

Why are you telling me this? Kathy thought. She had given Patrick the idea, but on condition that it became his idea. She had offered her child up for adoption. Now it was being unwrapped from a stranger's shawl, to show her how it had grown. The relationship between herself and Patrick had changed. Not romantically, at least not on her side: for Kathy power was no aphrodisiac. But she sensed Patrick moving on eggshells, for once the novice and not the expert. For once he was in a club with unfamiliar rules.

'Commander Special Forces lives by need-to-know. So he was very happy not to know. But four days ago I met the team he picked. How would they react? I had no idea.'

Kathy's curiosity got the better of her. 'How did you present it?'

'You know me – as part of a war game, of course. In the past forty-eight hours we had uncovered suggestions of a plot to remove the Prime Minister at some point during the next few months. But large parts of the plot were entirely opaque. We needed a team to put themselves into the shoes of the plotters. Game it. Figure out the missing pieces of the jigsaw. So that when the time comes, we can all do our duty. It was the thinnest of disguises, intentionally so. I needed to know whether we understood each other. To be honest, I felt sick waiting for their reply.'

'And?' she said.

'The four of them looked at each other. Then the captain

said, "Thank God one of you's got the bottle for it. We were wondering if we would have to do it on our own". '

'So you're sleeping again.'

'I am.' Patrick's gaze shifted, warning Kathy that the onus of the conversation was also about to shift. 'But they're not. The team is good. They've identified the need to move very fast. I'm inviting you and Zack to dinner this Friday. I'll make my pitch to him then – as my idea, of course. It will be good for the two of you to have the chance to talk it through afterwards, over the bank holiday weekend.'

'That fast?' Kathy gasped. 'How quickly do you expect to act?'

'Not quickly, but Zack will have some hard training. He'll need to put on a few kilos. We'll arrange acting school so he can walk like his brother and talk like his brother, and think like him too – albeit just for a few minutes. But I can't see us lighting the touch-paper for a while yet. BG will have to do something so horrific that the opposition parties agree to work together.'

'But does it have to be this weekend? We were planning…' Kathy bit her lip.

'Yes.' Patrick was quite firm. 'Zack's been videoing a few sketches of himself as Bob.'

'Yes, Troy thinks he can start his own YouTube channel, get a following and then get a contract. He's planning to show Troy what he's got next week. Oh, I see.'

Betrayal was stickier, messier, blacker stuff than Kathy had rationalised. It had got onto her fingers like fingerprint ink. She had persuaded herself vigorously that in no sense was she betraying Zack. Patrick would lay the whole idea out over dinner, persuasively no doubt: Zack could get rich (well, rich by Zack and Kathy's standards), give the acting performance of his life, do his country a favour and put the boot into his brother.

But Zack could walk away. Concealing that Kathy had come

up with the idea didn't restrain Zack's freedom. In fact, if he wanted to laugh the scheme out of the park as crazy, he'd suffer no embarrassment on Kathy's behalf.

While she had been thinking, she had missed something Patrick had said. It turned out to be about Cairstine, whether leaving her behind would be an issue. Kathy pointed out that it was something which she and Zack had already discussed, given Patrick's ambitions to post Kathy to DC.

'Good,' said Patrick, resuming his customary role as a chess-master of the universe. 'But I mention it now because I thought you might find it helpful, ahead of Friday, to ponder some options. We can whisk both of you out of the country for a new start somewhere else, once it's all done, if that's what you want. We could hardly do less. But strictly speaking, it wouldn't be necessary for *you* to end your Navy career so prematurely.'

'You mean Zack could do the whole thing on his own.'

'Might I speak objectively – like a benevolent relation, if you will? At this point your career prospects and Zack's are rather like chalk and cheese. You would be giving up a lot more than him. Bear in mind that it would be perfectly possible for us to connect the two of you in, say, DC, in some months' time. When any fuss has died down.'

'Meet him in his new, improved persona? Fall in love with each other all over again?'

'What a charming thought. Don't mention the possibility to my ex.'

'I'm not letting Zack sink or swim on his own. That really would be betrayal.'

Patrick's eyebrows circumflexed. 'Betrayal? Don't even think of it. You're Zack's most important champion and support, his rock. You're helping him rise to the professional opportunity of his life. He's fantastically lucky to have you.'

'Someone probably said something like that to Lady Macbeth, don't you think? Or Judas Iscariot.'

Patrick ended the conversation by squinting at the Lynx helicopter which had appeared some miles astern.

23

London, Tuesday 19/
Wednesday 20 May 2020

Returning to Putney close to 11pm, Kathy braced herself for ten minutes while Zack explained his latest idea for a Bob Grant video sketch. He reckoned he could put it on YouTube with only two other actors, a busty female and a Manuel-type from *Fawlty Towers*, but there was no point incurring that expense before he had three solid hits in the bag: this would be the first of them, he was sure. Kathy nodded and then buried herself in an unclassified report with six appendices entitled 'Winning Through Focus: Why Taskforces Fail' (aka WTF2). Zack failed to see how this could be more important than congratulating him on his creative genius, or discussing why Patrick Smath had invited both of them to dinner at The Shard in three days' time. However, he was wise enough to crack open another couple of beers and let she-whose-alarm-was-set-for-quarter-to-six do her thing.

The following day, Wednesday, Zack despaired of turning his inspiration into words. The idea was simple enough: desperate for relief from a ghastly international summit, Prime Minister Bob demands a massage. He is offered every variation imaginable – Swedish, Finnish, Indian, Native American and Thai – but he insists on a Great British massage, end of. By 2pm the comic ingredients remained unassembled, laughing at him instead of the other way around.

Rather than waste the afternoon Zack rallied his house-keeper energies instead. He summarised his progress in three sequential voicemails for Kathy, describing not finding a cross-head screwdriver in its proper place, cracking the light bulb casing inside the refrigerator and returning from the DIY store (a twenty-minute walk) with the wrong size of bulb. The third voicemail explained that he would seek a consolatory pint in The Rear Admiral. Zack omitted to mention that midweek The Engineer had a two-for-one happy 'hour' from four until seven.

Having lost Tuesday to *Vengeance*, Kathy's Wednesday was frantic. At first after the election it seemed that there would be nothing for the residents of Whitehall to do. New BG policies simply appeared, dropped out of the sky like pigeon shit. But for sustainable shit production on an industrial scale even the new lords of the manor needed the bureaucratic machine. The catch was their insistence that only a hand-picked few among the most senior civil servants – Patrick, for example, which in practice meant Kathy – could do the work.

When she got to the day's messages on her personal mobile it was gone seven-thirty in the evening. In London's permanent rush hour, the train home was still standing room only. Intermittent reception and endless train announcements meant that extracting even sixty per cent of the sense of the messages took Kathy from Waterloo to Clapham Junction, at which point she rolled her eyeballs. She had waded through a message from her bank and an offer on data bundles from her phone company before she got to Zack's three-voicemail-dirge left at 4.20pm. That was followed by three voiceless messages from his phone: at 5.23pm the sound of jostling hub-bub like a party; at 5.58pm a lot of people shouting; and finally a text at 7.18pm: 'With Alan. LBV. Come. Important. Zx'.

For most of the ten-minute walk from Putney station to Le Bon Vin, Kathy made an uncharacteristic spectacle of herself, shouting at the air.

Like anyone partnered to a sometimes-functioning alcoholic, Kathy knew The Rear Admiral's happy hours without having to be told. Important? she yelled at a passing piece of street furniture. Tell her about important. Yesterday in Gare Loch she had helped deliver an envelope which could kill millions of people, whose contents had been written by a certifiable idiot. Today her husband, mortally wounded by his inability to change a light bulb or string together enough jokes to fill an envelope, had got so happy before the end of happy hour that he had gone on the razzle, to the point of not knowing when he was pressing the speed dial on his phone. Having collided with Alan somewhere, the boisterous carousel had now ended up in LBV, whose lamentable *steak-frites* would be the excuse for no dinner on the table. Still, some of the day's frustrations had burst their dam and flowed towards the Thames by the time Kathy pushed open the wine bar's doors.

Entering Le Bon Vin, Kathy saw Alan at a table alone. His jacket was dishevelled and his head out of joint, with a dried streak of blood. Notwithstanding Alan's alarming appearance, what Kathy stared at first – it was so striking that she had no choice in the matter – was six customers wearing regulation yellow Bs stitched onto their clothing. Alan was wearing his B so that it clashed as loudly as possible with his cream jacket and grey and pink checked pants (a souvenir from Naples, Florida). He had started wearing a B since the election as a protest, even though no legislation had been passed. Something had happened to turn protest into compliance. By the time Zack appeared with two blood-stained dish-cloths and ice in a bucket, Kathy realised that her rage belonged outside.

Alan's silhouette was fighting the Battle of the Bulge. There was a price to pay for retiring to gorge on *raclette*, but Alan negotiated a handy discount by visiting his custom tailor once a year.

At fourteen Alan had discovered how handy it was, with girls and housemasters alike, to look intelligent. To borrow his own pejorative, the contents of Alan's forehead were pretty ordinary – enough for some kinds of banking, but with nothing to spare. However it was the forehead itself which did the trick. His eyebrows raced forward like forested ridges to join his nose, suggesting he was decisive. His eyes sat in shadowed ravines, conveying depth. The ridges and the squirrel-grey meadow of hair above had not thinned too much, and Alan's eyes could still flash with mackerel to show brilliance or pleasure – as they did now, seeing Kathy. This evening above the north-east ridge he was nursing a cut and a rivulet of clotted blood.

'What happened?' Kathy exclaimed.

'Nothing much,' Alan replied. 'Pretty ordinary stuff under this government.'

'A fire-bomb,' said Zack. 'Another one. Now you're here, Kathy, how about some *steak-frites*?'

At two in the afternoon Alan had led a protest in the local shopping centre, outside the shop taken over by The Vigilance. A core of two angry former bankers (Alan and his friend Deirdre) had been joined by, of all things, three nose-ringed activists from Labour for a Kinder, Gentler Britain – Alan thought their policies were nuts but at least LKGB were 'willing to get off their arses to save human rights'. Together the five had painted a giant yellow B on the blacked-out Vigilance shopfront. For the first half of the afternoon the atmosphere had been light-hearted.

The few Vigilance members who showed their faces appeared nonplussed, and the protestors tweeted away, joining with fellow protestors in the City, Croydon, Leeds and Edinburgh to bat back the predictable online abuse.

The idea behind the protest was to paint Bs on property paid for with bank loans and mortgages, starting with properties linked to BG. That way bankers could protest their stigmatisation and point out their usefulness (ultimately nearly every property in Britain would have a B on it), while the left-wing could uphold human rights and point to the cancerous spread of debt.

What really changed things was when four car-loads of Vigilance foot-soldiers arrived. At that point Alan texted Zack, 'We might need witnesses'. Soon after Zack got there, two police constables gave up trying to keep the disputing groups apart. So the mismatched gangs pressed into each other's space, bawling out abuse, spittle and promises to kick each other good and proper. Alan and his co-conspirators gave as good as they got ('at least we could spell the swear-words we were using') but they were outnumbered and surrounded, and Alan got knocked to the floor.

'I saw Alan disappear but I couldn't see what had happened. I couldn't understand why there weren't more police,' Zack said. 'In fact I was asking the constables why they hadn't called for reinforcements – they said they had, several times – when someone threw a fire-bomb through the shop window. Suddenly flames and electrical fumes were everywhere. Thank God the shopping centre's sprinklers came on. Everyone ran. Alan and I found each other in the car park. By then there were drones galore. I put my jacket over Alan's head and we came round the back way to here.' He lifted his right sleeve to show blood stains underneath.

Kathy's hand went to her mouth. 'Why didn't you call an

ambulance?'

Alan shook his head. 'It was nothing, Kathy, really – just superficial bleeding. Quite a lot of the ambulance service have joined The Vigilance too. Since the election, it's quite the thing to do. Just the ticket if you want promotion, or a quiet life.'

'So who threw the fire-bomb? LKGB?'

Alan shook his head. 'I don't believe they would. Besides, we were completely surrounded. None of us had room to throw a punch, let alone a fire-bomb. It had to be someone on the outside of the group. Maybe not someone who looked like part of The Vigilance, but someone they organised. Fire-bombs are their way of doing things. I think they did it themselves, but so it looked like us.'

'Inside a shopping centre there'll be video, that's for sure. Another bottle?' Zack offered. The two of them had finished a pinotage from Lammershoek. Alan decided to switch to water, so Zack retreated to the bar to get a glass of house red for himself, and a white wine spritzer for Kathy.

On his phone Alan pulled up the image of a face, half-hidden by a scarf. 'The Vigilance have already released a video still of the fire-bomber. I think it looks quite like me.'

Kathy grabbed the phone. 'No!' But it did look a bit like Alan – certainly the individual had the right forehead.

Alan shrugged. 'Photoshop, obviously.'

'But what's the point?' asked Kathy. 'To create trouble? Just for the hell of it?'

Alan gestured around the bar. 'Did you notice all the Bs when you came in?'

'I could hardly miss them. What's happened?'

'So you didn't catch this afternoon's announcement.'

Kathy closed her eyes. 'I've been up to my eyeballs. Annabel Wale is mad, but you knew that.'

'So, this from the Home Office, at half past four this afternoon.'

Kathy scrolled down on Alan's phone: it was an announcement from @BGGov. *Bankers and former bankers – to improve your safety and community relations, always wear your B in public places from tonight.* 'All right,' she said, 'but where's the policy statement? The Order in Council? Parliament hasn't even voted on the policy yet.'

Alan shook his head. 'That's the old world, Kathy. This is the policy – this is the legislation. It's a tweet. No, I tell a lie – they've also abolished human rights. Here's Bob himself, on the steps of Buckingham Palace:

> *British rights are defended by the British sovereign. That was good enough for Magna Carta, and it's good enough today. That's why I'm delighted to say that the Prince Regent has agreed, when he succeeds to the throne, to assume the new title, Defender of Rights. Claiming bogus international 'rights' is stabbing this great country in the back. The lawyers' gravy train is over. Britain's Great! End of!*

Kathy's head swam.

Zack reclaimed his seat. 'Time for some light relief? I think so.' He flipped the lid on his own phone and went to the *Guardian's* website. 'Check that out.' *That* was an article with the title, 'If your grandmother can't remember the Sixties, maybe she's still there.' Zack was hooting. 'Recreational drugs are turning out to be a big problem with the new generation of old people. The thing is, if you got into them, it makes sense to do them in your seventies. I mean, you've got the money, you've got the time and you've got bugger all else to do. Why pollute the planet taking holidays? It's not as if they aren't popping a dozen different pills anyway.'

Cairstine taking illegal drugs at 78? Kathy couldn't work out whether the idea was more or less nuts than Jimmy Keohane's pretend dementia. 'Of course!' she snorted. 'And I know who Cairstine's dealer is – Meghan.'

'No, Kath, here's the thing. The article says, in eighty-two per cent of cases, the nearest and dearest haven't a clue it's going on, and when memory loss kicks in, the old druggie can't remember what they've taken or where they've put their gear.'

Kathy's memory wasn't perfect but she knew exactly where she had left her rage outside LBV's door. She had her hands back on it in less time than Zack would have needed to recite all the lines he had ever spoken on a West End stage – four.

24

London, Thursday 21 May 2020

The first dinner anyone can fix between Angela and me is weeks away, so I've given the Bills a bollocking, basting the offending parts of their anatomies with *piri piri* sauce. Annabel had a good tip to make up for the wait – get Angela round late one evening for a glass of bubbly in the Cabinet Room. So that's what we've just done, the two of us alone, me in the Prime Minister's chair (the one with arms in front of the clock), her opposite with her stockinged feet up on the table. We compare notes on how yesterday's Prime Minister's Questions from the Red Lion came over. A fortnight into the BG government and the ratings haven't dipped yet. What's on Angela's mind is drones, and Europe.

'Zaf is totally clear on our drones policy. Trust me, he and I went through it ten days ago. He'll be announcing it in a couple of weeks. For three years we'll only allow two big commercial fleets – Shock News for media and news, and Gargantua for deliveries.'

'We think it should be five years. We discussed five years.' Angela's wearing a white jacket and trousers and a black shirt buttoned low. Tonight her orange curls are tight and high.

'We did, but Zaf has got to make the policy stack up as a trial period, balancing new services with the public's safety. Three years is the most that the civil servants can come up with, to work out safe new rules of the air. Then we let everybody compete. But by then you and Gargantua should be so far ahead of your competitors – imagine, three years with no other media organisation allowed to use drones! Not even the Beeb.'

'OK, but until you get the policy out there, we can't move. Until then that's staying top of my commercial agenda. Top of my viewers' and readers' worry list is Europe.'

'I hope you're not worried?' I ask. 'We've ripped up the single market rule book already and no-one's done anything about it. Result!'

'Up to a point. But everyone knows a showdown is coming.'

I begin, 'After the Tory Brexit fiasco we haven't come all this way to bottle it...'

'That's for sure. That's so for sure.' She's distracted now, speaking as if to one of her five hundred best friends.

It's tough to have better information than Angela but sometimes I do. 'The Polish prime minister and Ducros will be in Toulouse tomorrow. Airbus will announce moving wing manufacture from Broughton to Katowice in Poland, and R&D from Filton to Toulouse. That's ten thousand jobs gone directly, a multiple of that in the supply chain.'

'What's Ducros doing there? Airbus is supposed to be an independent company.'

'He'll announce big infrastructure works to move the wings. The A380 wings are huge motherfuckers. Plus some European Defence Corps contracts. He's been pushing European defence hard ever since Britain got out of the way.'

'Your plan?'

'Arrests at dawn tomorrow for the CEOs of our major banks. They'll get bail, but still.'

'Our cameras will be there?'

'Of course.'

'That'll keep Airbus off the top of the news but our readers are still going to want our European push-back.'

I roll up my shirt-sleeve to my left elbow, showing her the scar from the stabbing. 'Don't wind me up. We'll be pushing back.'

A smile of acknowledgement flickers over vermilion lip gloss, then catches fire and becomes a grin. 'I know you will, Bob.' Suddenly she says, 'Look around.'

Both of us do. We pretend not to be, but we're awestruck by all the dice that history has rolled at this table. *I have nothing to offer but blood, toil, tears and sweat.* That was eighty years ago, almost to the day, in this exact room.

'Remember that day in 2010?' Angela says.

'Four weeks after the election. In your office at Shock News.'

'That day David Cameron and Nick Clegg were making love here, and in the garden downstairs.'

'I'd failed to win my seat with UKIP.'

'And I told you that you could be prime minister. No-one had ever told you that before.' Angela's ready to go. She knocks back her drink and climbs back into her Maison Margiela toeless ankle boots. I show her to the stairs where one of the Bills takes her out the back way, through the Cabinet Office.

I don't tell her. Who would? Everyone likes to think they're the first, and what harm does it do? But that wasn't the first time someone told me I could be prime minister. My first time was when I was about to turn sixteen. I had got the earring but not yet the knife wound. The guy who beat Angela to it was seventeen, and his name was Jules.

25

London, November/December 1994

I'm five foot ten, an inch taller than Jack. I pretty much shot up to that height when I was thirteen, which made me taller than Jack, even though he was fifteen months older. Puppy-turned-into-a-beanstalk wasn't a look I fancied, but protein shakes, doing weights and shaving my head fixed that. Acne was number two (as in Jack got it but I didn't). I'm cleverer with my hands than with my feet, so I was more rugby than football. I'm even better with my brains, so fly half in the under-sixteens was perfect. When it was time for the under-eighteens there were too many bigger and taller players so teams were less interested. I guess that was mutual.

When I was fifteen, towards the end of November we get thrashed at a school near Windsor Castle with boys in penguin get-ups and heated changing rooms. Twenty minutes into the game a tear in my hamstring starts killing me. From then I'm about thirty per cent, if that. By the second half I'm doing more harm than good, so I come off.

The only guy watching the game and I exchange words. He's about seventeen, six-foot, a balletic build – too shapely and dent-free to be a rugby player. His skin is the colour of the outside of a Mars bar (mine's a pale version of the nougat inside) so he sticks out from his white school-mates. I look up and down his lambswool pullover, pre-washed jeans and calfskin loafers with no socks as he stands on the muddy grass. My school gets thrashed so badly there isn't much to say about the game, but at the end the Mars bar offers to drive me home. It would save a journey on the world's slowest train, plus a couple of buses, but is this for real? My face says as much.

'Bermondsey, right? Your school's there, right? That's why I came to watch the game. We've just got a new place there.'

Well – la di da. One of the penthouses on the river, obviously. Well, look at it another way – maybe I do a recce and turn the place over sometime. 'All right then,' I say, putting my hand out. 'I'm Bob.'

'I'm Jules,' says Jules.

Fuck me, his car turns out to be a white Sierra RS500 Cosworth. He goes up even more in my estimation when he kills a really wanky song on the radio – East 17 trying for a Christmas number one with *Stay Another Day!* – in favour of Carter USM's *Glam Rock Cops*. The car's got more speakers than Hyde Park – and by the time we've gone half a mile beyond my local Tesco and arrive at a boat in the new marina, I'm almost ready to join his weekend love nest. Almost.

Jules is gay – he says so pretty much straight up – but that turns out not to be what's going down. He got caught with a few Es. The school has a new gaffer who is determined to be a stinker on drugs, so Jules has been suspended. He might get back in in January but that depends on Dad pausing for breath long enough to persuade the gaffer to do the right thing. Dad is coining it in Singapore, third generation Old Etonian, banker; Mum was Congolese but dropped out of Jules's life while he was in prep school (whatever that may be). This winter will be a bore because in a few weeks' time skiing could have been an option, but the house in Switzerland has been rented. Gimme a minute while I burst into tears.

So Jules has just got himself this floating base in Bermondsey with a residential mooring – running water, power, phone line, the lot. Call it a cross between an unloved canal boat and a Victorian warehouse. In it he plans to trade some stocks and shares, maybe some options, because the gaffer might not take him back or dad might not get his arse in gear for his only son. The lettering across the stern says MEERMIN, Dordrecht.

'So the boat just stays here all the time, does it? And you own it?' I say, as Jules unlocks a padlock the size of his fist. He opens a hatch into a space three times the size of my ma's flat – two decks, three bedrooms, full-size kitchen, study, living room, you name it.

'Yes. My dad bought it but in some kind of trust for me. Don't ask, it's all about tax, or alimony. What do you think?'

I think my life has just changed, but let's take it easy or I might scare Jules off.

'I live about ten minutes that way,' I say, pointing at the large council estate. 'Looks to me like you're sorted. Maybe catch you around some time – go for a drink.'

'That would be great. I don't want to go into a Millwall pub by mistake.'

I laugh. 'There aren't any others, really. But if you get shot of those jeans and keep your mouth shut, you can fix it all with the help of a hoodie and some trainers. Black skin goes down better here than where you were.' Jules looks at me, so I go on, 'I'm a touch tantastic myself. Apparently my dad was half-Egyptian. That'll definitely help me pick him out in a line up.'

We swap phone numbers. Jules has a to-die-for Nokia 232, of course. I saw one the other day at Carphone Warehouse – £50 new or half that with an airtime contract. They might as well have put a sign in the window saying 'not for the likes of you'.

***

Ten days later Jules hears that the school will take him back in January, and we meet for a drink in the Prince of Wales. He's taken my tailoring advice but I buy the first round with his money, because his accent will cut through the chatter here like a foghorn. He asks what's up with me, and then suggests I move into one of the spare rooms on MEERMIN. I realise that he fancies me but I reckon I can handle it. He'll be at school most of the time, and whatever he wants he can't be short of it there. I say yes; my heart is pounding because there's a much bigger prize.

I'll buy a sleeping bag and just bring clothes. I ask Jules to teach me how to trade stocks and shares. If I can hack it, I'll drop out and earn both of us some money while he parades around school in a penguin suit. Jules thinks someone smart with a modem, a landline, a mobile phone and time to kill has an advantage, if they know what they're doing. He tells me about Bloomberg terminals. It seems I don't have to be smarter than the American bankers with those, which suits me – I'm confident but not crazy. I just have to be nimbler than pimply pension fund clerks and perma-tanned golfers who get to the share prices in the *Daily Telegraph* after lunch.

I'm so up for it. 'It gets me out of our shit-hole and beats getting up at 5.30am in the morning to fix stalls in the market for a fiver.'

'Won't your parents mind?' Jules asks. 'You leaving home, living on a boat?'

'What parents?' I reply. 'The last man to live in our council flat was a skag head. I threw him out six months ago – that was one of the benefits of getting tall and going to the gym. My ma is out of her tree half the time. She thinks her main job is making sure that the fridge is empty. Then there's my brother, Jackshit.

Well, Jack, technically. He does my head in as well. He's older but he just kind of lets it all happen? He's not bringing in anything, and says he wants to go to uni. Of course Jackshit was nowhere to be seen when I told skag head to take a hike.'

I slip a hand down into my boots and take out a knife. 'In case skag head and his mates try to jump me one night,' I explain. Jules is a little pale. I buy the second round.

For all that our backgrounds are different, there's funny ways they are the same. We both learned to drive when we were fifteen. In Jules's case that happened on the country estates of friends. 'When you're a tart at Eton you get to choose where to spend your holidays,' he explains. He's pretty enough for it, I can see that, but I don't want to know any more.

To get to drive, me and my friends have a different thing going with the assistant manager at Tesco. He can't be arsed with clamping commuter cars from Kent which get left all day in his car park – it's far too much grief and the cars are back the following week. So he tells us which ones to lift, and turns a deaf ear when we set off the alarms – nice.

Nice is also this rave in south London Jules and I are going to for New Year's (supernice is that Jules will have an ample supply of readies). Soon we'll see if I can make some of my own from stock trading. Over the holidays we spend two days together travelling financially back in time, working out trades which might have been worth doing in the week before Christmas. I learn fast.

Other times our journeys are in different parts of the Milky Way. I remember the time Jules announced, 'William is coming to our school next September. Maybe to my house.'

'William who?'

'Prince William. I saw Diana leaving our house a few weeks ago. I'll be in my last year. The house master might ask me to look after him.'

A brown gay boy looking after Prince William? Dream on, my friend. Now William's mother's another story. Jules's skin is really soft and smells of coffee grounds. That and his pop star haircut for New Year's Eve – part romantic flop-over with highlights and part number two on the side – they might be just a princess's thing. It seems she might like a bit of dark. Go on, you could always swing the other way for your country.

26

London, January 1995

January dives down to a record -27°C in the Highlands and wraps the north of England in duvets of snow. But London thaws out, so that by the end of the month the capital is a giant leaking municipal swimming pool with puddles in the changing rooms. Jules is stopping over this Saturday evening. School is normal, he says, although another boy got handed over to the police for dealing. As for my stocks and options, I'm up about 250 quid on the month. Before you open your gob, consider what I started with.

I swear I hear the Cosworth but it's a good twenty-five minutes later when MEERMIN's hatch bangs open and Jules steps inside, his leather satchel at the ready. The temperature drops ten degrees in as many seconds. I'm watching National Lottery Live with my numbers in my hand – everyone I know is doing the same, the Lottery's less than three months old. Jules is bemused. 'The head of maths says we should call the Lottery the stupid tax. If you're gagging to make a donation to the government, just write them a cheque.'

Jules's head of maths can't add one and one. One, who else is giving me or anyone I know the chance to be a millionaire? Two, horse-racing, the football pools, whatever, he's against them, right? Because he's against anything where my chances of winning are as good as his. Where he comes from, that's not how the world should tilt.

Jules tries to throw the point back. 'The chance of winning the jackpot is one in forty-five million. You've got more chance of becoming prime minister.'

'What?'

'There are forty-five million voters. Two or three of them will become prime minister. Much better odds.'

'Who the fuck wants to be prime minister? I'd rather win the jackpot.'

'Clarence, Archibald and Harvey. That's just in my house, and school's got about thirty houses. You're smarter than any of them, so you could become prime minister. Definitely.' Jules starts running the shower. Tonight the shower will take five minutes to achieve a warm piddle.

Prime minister? Jules is taking the piss. He shrugs his shoulders. 'But I never said the odds were fair. We're up to eighteen now – prime ministers from Eton, that is.'

Over the last month I've kind of had it up to here with Eton. Each time it's something else – we're special at this, and then that, and then the other. Fuck me, if any school in England tailors a special jacket and invents first, second and third teams for base jumping, it will be Eton. And they'll invent peculiar rules so that no other school can beat them. The Field Game, the Wall Game – if the battle of Waterloo was won on the playing fields of Eton, it was because nobody from Eton thought to play by the same rules as everybody else.

As usual Jules is in the shower for twenty minutes – the fastest I've seen is fifteen – which makes him the cleanest boy I know. A plastic shower tray is rigged up in a corner of a cabin, screwed to wooden floorboards. Around it manky curtains and a heat-as-you-go electric box on the wall don't stand a chance against tonight's weather. I can hear the fan heater on full blast. The shower tray drains into the bilges but however you shower, you'll wet the planking.

The shower goes quiet and then Jules comes out, towelling his head with his right hand and clutching a YSL toiletries bag in his left. He's gagging for me to give him a once-over, so I do. I take in the whole six feet of waxed mahogany sculpture – shoulders tapering to the waist like a diagram in a geometry book from the 1950s, dozing pythons for hamstrings. And I mean waxed – no hair anywhere.

'What's your tattoo?' I ask. He shows me six letters, FREUDE, curving round his butt like the crown on the Statue of Liberty. 'Like the psychologist?'

Jules laughs. 'No, it's the German word for joy. Get it?'

So do I get it? Meaning, of course, do I get any joy from that particular aperture? I want to say – is that any of your fucking business, really? You're pushing your luck there – count yourself lucky I don't punch you in the mouth. But help yourself to the following nuggets for free. Jules doesn't trek to the south-eastern edge of the known universe one weekend in three because I whisper sweet nothings in his ear (not my style, really). Plus his anus gets worked over plenty in Slough. To cap it all, he's not coming for the quality of the shower. I know, I used their changing rooms after the game. Let's put it this way – it does take me a while to get it, if by 'get it' you mean understand what's really going on.

***

It's a fickle Friday night in early March. Half an hour ago it was mild, now it's nippy. Jack is sitting on one of the cast iron marina benches, ten yards from MEERMIN. We cycled here from the cinema complex in four minutes. He's minding our bikes and supposedly keeping an eye out. At least six cigarettes in the packet of Marlboros I bought him to keep him quiet have died already (he's still whingeing).

When it was mild we bought tickets to *Star Trek Generations* at Surrey Quays – the late show. We walked in through the lobby – in front of the security cameras, natch – and slipped out through an unarmed fire exit. We'll be back in time to exit through the lobby. This job is the cushiest doddle ever – for God's sake, we're breaking in because Jules wants a favour – but oh no, that's still big drama for Jack. Jackshit likes drama – he wants to go to uni to study it.

I pull on my gloves and fill the external burglar alarm with a long blast of cavity wall expanding foam and open the padlocked hatch doors with my key. I chuck that padlock and key into the dock and scatter the innards of a different smashed padlock on the deck.

It takes me fifteen minutes rather than Jules's ten to unscrew the shower tray and slide it to one side (I assume he spent a few minutes having a shower). I lift the cut plank in the decking, check out what I find and decide what kind of scene to leave – innocence or violation? Violation, naturally. I empty a few drawers onto the floor. In half an hour I'm done, with the stash re-wrapped to keep it safe from Jack's curious eyes. I set the alarm off as I leave but the foam has well and truly set. A dead cat on a sofa would create more excitement. We cycle back to the cinema via what Jack calls home – I need him to store the package for a couple of days.

When the movie finishes we nurse a couple of late TGIF pints in Spice Island, watching the Thames surge inland from the North Sea. A boaty told me the tide peaks at Teddington an hour later than here, but it doesn't go on to Eton because the

Teddington lock stops it.

Jack says, 'Tell me the story,' so I do. Jules is dealing. Nothing super-heavy – just Es from what I've seen in the stash – but visiting a boat in the marina every two or three weeks suits him well. He revs in, visits his supplier and then drops in on MEERMIN to sort out his cash and working capital like any businessman. In this case they're in a compartment under the shower tray. He decides MEERMIN will be less conspicuous if someone lives on her, sees that a school from this neck of the woods is playing, comes over and scores lucky me. I'm happy as anything, learning a trade, out of school, out of home. I tell Jack I can't understand how he still stands it.

He says, 'Sunday's ma's birthday.'

'So? She'll stagger in at four or six from her night out, and expect you to get her eggs and bacon and beans when you get up. The fridge will be empty, so you'll get the shit bacon from the Muslim corner shop. Why are you playing her game?'

'It will be her fiftieth. Come on.'

I roll my eyeballs and get back to the story. Two weeks ago that bank on the telly goes down – Barings. A billion dollar loss run up by a trader in Singapore while no-one was watching. Jules's dad was supposed to be watching so he vanishes into the night (to Bali, if you believe Jules) with not a word to anyone. Bali beats bail, that's for sure. Jules hears it all from the school after the police in Singapore phone up. Oh and by the way says the housemaster, in a most nicey-nicey way, while your trauma as a young person with a parent on the run from the police is *absolutely* top of our mind, come to think of it your dad is behind on the fees. Since his employer is now bankrupt, come September when you start your last year, there won't be the usual financial contribution from them. Correction – when you start what would have been your last year. Doesn't time fly when you're enjoying yourself?

That weekend Jules is definitely the worse for wear – who wouldn't be? – so he gets caught. The gaffer's having no dealing, least of all from someone who isn't able to pay the fees, so it's straight on the phone to the Old Bill. There's no posh parent to bail him out. He sends me a text message: waiting to be nicked, ha ha what crap, don't forget the shower tray needs a good clean.

Jack's not the sharpest tool in the box but he gets there. 'Jules just asked you to clean out his stash. He didn't say anything about burgling the boat.'

I shrug. 'I've been living on the boat. Do I fancy being done as his accomplice?'

'Instead you're going to report being burgled.'

'Yeah. In an hour or so, when I get back. Like any good citizen. We're sweet – we were at the pictures.'

'Did you put the shower tray back?'

'No, on account of it being a burglary, not a visit from Keep Britain Tidy.'

Jack starts pacing around. 'Like, they're burglars and they didn't take your computer.'

'They're suppliers. Maybe they're owed money. They knew what they were looking for.'

'You've stuffed him, you know? You're such a shit, I can't believe I have you for a brother.'

'I've learned to look after myself.'

'You never look after anyone else.'

We have a tussle outside and then stop. 'Look at yourself!' I say. 'You don't even know who I'm rabbiting on about. Trust me, he's got suitcases full of pounds looking after him. And talking about looking after ma, what use were you when it came to skag head? Jackshit by name, Jackshit by nature.'

It turns out badly for Jules. He's in jail on remand – imagine how FREUDE goes down there. I go see him and tell him it will only be for a few weeks if that. I keep his spirits up with how my trading is doing: with £3,000 to play with from underneath the shower (it was in cash and Es), my results are starting to add up. But Jules is wilting. Liquidators have seized the car – it was on some under-the-counter finance deal his dad had fixed at the bank. The cops didn't find too much on him, but there were traces in the car. Plus they're throwing the book at him for driving without insurance.

The last time I see Jules is in Belmarsh. He tells me, 'There's always a way out,' but his heart is caught in a bear-trap a long way away from the edge of a dark forest. The forest has been growing for a long time.

The last time we speak he's ended up at Chelmsford. I ask if it's a low security prison. He replies, 'Essex is a low security prison'. I guess it's his way of saying that there's nothing for him outside. I say no-one has come for the boat yet, but we know it's a matter of time. It's also a matter of time – just a few weeks – for Jules to work out how to get into the art room after hours and hang himself. Put it down as part of the havoc created by his dad.

Whom you will have spotted was a banker. Traders play the markets with their own money, but bankers use other people's, losing over a billion dollars of it in Barings' case. They think the rest of us will never learn. Maybe one day everyone will get the shock of their life and we will.

27

London, Friday 22 May 2020

Dinner at the Shard needed preparation on all sides. Patrick's timetable included cover for one of his increasing number of off-the-radar meetings. Kathy imagined him stepping into a time warp – rolling up the collar of his tan raincoat, slipping into the public toilets at Charing Cross station to put on a moustache, before trysting at the quiet members' bar in the Royal Society of the Arts with the leader of the special forces team. But she didn't know.

Kathy had left Zack a note about his light grey suit which she had ironed. Zack had been solicitous and hugely apologetic after Kathy's explosion at Le Bon Vin, mortified by his childish regurgitation of fancy theories about Cairstine's 'hallucinations'.

In the car with Patrick, Kathy scrolled through the news. The bank CEO arrests were still attracting huge volumes of comment, mostly ecstatic: the Metropolitan police had well and truly brought the 'perp walk' across the Atlantic. Half an hour ago a trade union leader had vowed that the families of Broughton, 'man, woman and child', would lie in the path of any trucks attempting to remove manufacturing equipment.

'Magnificent. And if they win, they make wings for what?' was Patrick's response. 'Policy everywhere is a total fuck-up. Can nobody think any more?'

'The French consul is in Filton announcing plans to build "the best English grammar school" for families who relocate to Toulouse.'

Zack was standing outside the podium of the Shard having a vape when Terence dropped her and Patrick off at 8.20pm. With the light grey double-breasted he wore a light blue collarless shirt and a bold blue Los Angeles Dodgers baseball cap (to divert attention from his shaved head). The outfit gelled in an improbable way. Kathy felt under-dressed in her officer daywear; Patrick had changed into a striking Italian suit in white and metallic tones. He was the Shard in miniature, elegant, wealthy and ridiculously clean, the suit's colours matching the glint in his hair and rising to a commanding peak.

Watching 'her two men' together, Kathy knew that Zack was a decent human being through and through. In the last analysis she had no idea whether Patrick was a decent human being. He got within touching distance, but somehow there was always smoke and mirrors.

Patrick guided them effortlessly through the first course and mains, ordering unusual wines like a gourmet Riesling by the glass. The restaurant was half way up the Shard, so their bread rolls and extra virgin olive oil sat on a level with the top of the Walkie-Talkie. The restaurant's tables were close together, so their conversation was laced with generous helpings of a dog-walker's failings in Milwaukee and a pianist daughter's triumphs in Shanghai.

Had Patrick made a mistake with the venue? Of course there was the view, but how would he raise a deeply secret proposal in such cramped surroundings? He would have a plan, Kathy didn't doubt that for a minute. For the time being Patrick seemed content to chew the fat with Zack in a mates-together, TGIF way. They compared notes on Richard Deshaye films, Patrick's favourite being *A Long Afternoon in Paradise*. Still, Zack wasn't going to say yes to what Patrick had in mind simply because the wine cost £25 a glass.

Their table was on the east side so not positioned for any sunset. However they had an unimpeded view out towards Canary Wharf and Greenwich. Kathy watched the surface of the Thames being dimpled by the passing of party boats. Even at this hour, the railway lines out of London Bridge writhed with maggots – trains with white tops bearing their cargoes of decay into and out of Britain's big apple.

At a certain point Patrick glanced at his watch and pushed his seat back. 'We're having dessert upstairs.'

***

The transfer to the Shard's topmost lift, a metalled and mirrored walk-in wardrobe, took place on the thirty-third floor. Patrick and his guests were welcomed by an assistant manager in a purple jacket, but she made no move to ascend with them. Inside the lift were three buttons: 32, 33 and 68. Kathy's ears popped. The welcome party on level 68 was different – two Metropolitan police officers with bullet-proof vests and machine-pistols. The visitors climbed the stairs to floor 69. Kathy had never been to the viewing decks at the Shard before, but she grasped immediately that no-one else was there: Patrick had booked a private view. The £25 glasses of wine hadn't been the show; they had simply been the programme on sale in the foyer. Zack gawped.

Level 69 provided a wooden-planked viewing platform about twenty yards square. Steel struts painted white enclosed the space inside a four-sided prism of sloping glass three storeys high. The clouds rolled lower, oblivious to the Shard's impertinent attempt to pierce them. After a few minutes, Patrick led his guests up more stairs to the Sky Deck.

Kathy emerged on level 72 facing north. The Sky Deck – cool and spattered with rain in places – was still a decent size. Now the Walkie-Talkie was half her altitude. Above her, sloping panes reached beyond lagged pipes to the skyscraper's broken apex. At each of the four corners, the missing glass let the weather in.

On a bar in brushed aluminium, complete with cappuccino machine, sat a bottle of champagne in an ice bucket with three glasses. They would be serving themselves. Apart from the armed police four levels down, Patrick, Zack and Kathy were the only ones present.

Patrick cracked open the champagne. Quietly they toasted their respective demons. 'May I let both of you into a childhood secret?' he continued. 'Ever since I was six I've wanted to be in one of those movies where someone is up against the clock and has to save the world.' He glanced at his watch. 'So now, Zack, I have fifty-two minutes to do that. To convince you that Britain needs you. Ordinary people need you. Decency, common sense and respect need you. Maybe the world needs you.'

Kathy watched Zack smile, trying to brush the words off. She knew Zack. Yes, his ego needed stroking, especially with the way his career had been going. But this couldn't be an appeal to ego (something Patrick could do falling off a log); her boss was having to go out on a limb, to appeal to something he knew much less well – a decent ordinary man.

'Psychologists warned us that Bob is a dangerously unpredictable man. I think you know that better than any of us. He is part of a mindless politics which has weakened every democracy in the world. That mindlessness is dangerous. Ask him how the government will avert any of the many impending disasters? I have. Bob grins and says, "Britain's Great. End of".'

Zack winced. Patrick continued.

'You know you are watching the rule of law being torn up, tweet by tweet, cheeky grin by cheeky grin. But then you read independent journalism – that's rare now. Too many fellow citizens send each other streams of lies as well as selfies with cats.

'You helped us role-play what might happen to this country's security if BG were elected. You helped us wake up. But the scenarios we gave you were too tame.

'Let me stick to what I know – defence. In another couple of weeks, the Prince Regent will ride out on his horse and take the salute on Horse Guards Parade. The pageantry, the monarchy, the horse – it's a ceremony, one piece among many in our national theatre. A theatre in which we prove to ourselves that Britain is always Britain, that our summer weather is always our summer weather, that our country hasn't changed and that people, beer and walks in the country are safe.

'But a few days before the parade, ten of our generals, admirals and air marshals will retire early, their mouths stuffed shut with gold. The papers have already been signed. A wave of promotions will be announced, a generation of fresh young names, and our first black brigadier. Annabel Wale will announce a new fleet of sea-skimming boats, equipped with missiles and drones, to protect our coasts from drug-dealers, immigrants and fishing boats from France and Spain. It will all be terribly popular, not least in our shipyards. And the government will open a new shipyard in Wales.

'Among those promoted will be a new Chief of the Defence Staff. My uniformed colleagues are certain it will be Hugo Tremayne. Hugo trains every day like an Olympic athlete. His sport is inventing with intuitive brilliance what his bosses want to hear. He has acclaimed General Wale as a genius: creating the Vigilance and putting it alongside the armed forces has solved at a stroke the Army's inability to recruit reserves.

'I've warned Hugo that if he salivates any more over the prospect of additional gold braid, he will qualify for a submariner's badge. Besides, he and his uniformed brethren have failed to notice another possibility. Integrating the Vigilance as the fourth armed service means that the person who General Wale may put forward to be CDS might be General Wale.

'Why should you care, Zack, about any of these possibilities? Tonight, with the cloud coming down, we can just about see Greenwich. That's about five miles. So suppose a single hydrogen bomb exploded right where we're standing. In 1955, fifteen years before I was born, my predecessors did this calculation for a ten-megaton blast.'

Patrick pointed in a circle. 'From Buckingham Palace in the west to the Emirates Stadium, to Canary Wharf, to Clapham Common – within the greater part of what we can see, everyone and everything would be completely devastated. In a second, gone. The heat flash could start anything up to 100,000 fires, covering a radius of sixty miles. That's Oxford, Brighton, Canterbury and Ipswich.

'Now our altitude is quite low, about one thousand feet. The person with their finger on the trigger would have a choice. An air burst, perhaps at five or six times this height, would maximise blast destruction but minimise ground radioactivity. The fireball doesn't touch the ground and the radioactivity is vomited into the upper atmosphere, coming down who knows when and who knows where. But with a burst at our altitude or lower, central London would become a crater one mile across and three hundred feet deep, while millions of tons of stones and powder and dust would fall in a lethal plume from here to Amsterdam.

'If that is what one hydrogen bomb can do, each of our *Vanguard* submarines carries forty. A single Trident missile carries nearly a dozen. So now then, what does it take to order a launch in our well-ordered country, with driving on the left, free healthcare, two-for-one-offers and marching bands?

'An order to launch requires the concurrence of two people – the Prime Minister and the CDS. So it is no exaggeration to say that within two weeks from now, not only will your brother's finger be on the trigger, but the safeguard envisaged by our system of government will be gone. Our constitution is made out of old hopes and sealing wax. The barbarians have come with oxy-acetylene torches.

'Did Kathy tell you, Zack, that when you are admitted into the world of national intelligence, the experts hammer home the difference between secrets and mysteries. I have been telling you secrets: things which can be found out and known, some of which will be public within two weeks. Secrets can leak, but a mystery cannot. A mystery is something which cannot be known until it is too late. Within Bob, does there lurk the capacity, in certain circumstances, to order a first strike – to unleash Armageddon? That is a mystery. I wonder what you think.'

***

One thought in Kathy's mind soared like the Shard to a place high above other perceptions. It was a sense of bone marrow coldness when she recognised herself as co-author, perhaps even lead author, of what was happening. She felt distant and apart.

In part the feeling was trivial. Had the event been hers to organise, she would have provided something non-alcoholic to drink in the eagle's nest. But since Patrick had organised things himself, the only refreshment to hand was Mumm Cordon Rouge and (no surprise here) she was the designated driver.

Patrick would offer them a lift, but she and Zack would need to talk.

Downstairs she had had one glass of the remarkable Riesling. For the rest of the time she had been on water. She was experiencing two separations at the same time. One was the widening gap between herself, standing on the bank of sobriety, and Patrick and Zack, getting increasingly intoxicated with ideas.

But the other separation Kathy felt within herself. Someone unfamiliar inside her had made a decisive intervention in Zack's life – frankly, in her country's life – and set events in motion which could be tough on Cairstine.

How had Zack taken the flow of words which Patrick had thrown his way? Over dinner, Zack had been ebullient, relishing the flattery of attention wrapped up in camaraderie. When he had arrived at the viewing gallery she had seen him puff up. Then he had stiffened at Patrick's portrayal of peril and, reading the winces on Zack's face, he had flinched from memories of the brother he despised. Well Zack, she thought sardonically for a moment, if that's what it takes to realise *your* potential – merely that someone asks you to save the world…

But none of that paid enough attention to why she had married him. In truth, the world did not have so many decent, likeable men. He might be under the cosh of his chosen career, smoking and drinking far too much; but Zack was one of those men. That man could say no, possibly should say no, to Patrick's request.

Kathy cut in when the discussion turned to what would happen if Zack said yes, but the chance to impersonate his brother never arose. 'After six months you pay up and move both of us to Canada anyway.' This was a decision to leave behind the chessmaster's board as well as her mother. If she was half as good as Patrick thought, the Royal Navy could not be the only place where she could make something of herself.

The details of safe houses and clean phones and acting lessons (Patrick referred to them as 'coaching" and 'masterclasses') bored her, so her mind wandered from them. Leaving Cairstine would be… tough. But possibly healthy. There had to be appropriate provision, of course. She rejoined the conversation when it turned to financials – how much per month in the safe house, how much at the end, what would be provided in Canada. Plus a meritorious exit package for herself from the Navy.

Patrick's words had the splendour of the Niagara river, tugging Zack towards events visible only as a cloud of mist in the distance. Suppose that right now, Zack was close to saying 'Yes'. Yet back at Walsingham Road, the ordinariness (borrowing Alan's word) of Zack's life, his surroundings, his ambitions and his career to date would swarm back into his mind like rats up a drainpipe. Those rats could eat memories of the Shard for breakfast. By the time Zack plugged in the kettle in the morning, his answer might be 'No'.

Kathy knew her Patrick. With stakes so high, Patrick would never depend only on fine words and hand-waving. He would have organised something else, something which would rock Zack to his core.

Voilà, a photograph, a black and white glossy as if from a star's portfolio. Kathy and Zack had to do a triple take. It wasn't Richard Deshaye and it wasn't Zack; it was an ingenious fusion of the two – Zack with leaner cheeks, straightened hair and Deshaye's eyebrows.

'From the pricey end of the Witness Protection Programme,' Patrick declared. 'Cosmetic surgery. The chance not to look like your brother. To have your own face, for the first time since you were fifteen months old.'

Zack said, 'I'm overwhelmed, how could I not be? Both of us.

You want me to hide away for up to six months, to train and be ready to impersonate my brother, and then the two of us make new lives in another country. I'm blown away that you think I could carry it off. I do get that lives could be at stake, more lives than I can imagine. You're giving us the long weekend to think about it – we'll need it, for sure.'

On the Shard's glass skin the moon rose a quarter of an inch. Patrick ended the silence with, 'Of course you would choose your own look, this is just a first go. Pin it up in the kitchen and see what you think in the morning.'

Maybe the consummate professional would defeat the rats in the morning.

28

London, Friday 22 May 2020 (evening)

The traffic heading west for the holiday weekend had been in full spate since mid-afternoon and yet, gone half past nine, it had only partly abated. Zack and Kathy's journey home was scratchy and temperamental. Zigzagging cyclists, fluorescent or black, didn't help. Glancing sideways at Zack, she saw he was in the other world into which she had catapulted him, staring at his possible Richard Deshaye face.

Zack lowered the passenger window to exhale a big vape. 'If we say yes...'

'If you say yes,' said Kathy.

'If *we* say yes' Zack kissed her on the cheek. 'He says he's discussed with you some help on Cairstine.'

'Because it was going to come up anyway if we moved to Washington. Apparently there's a retired nurse who could visit. She's trusted, she used to work at Faslane. As it happens, her name's Meghan.'

'Wow.'

'It is a bit freaky, but the point is she's a mental health specialist. I mean, I guess it's not surprising Faslane has them, with all those three-month tours away from family and friends.'

'With hydrogen bombs to make up for it.'

'Cairstine's explosions will be nothing to her then!' They both laughed.

Uncharacteristically, Kathy poured out some expletives. Behind them a police car had switched on its flashing lights. Kathy was doing twenty miles an hour and left plenty of room for the car to pass. Instead of overtaking the police car flashed its headlights. As Kathy pulled over they both started at an unfamiliar chirp inside the car. Patrick had given Zack a clean phone, to call at some point over the weekend with his 'yes' or 'no'. It was vibrating next to the hand brake. Zack took the call as the car came to a halt. Within seconds, without Zack saying anything more than 'Hello', Kathy knew that something was badly wrong.

Zack looked up. 'Patrick. Something bad has happened. He wouldn't say what. He's asking us to follow the police.'

The words from the officer through Kathy's lowered window were the same. They set off in convoy towards Wandsworth.

'How did the police know where we were?' Zack mused.

That was simple enough: the new phone. What bothered Kathy more was what bad thing could have happened, and why would the permanent secretary of the Ministry of Defence be so early in the loop on it?

The descending clouds they had watched from the Shard unleashed a spattering of rain, a down payment on what would come within the hour. Kathy could have sworn their route was circuitous, but it was night in Wandsworth, a part of London neither of them knew. One Shell station with a 24-hour shop could look like another. Somewhere they turned into an office park. Lit by street lighting were offices on three sides – a six-storey 1960s concrete flat-roof, a more recent eight-storey building with sloping tiles and finally a recent twelve-storey development complete with a half-hearted atrium. They parked behind their escort on the fourth side.

'That's Patrick's car,' pointed Kathy. Apart from a soft glow from the dashboard, the car was dark.

The side where they had pulled up was a four-storey open roof car park of the same vintage as the 1960s office building, with more blue lights, police floodlights and forensic screens blocking the entrance. The low level fluorescent lighting showed few cars parked above them. Giant shadows were cast by a police floodlight on the roof level. The shadows moved as someone on the roof peered at them over the four-foot perimeter wall. As they got out of the car, a suited figure – Patrick – emerged from behind the screens and headed towards them. The lighting turned his hair into a silver halo. A uniformed officer made to follow but Patrick turned him back.

'I'm sorry you've got me again,' he said, breathing heavily. He clasped their wrists, one each. 'I'm even sorrier about the news. The Vigilance have got Alan – your neighbour. Got him and thrown him down from the car park. He died instantly.'

Kathy let out a shriek and burst into tears, hugging Zack and pounding him with her fists. His own tears mingled with hers.

Raindrops tapped a hundred questions on the windscreen. 'Why don't we sit in your car?' Patrick suggested. 'Terence can get us some teas from the petrol station.'

***

They raided the glove compartment for Kleenex. Ten minutes later they had calmed down enough to sip hot tea from Styrofoam cups, Kathy and Zack sitting in the front of their own car and Patrick in the back, the scene a dark counterpoint to the three of them opening champagne on top of the world an hour before. When she surfaced, Kathy seemed unnaturally cold and brittle.

Someone had to speak, so Zack did. 'All my life I've been

running from my brother and searching for a mission. Now I've got my mission.'

'Not yet you haven't,' said Kathy, looking at Patrick. She was hoarse, so the words came out with painful slowness. 'Both of us need to know how the permanent secretary of the MOD comes to know within minutes about a retired banker falling from a car park in Wandsworth? So fast that even his private secretary hasn't a clue.'

Silence lay between them for a minute. Zack's expression turned from puzzled to concerned.

'Kathy.' Patrick paused, calm as always. 'You seem to be wondering – why don't you just spell out what you're wondering?'

She shook her head. Her throat was clamped tight, as if in a vice.

'OK, well let me spit it out. Kathy may be suggesting that the only way I would have known so quickly about Alan's death is if I had arranged it, in order to help both of you make up your minds. Kathy, is that fair?'

Kathy nodded stiffly.

'I understand the question. I even grasp the reason for asking it, mistaken though it is. The answer is simple enough. More or less from the day we started working on our embryonic operation, 102A Walsingham Road has been watched continuously, for your protection and ours. Kathy, you are sufficiently trained to appreciate that none of this is hostile – quite the opposite. With so significant a mission, making mistakes is simply not an option.'

A second nod, slightly longer.

'At 7.45pm tonight a car pulled up outside 104. It contained representatives of the Vigilance. After an altercation, Alan got into the car. Of course we were aware that he was not just a neighbour but a close friend, and that his image had been circulated by the Vigilance after the firebomb on Wednesday.

About ten minutes before you and I, Kathy, set off for dinner the watchers asked me whether they should follow. I said yes.'

'Follow, but not intervene,' Kathy whispered.

'Correct. As you see, the car park was nearly empty so the team could not follow in without being noticed. When they saw a body fall they contacted the police. By then we were in the Shard. I only caught up with developments on my way home. As soon as I knew, I asked them to find you to meet me here.'

'Which happened within minutes because we were being tracked.'

'Yes.'

'We took a circuitous route so that you could get here first.'

'Probably.'

'They're bastards!' exclaimed Zack. 'We have to stop them.'

Kathy sighed and closed her eyes. When she opened them, she turned on the windscreen wipers and studied the figures moving round the forensic screen. 'I need to see Alan's body,' she said. 'Don't lie to me, I can see it's still there.'

Patrick sat up like a startled rabbit. 'You don't need to see the body, believe me.'

'Someone needs to identify him. You can't, and you won't want the watchers coming out of the shadows.' Kathy pushed the driver's door open.

Patrick reached out as if to stop her. 'Of course, but see him in the morgue tomorrow. The police haven't finished … you need some rest, Kathy, you've had so much to take in in one day.'

Suddenly Kathy exploded. 'I'm a naval officer, Patrick Smath! For once, stop telling me what I can do and let me tell you what I can do. I've seen a mother and baby drown in the Mediterranean as far from me as you are now. Zack, this doesn't need you – one person is enough to identify.

***

Patrick nodded, and the officer at the screen explained that a man had fallen from the roof onto the automatic ticket barrier, with extensive consequent damage to his internal organs. Kathy braced herself.

The grey and pink checked pants were stained with blood. The front of the midriff had been gouged open and its contents disgorged, creating a cocktail of blood, urine and faeces. The ridges and ravines of the man's face were largely untouched. The helpless eyes drew Kathy like silent beggars. She turned away to see Zack retching.

'I'm sorry, ma'am. Was the victim your neighbour, Alan Tinker?'

Kathy nodded.

The blue jacket bore the crest of a posh club as well as the regulation B. The rib cage had cracked under sharply angular wounds about two inches long. Next to the body the police were assembling parts representing about two-thirds of a black, metallic equilateral triangle – a Vigilance drone.

The officer pointed to the fractured chest. 'The ribs are cracked in two places from the drone being flown into the victim at speed. But the victim managed to strike back, hence the fragments.'

Kathy's organised self did the deductions. 'Assuming this was on the top level of the car park, Alan would have collapsed. He was fit but in his seventies. His bones and his balance were brittle. So how did he get over a four-foot wall?'

'With help,' surmised the officer. 'We're searching for fingerprints or trace material.'

When Zack had finished retching, he turned to Patrick. 'I'm in,' he said.

PART THREE

Stormstruck and split

29

Helsinki, Tuesday 26 May 2020

Le Conseil des Ministres, prenant note avec satisfaction des progrès qui lui sont communiqués lors de l'établissement du Corps de Défense Européen, a approuvé les déploiements initiaux suivants, à effet immédiat:
- *un régiment d'infanterie à la Roumanie (Galat i);*
- *un bataillon anti-char à la Lituanie (Paneve ž ys); et*
- *un bataillon de parachutistes et un bataillon du génie à la France (Pas de Calais).*

The Council of Ministers, taking note with satisfaction of the progress reported to it in establishing the European Defence Corps, has approved the following initial deployments effective immediately:
- one regiment of infantry to Romania (Galat i);
- one anti-tank battalion to Lithuania (Paneve ž ys); and
- one parachute battalion and one engineer battalion to France (Pas de Calais).

30

Brixham, Friday 29 May 2020

The double bed is made for one and a half, but the wooden frame is sturdy and the sheets ironed. I grab a handful of duvet and inhale good housekeeping – freshness without chemicals, smoothness without hairs and no lumpiness from having been ripped out of plastic in the last twenty-four hours. The idea that others have been in the care of my hosts and were well looked after is comforting.

The bedroom was also made for one and a half. The duvet's overhang touches the walls of the room and the wardrobe is in the corridor. But the head of the bed presses against full-length sash windows. Through them, a trawler is making her way home, trailing seagulls like a bridal veil. The gulls are muted by double glazing.

The house is like others in the row, tightly-packed, converted into holiday apartments overlooking Brixham harbour. But the wardrobe comes ready-stocked with size nine shoes with one-inch raised heels. The freezer has meals in Tupperware containers labelled by the day. Instead of a dining table there is a barbell, clips and three sets of weights in lavender and pink on a rubber mat: the friendly colours are unconvincing. On the small breakfast bar are instructions and a bag of powdered whey.

This flat is the meat in the sandwich. I'm told I have a support team who will use the triple-locked loft flat, although I won't see them every day. Audrey, the housekeeper, is on the ground floor. She's an energetic fifty-year-old who scoots up and down the stairs like an advertisement for Lucozade. I'm sure the surveillance she provides will give the eyes and ears in the loft a run for their money. Apparently the loft contents are 'very whizzy', with several of the flower-baskets on nearby lamp-posts 'playing on our team'.

I glance in the mirror in the shower room (large but no bath, digital scales to measure my progress towards another nine kilos). Next to the mirror four A4 faces have been Blu-tacked to stare back at me from laminated card. One is of Bob taken as if from a lens embedded in the shaving mirror at No 10. The other three are 'as ifs': the photo of me with Richard Deshaye's eyebrows and two other digital imaginings of me with variations in surgery and hairstyle. I take off my Zack-ish curls and enter the pine-floored living room wig in hand. This morning was too much of a rush for a once-over with the Phillips clipper.

Looking out onto the harbour is a squat, dumpy woman older than Audrey, in a feminist T-shirt, trousers and a well-worn gilet. She's short, not more than five feet tops.

'Mary Lee Gannon,' she says, holding out her hand. 'Tea?'

A review of something experimental which a Lee Gannon had directed comes back to me dimly. While the kettle boils I venture that I had expected a 'safe house' either to be forty minutes' walk from the nearest habitation or a terraced house in a nondescript suburb – a stone unfindable in a large wasteland or on a pebbly beach.

'Really?' Mary replies. 'Do you watch spy fiction?'

'Some,' I respond cautiously.

'Then enjoy your first homework,' she says, tossing across the kitchen counter a TV script. It's episode one of *London Spy*,

Tom Rob Smith's thriller spun off from a secret agent who died inside his own luggage. 'Study the scene where Danny's going to throw his phone into the Thames, also the dialogue from page twelve with Scottie. Then pick another section you like. We – or whoever is paying you – have taken over the church hall from eleven till three for the duration. Out the front door, right and then left, about five minutes' walk. Look for the church tower. When they wrote the cheque for the hire fee, I expect the vicar absconded to Barbados.'

'I'm still surprised to be in Brixham.'

Mary's eyes roll. 'Because it's full of here today, gone tomorrow holiday-makers. And this is retirement country. Which you're in because I'm retired. Fifteen minutes' drive away in' – Mary swivels, her index finger at the ready –'some direction. I value my privacy. And you are with someone retired, because – so I'm informed – we may be working together for four days or four weeks or four months. Very strange. But let me tell you that in November, I'll be with my grandchildren in New Zealand. If you haven't done your big show by then, you'll do it without me.'

Mary puts down her empty mug and pivots a large behind off a kitchen stool. 'This assignment's crazy, but isn't that what retirement's for? You're to learn to be your brother, but there's no script. I don't know what you are going to do as your brother – go on breakfast TV, chair the Cabinet or invade a small country? On that front the amount of help I have is one thing only – that you won't have to be him for more than thirty minutes, and for anything beyond polite conversation the words will be given to you. But then they tell me, you're not only his brother, but an actor, albeit one of whom we have never heard. Someone thought this might make our job easier.'

I feel brusquely ruffled. 'Well, it might.'

'We'll see. See you in the church hall in ninety minutes?'

With which she heaves herself out of my life, for now.

As I finish my tea I'm thinking myself into Danny's head. I trust that Mary will recognise my professionalism. Imagine trying to do what I'm going to do with someone who *wasn't* an actor! We need to establish mutual respect, but it shouldn't take us an hour (if that) to get out of the suburbs of technique and into the crevasses of Bob's character.

That morning we act different portions of *London Spy*, often the same bit several times. Sometimes I'm a twenty-something Danny, sometimes I'm Scottie, the wizened civil servant to whom he pours out his story, and whose love for Danny goes unnoticed. Mary plays opposite me, she directs, she breaks into improvisation, all the time watching with something on her face. Is it a frown? A scowl? I can't tell.

We start the afternoon with a DVD of silent video clips of Bob, walking, talking, sitting, standing. I'm glad we're on to the real thing. For one thing I've got used to an extra inch in my observation of the world, which I resent. From thirteen I've told myself that the difference in our heights is nothing. I'm annoyed to discover that I was wrong. She gets me to move like Bob, doing the things we've just watched.

Then we listen to audio clips – short bursts of my brother in conversation, on the phone, canvassing in the street, Prime Minister's Questions in the Red Lion, interviews, announcements, speeches, the lot. After each clip she asks me to say a few sentences. It's childish stuff and it's dragging.

By the end of the afternoon my confidence and my temper are slipping. I stand over her and glower. 'You may be here for the money but I'm here because my friend had his ribs smashed and got dropped off a four-storey block. Just get over treating me like some shit acting student. Or do you do that with all your actors?'

Mary doesn't move an inch. 'So, you can do temper. Patrick wondered about that – it seems Bob can do quite a rage.' She looks up at me. 'Tomorrow you and I need to have a talk,' she says. 'Your acting's not shit, but when you're acting your brother you are shit. Both of us need to sleep on it and figure out why that is.'

Dinner is Tupperware chicken *tikka masala* (Friday). Weirdly, *London Spy* is re-running on Sky – maybe she chose that play so I could see what good looks like? I nurse my grievances with that and a rosé from the Co-op's chill cabinet. I don't know what Mary's problem is but I *know* my brother. Not just his back story but my hacker's back door into his soul. Something I've never shared with anybody. Mary Lee Gannon, stand by to be blown away.

31

London, May 1997

Saturday morning. May 1997, the dawn of cool Britannia. Sellotaped to my bedroom mirror is the question, *What is revealed, and concealed, about the character of Macbeth by the scene in which we first meet him?* I'm cramming for my English and history re-takes at an FE/FF college. FE as in 'further education', FF as in 'fixing failures'. They're fixing me so I don't mind. Drama at uni will be my way out of an estate where all the blocks are named after Shakespeare's plays. The confusion between the two parts of *Henry IV* is massive.

I try to get out of my bedroom but fly half legs block the way. Bob is propped against the hall radiator with a can of Tennents Super clutched precariously in his fist. A dead one lies by his side on the weather-beaten carpet. Early showers of 9% lager, clearing later, some risk of cigarette ash after dark – that's the kind of weather the carpet has seen over the years.

This must be Bob's first night at home since he went to live on that boat two years ago. That didn't last nine months. Still, the money he nicked got him a flat-share.

Ma got in about three this morning. Getting her key in the lock takes ten minutes, but she does insist on banging a bottle of Château Shit against the door-knocker at the same time. That's her out – as in 'unconscious' – till lunchtime. I didn't hear Bob let himself in after three, so he might be half-sober.

'Jack,' he says, waving dregs of lager in my direction. He adjusts his limb position so I can get out of the bedroom.

Will getting to the bathroom be worth the bother if he's thrown up in the sink? Thanks to the half-sober bit, the bathroom's fine. I pick ma's polyester dressing gown off the bathroom floor and wear it into the kitchen. In England the answer is always the kettle and a bacon sarnie. Like hell am I going to the corner shop to get Bob breakfast, though, if that's why he's come round. I assert this vigorously but of course I do. Twenty minutes later his three strips of bacon lie fraternally alongside mine, deliquescing white gunk into the pan.

Bob starts fishing for £50 from the emergency stash that he knows I keep. Well, someone has to – and someone has to keep moving it around to stop ma finding it. I tell him to eff off, who's the one who keeps bending my ear about how much money he's making? But he's fishing out of habit, not need. Money isn't the reason he's come round.

'You definitely going, Jack?' he says.

'Going where?'

'To the University of the…'

'…Elephant and Castle.' I voice Bob's sarcasm for him. 'You found your way out; this is mine.'

'More classrooms and no money is *out*?'

The fact that it makes no sense to him may be the reason why I'm doing it, but I don't say so. Instead I serve up on the kitchen table. Bob's left arm reaches for ketchup, exposing his scar. 'I'm hoping you haven't got any more of those,' I say, pointing.

'No,' he replies. His eyes light up at an unopened two litres of Coke in the fridge. He pours himself some. 'Do you want to know how I really got that?'

Do I look like I give a shit? But he's going to tell me. This is the reason he has come round: I'm to see one more time his certificates from the University of Life.

'I make it a few months after Jules tops himself. People come for the boat, I get into a flat-share. I start to make some money doing what I learned from Jules, and reading up. Did I tell you I started reading the *Financial Times*?'

I groan inwardly and start another roll-up. Only thirty-five times, mate. I guess a paper full of numbers is no bad choice for a useless speller.

'Yeah, I'm getting a proper head on my shoulders. In '95 the markets are stonking. In '96 not so bad. And this year so far – pretty good. They're going to turn, markets always do. It's like the two halves of a game, except you don't know when the ref's going to blow the whistle. Punters keep cheering and whistling, thinking this is the life, except they've never seen the players change ends. When that happens they're stuffed.

'Anyway I'm not reading the pink 'un in 1995, I'm hanging out with mates who are still in school. I'm showing off some of the money, nothing too heavy, but the attention's cool. A few guys from the gangs hang round. A bit is respect, we've all shown we can fuck the system and do our own thing. And a bit is they're sniffing around to see if I am dealing, and if I am and it isn't drugs, what the fuck is it, and is it something they want a slice of. And Tel, the kid who ends up on the slab, he's one of those. You remember Tel? For a youngster he had a lot of mouth.'

When Bob tells a story, he tells a story. He has to be the centre of attention. To be honest, it gets on my tits. 'Yeah, Bob, I got it. You're with Tel, his gang are somewhere else, another gang jumps you, six against two, heroes all round except one of you dies – and that's Tel. Needless to say, the Old Bill and the CCTV caught nothing.'

'You remember well, Jack. Maybe that's why you want to

become an actor, all that remembering they have to do.' Bob cuffs me on the cheek, not friendly, not unfriendly. 'When someone makes up a nice story, someone remembering it is appreciated. Put a bit more energy into it when you're on the big stage, though? They need to hear you in the cheap seats.' He scrapes back his chair and picks up his plate. 'Thanks for the brekkie, I appreciated that and all.'

He puts rind into the bin and the plate into the sink, letting the hot tap run. 'There weren't no gangs that evening, just Tel and I. We had an argy-bargy. He was a bit of a racist cunt, as it goes. He pulled a knife but didn't know what the fuck he was doing. Neither did I, but I thought I did. I grabbed his knife and stabbed him. Fuck me he bled so much, it was all over my shoes. I thought about it, picked up the blade, ran off towards a call box, cut myself and chucked the knife. I dialled an ambulance. When they asked me if anyone else was in trouble, I said no.'

The hot tap makes gurgling sounds. I'm feeling feverish and sick. My brother thought about it and left Tel to bleed to death. He's conned me, he's conned all of us. He's lived this lie for a year and a half, effortlessly.

Bob finishes the torture. ''Course they questioned me about that later, why I said there was no-one else. But I was faint, wasn't I? Losing blood, didn't understand, saw Tel showing a clean pair of heels. Must've got confused.'

Bob's hand has landed on my arm. I back away.

'I didn't figure on telling anyone,' Bob says, 'but you're my bro. You want go to college and do make-believe, good luck to you. Why would I tell you what to do? But when the make-believe bits are over, you might need somebody's help to see the world how it really is, not how you fancy-pants imagine it might be. Guess what? That somebody might just be a shit-bag like me.'

Ma wakes up gone two o'clock. She sees two plates in the sink and vomit in the bathroom. The vomit's mine but fortunately the little carroty bits come without ID. I threw up after Bob left, craving the sweet relief of toxin that's gone. I tell her Bob came round. I also tell her I'm going to be finding myself a stage name.

She smiles. 'You're a nice boy, Jack,' she coos. 'Choose something nice.'

'So fucking nice I'll make it my real name.'

32

Brixham, Saturday 30 May 2020

On Saturday morning I'm cut with a scalpel by Tadeusz, who is to be my digital ghoster, and then slain with an axe by Mary. Tad introduces himself after my work-out with the trainer. He is a pimply twenty-year-old, the sides of whose spectacles are fat and the colour of custard. Somehow he hasn't joined the Vigilance. Tad is to see me twice a week to re-arrange my digital footprint, so that on the beach of social media my track will stagger erratically towards the water's edge. He adds short posts dated a few months ago to allude to a possible directing contract somewhere hot. A couple of pictures show cautious experimentation with beard growth. More recently I make a lame joke about becoming a tax exile and 'like' *Islam for Dummies* – all with the appropriate metadata, of course.

A few bits I have to do in person – a row with Troy, for example, in which we will fire each other in clouds of telephonic spittle. The plan is marvellous. Troy will decipher the fake row in a flash: if Zack, the lowest of the low, is dispensing with his services, then a contract is in the offing and Troy's ten per cent is about to be stolen. In the meantime Tad will create some desultory gossip among my acquaintances that *finally* something might be happening for Zack, one year tax-free in a Middle East country which is burning money to create the incense of cultural capital.

It's nothing of artistic interest but tax-free moolah in the bank, but keep it quiet because Troy will be on it like a truffle hound.

The scalpel moment comes when Tad explains how easy the job is, because apart from Kathy I have no real friends.

An hour later Mary completes the job. Archie, her Labrador, scampers ahead of us on the concrete slipways built to embark soldiers for D-Day. We walk the length of Brixham's breakwater. It's almost June but the locals aren't fooled: English coastal wind chill is showing what it can do. I have my wig and Saltrock hoodie on. Still, the breakwater, a mile away and extending half a mile from the shoreline, should afford us privacy. I tell Mary the true story of Bob's scar – a story I've never told anyone before. I'm glad the wind whips my shameful words away.

Except that for a few seconds we're not alone. A windsurfer blasts past ten feet from us at the speed of a motorbike, heading out into the Channel. The speed comes from a sail twice my height, held taut by the weight of the surfer's body adjusting to the south-westerly gusts. She is being filmed from a drone which misses us by inches, paralleling the surfer's track, both moving with no sound except for the hiss of the surfboard's wake. We watch both recede and vanish.

Mary uses her walking stick to ease herself into a sitting position on the breakwater's edge, so I follow her. Archie climbs into her lap. 'That's a big story to carry around on your own – for how long?'

'More than twenty years.'

'Obviously, it might be true. I've no magic window into that, since I wasn't there.'

Where's she going? Of course she wasn't there.

'And you weren't there either, when the fight happened.'

She's not just getting under my skin, she's drawing blood. I've shared something profoundly private and distressing about the person I have to become, and her reaction isn't anything I could have anticipated. 'No,' I protest. 'But Bob's my brother. I've known him since I was this high. He told me. He didn't have to, but he did.'

And so to the axe blow. 'What strikes me as important about the story you have told, given the work we have to do, is that you so very badly want it to be true.'

Why would I want a fifteen-year-old, any fifteen-year-old, to die on London's streets? To faint and bleed to death at my brother's callous hands? How could I want a story which made me physically sick to be true? I nearly hit her, and we argue for forty minutes.

Then, with the slow purposefulness of a salvage master righting a wrecked ship, Mary persuades me to entertain the possibility that thousands upon thousands of gallons of certainty which have seeped into my holds during childhood and ballasted my adult life should be pumped out.

Mary says that the path to my succeeding in my mission is blocked by unhelpful certainties. I'm convinced that I know my brother deeply. And most likely, once upon a time we did understand each other and were close. But then *not* being him – not in appearance, not in name and certainly not in character – became the foundation on which I built three decades of my identity. A foundation whose certainty we now need to disturb, because – says Mary – it's obstructing my seeing him as he actually is. A wrinkling of his brow, edges like flint in his voice, the swoop of his shoulders: I see what I know is there, not what's there.

'You want me to change my beliefs about Bob. You want me to believe something else killed Tel.'

Mary shakes her head emphatically. 'No! I've told you already. How would I know? Believe the story but *don't hold on so tight*.' She clenches both fists and then unbends her fingers.

'Something else might be true.' She taps her forehead. 'Acting with a closed mind is acting with closed eyes.'

'So what else might be true about Tel?'

'Lots of things. The obvious one is that Bob made up a story which he wanted you to believe. He comes one night for no very apparent reason. There isn't much love lost between the two of you yet he trusts you with something which, if true, he has every reason to keep to himself. It's ghastly. Because it's ghastly you believe it. Your brother knows you well enough to work that out.

'Maybe there's nothing accidental about the timing. You are about to go to university, a chance he probably won't have. Of course, Bob makes very loud noises indeed to say you are the foolish one. We all do this. What's Bob's payoff? The story will big him up in your eyes – big in hate rather than admiration, but needs must. Also, he gets to pull the wool over your eyes – you might go to university but he is smarter. But there's got to be a payoff for you as well, or else you wouldn't have clutched the story so tightly for twenty-five years. Is this the payoff: however poorly things go in your life, you will never, ever, be as bad as your brother?'

'That could be. I've never thought about it like that.' A cast iron bollard which can carry the weight of my world appears, and I sit on it. Where in a life do you find the rewind button?

A few minutes of silence lie between us before Mary wraps up. 'One final thing. Stop thinking that you're being asked to play the "real" Bob, some essence of Bob that starts with his secrets and seeps outward. It's a natural mistake, but there would be no point in substituting you for your brother if you were going to be exactly the same. No-one's asking you to live as Bob for several months without being noticed. Your challenge is to do something – we don't know what – which he would *never* do, and have people say, "Bob, what the fuck?" and not, "Who are you?"'

33

London, Tuesday 2 June 2020

From the BBC's lunchtime news:

The Archbishop of Canterbury, the Most Reverend Justin Welby, wore a 'B' at the funeral this morning of murdered banker, Alan Tinker. At the request of the Lord Mayor, the funeral was held at St Paul's Cathedral. All the banks in the City were represented.

The Archbishop told a packed congregation that Jesus had mixed with the disreputable money-men of his day as well as with the poor. Moreover he died when the government washed its hands of the consequences of mob rule.

Alan Tinker, 73, fell to his death in a car park in Wandsworth on 22 May. Parts of a Vigilance drone were found at the scene. A police spokeswoman said that investigations continue. 'The drone may well have come to Mr Tinker's aid but succumbed to the ferocity of his assailants.'

Archbishop Welby worked for many years in corporate finance and served on the Parliamentary Commission on Banking Standards. His office did not know whether he would be permitted to wear a 'B' on state occasions. Although the Archbishop and Mr Tinker both studied at Eton, their periods there did not overlap.

34

Brussels, Thursday 11 June 2020

From the weekly media briefing by the President of the European Commission:

JOURNALIST 1: What about the new directive on minimum qualifications for high office?

DUCROS: I find it not that interesting.

JOURNALIST 1: In future members of the Commission and heads of national governments will need a minimum of three years' full-time education post-18.

DUCROS: It's nothing, right? Currently many of those individuals have doctorates. It's just a minimum standard.

JOURNALIST 1: All the twenty-seven present heads of national governments meet this requirement?

DUCROS: They exceed it in all cases.

JOURNALIST 1: So why bother?

DUCROS: We have no crystal ball, heh? Who knows who might apply to join in the future, or seek to head up a government?

JOURNALIST 2: I get it. Bob Grant doesn't pass the test.

DUCROS: Please, be serious. The UK is not even a member. Though certainly, if it wished to rejoin, it would have to find a prime minister with at least three years' post-18 education. But frankly, some things are too unlikely to talk about. Mr Grant getting five more years' education, I mean to say.

35

London Friday 19 June 2020

Defence secrets were circles within circles. ACERBIC was one of the smallest and Patrick was its custodian. He initiated newcomers into ACERBIC's mysteries. For Kathy that meant two or three times a year finding an hour for Patrick to descend into the Main Building's bowels. Jennifer, the new Chief of the Defence Staff, or CDS, would be 'done' at three o'clock that afternoon. Bob's indoctrination had been postponed three times but should take place finally on Monday.

As to what ACERBIC's secret was, Kathy had no clue. Could she have pierced the veil? For example, could she have noticed how inactive ACERBIC was? There was no 'traffic' – no digitally sealed 'eyes only' ACERBIC messages for her boss. She was sure that the Prime Minister and the CDS wouldn't be communicating with Patrick on some gadget in a sock drawer. She knew secret gadgets froze, needed re-booting and disappeared up their own backsides at least as often as their everyday cousins. In real life James Bond would need not just Q but R, S and T (repairs, support and technical assistance); in Patrick's case she'd be the one phoning for help.

Besides, secret circles were forming and disbanding all the time. The most recent was WHITE GHOST: the destruction of any embarrassing monitoring which the intelligence agencies had done on BG before the election. After 7 May a blizzard of secret messages had flown back and forth for five days. (Patrick had commented that the only embarrassment which the agencies needed to cover up was how little they had done on the Vigilance.) But in all Kathy's time as Patrick's right hand, ACERBIC appeared to be a silent community: they had nothing to say to each other. She assumed the whole thing belonged to the tangled knot of Government War Book procedures invoked in the run-up to Armageddon.

'At ease,' said Jennifer, standing Kathy down from her salute. The new CDS had cheeks like scones smeared with cream and jam, and a grin like someone who had scoffed a plate of them. Nicknamed 'Jennifer' during officer training at Sandhurst, the full name of Patrick's military twin was Hugo Eccles Montcalm Tremayne. Sadly for the CDS, even his startling promotion last week from two-star general to four hadn't caused the nickname to fall off. 'Patrick about? I thought we might mosey on down together.'

'He'll be right along, sir. I'm sure he will enjoy that.'

'Excellent. I can't wait to find out what all this ACERBIC stuff is about.' Jennifer parked both his behind and his peaked cap with red band and gold braid on Patrick's desk, and helped himself to a *Daily Telegraph*.

Contemplating the man in front of her, Kathy reckoned it would not take long for the paunch to grow from two stars to four as well. Mind you, the days of having to go to the right school (Patrick's) to reach the top of the Army had long gone: Jennifer had attended Sherborne.

Jennifer and Patrick were like the Archbishops of Canterbury and York: separate and equal, but not quite equal. For most purposes, Jennifer had the edge. For one thing his was the second finger on the nuclear trigger, alongside the Prime Minister's. If the country was going to hell in a handcart, Jennifer was in the firing line – literally. Patrick wasn't. On the other hand, Patrick had the brains and the spider's web of contacts into Number Ten and other ministries.

Patrick swept round the corner. 'You're a lucky man, Jennifer – double promotion, lunch at the Palace and the front page of the *Telegraph* all in a fortnight. Mind it doesn't all go to your head.'

'Patrick!' the CDS exclaimed. Two weeks before he would have said 'Smath'. 'You're a good man. I thought we'd go down together. The new leadership team – being visible – working together. You know how people talk in this building.'

'What an instinct for leadership you have, Jennifer. How envious I am.' Patrick elicited the desired puffing up of the scone-like cheeks. Then the two men were gone, although one had forgotten his hat.

Kathy never forgot Jennifer's re-appearance forty minutes later, when both of them had surfaced from the building's blast-protected womb with doors of eighteen-inch steel. The cream and the jam had been wiped off the scones with wire wool. It was as if the Archbishop of Canterbury had reached that position and only just been told about the crucifixion. The Archbishop of York, on the other hand, remained totally inscrutable – except for the fraction of a moment in which Patrick looked across to his private secretary and self-satisfaction danced a conga across his lips.

When Kathy and Patrick were alone she said, 'I'm going to the safe house at the weekend.'

'I know. Zack's really looking forward to it. His coach says he's doing very well.'

'You'd tell me that even if it wasn't true.'

'Mmm, but it also happens to be true. Ideally she'd like

another two weeks, which I said looked possible. However we'll get scarcely any warning when the right moment comes. She's incredibly thorough. They've devoured footage of Bob greeting visitors in his office, or arriving at the beginning of Cabinet. Fortunately Bob hasn't the faintest idea that we've got cameras rolling on him most hours of the day.'

'CDS looked shocked when he came back from the ACERBIC briefing.'

The secretive mandarin ignored her reference. 'I did my best to look shocked when the Deputy Prime Minister confirmed he was the choice. The man's a fool. That's why they picked him, of course.'

Patrick paused to look Kathy in the eye. 'Kathy, please understand it's my job to give this one last try. Everything I've seen tells me your future here is incredibly bright. Let Zack go to Canada on his own and you'll be out there on your new posting within six weeks. We'll even switch the posting from Washington to Ottawa.'

A surge of emotion, pride as well as patriotism, caught Kathy by surprise. 'It's taken a while for the penny to drop, but here I am, at last thinking that I might be as good as you've always said. But if that's right, then I'll be able to make things work out in Canada, and not just in the Navy. Besides, it's getting fucking scary round here, don't you think? Maybe you're so used to politicians that you don't notice it as much, but I can't get over Alan. Things could go really pear-shaped. For the first time today I thought: don't be an idiot, Canada's the place to be.'

The aluminium in Patrick's eyes softened. 'I had to try but I'm not surprised. Go for it, girl. Be proud: you've already devised our best chance to save our country. Zack and I just need to walk on stage and say the right lines.'

36

Brixham, Friday 19 June 2020

It's the end of week three. Mary Lee Gannon deploys the church hall keys with practised ease. Archie darts in through the door of the eighteenth-century church hall to curl up in a corner with some sun.

The wooden hall floor showed its age until it was covered in the chaotic psychedelic marks of a dozen coloured chalks. Obviously at various points during rehearsals I have thrown several plates of pasta, a cheese board, some large trays, a tureen of soup and a wedding cake onto the splintering boards, and Mary has chalked the spill of each in a different colour.

The second week was painful, occasionally hilarious. I kept tripping up over Bob's way of saying 'the Vigilance', so one morning we stood with clipboards and a miniature recorder at the seafront, beside the replica Golden Hind and at Paignton Railway Station – anywhere with tourists from different places – getting them to say 'the Vigilance' as many times as we could. 'Excuse me, ma'am, doing a quick survey for the Department for Employment. What do you think about the new things the government is doing to get young people to volunteer and learn new skills?'

'Ooh yes, the Vigilance, I think it's ever such a good idea. Walking about we feel safer, don't we, Harry? Yes, both of us do.'

Since then we've been doing what we're doing now, watching video of Bob interacting with people. A long list of people, from Cabinet colleagues and Shima Patterson to the four 'Bills', to this lady, a black woman, a doorkeeper at No 10. I'm memorising and practising what he does with each.

The first few times we watch without sound. Bob comes down the stairs at No 10 followed by one of the Bills, the young sexy one (Francine Ellis – I know their names even if my brother doesn't. She does Pilates and as an actor I approve). We spent an hour watching six minutes of Bob and Francine last week. Now we're watching him look up, grin and embrace Aude.

'He's started winking at her with his left eye, just as he reaches the bottom step,' I say. 'Not a deliberate wink, something brief, probably subconscious. Two weeks ago he wasn't doing that, or the embracing.'

Mary has been making her own notes. 'Yes. It's so slight that overly copying it would be over the top. Just file it away and trust your own subconscious.'

Then we listen with sound, repeating from the beginning another five or maybe ten times until Mary says, 'OK, we're ready,' and I come down the steps at No 10. The white chalk marks are the steps, Mary is Aude standing by the door or polishing brass. Then we do bite-sized improvisation: Aude and Bob discussing the football, or me taking her into my office because she's had bad news at hospital. Each time three or four minutes' worth, hellos, goodbyes, distance, body language.

I've thrown into Brixham harbour the idea that I know anything about the person I'm studying. Forty-one years of brother-to-brother emotions, made worse by Bob becoming a figure in the media whom I loathed more and more, did indeed turn out to be a block.

'You're really getting it now,' Mary said at the start of this week. 'Imagine you had to impersonate President Trump, and the sight and sound of him made you ill – how big a block would that be? What you're doing is harder – you've got forty-one years of knowledge to get over as well.'

'It's not that bad,' I pointed out. 'We were only on speaking terms for twenty-eight.'

Today I walk down the steps at No 10 (the white chalk marks) and at the bottom announce, 'BG is committed to landing a white horse on the moon. Britain's Great! End of.' The point which she made on the breakwater we are now grinding out in practice: I won't be trying to pass myself off as Bob for weeks without anyone noticing. It will be short and sharp: in less than an hour to say or do something left field – like promise to land a white horse on the moon – and have those around me say, 'What the fuck, Bob?' and not, 'Who are you?' The real white horse on the moon will be handed to me by Patrick and his script writers.

Finally, there's the homework that's more like getting ready to be a spy than preening to go on stage. Now most evenings I spend a couple of hours with Howard, on top of my sessions with Tad the digital ghoster or Gary the personal trainer. Howard is my height and probably my age but thinning on top, with chemistry-teacher glasses and an Adam's apple which bounces around like he's trying to semaphore. He wears shirts so frayed I worry they'll come apart during our sessions. I guess he's the closest I'll ever knowingly come to some kind of spy.

Each evening he opens up his briefcase and takes out his tablet to spread his wares; like a travelling salesman, he puts the new stuff out first. Typically we spend half an hour studying photos or clips with audio of new individuals I need to recognise. Then he syncs these to my tablet and we spend the next forty-five minutes in quiz mode. Which of the Bills has just had a baby? Who are Annabel Wale's junior ministers? Whose picture is this? What's their job? What do I call them? When did they join BG? When Angela Deil calls, how do I answer the phone? Do I flirt, and if so how much?

It was the evening we spent time on Nassia Sotiris which really churned me up inside. The last image of her, in the entrance hall at Number Ten, was date-stamped 202006171810Z – 7.10pm in summer time on Wednesday. I can't help being surprised, even jealous, at how long she and Bob have stayed connected. Yes, I'm trying to throw my old knowledge of Bob away, but surely he's not clever enough – not classy enough – for her? The way she pressed her business card into my hand I can feel as if it was yesterday.

Whatever Mary says, parts of this do feel like stepping into my brother's skin. Two nights ago I dreamt that Howard would show up with my picture – Zack in his scruffy clothes and curls – together with what Bob thinks of me. When I get the heebie-jeebies like this, I think about Alan and what all this is for. Sometimes I say to Alan, 'Take a look at me now. Even you can't call what I'm doing *ordinary*.' Of course, Howard never produces my picture. Someone I'm not going to meet at curtain up is myself.

***

Mary knows Kathy's coming down and I have the weekend off, so she suggests we finish early with a couple of pints. Now we're getting on and I jump at the company.

We enter the Maritime Inn under the watch of a naval officer from Nelson's time who peers at the harbour through a telescope. Mary returns from the bar with two amber pints of Topsail. I gawp at a ceiling entirely covered in mugs hanging from hooks as well as suspended beer glasses, chamber pots, bedpans, ceramics and metalware. The Maritime Inn also boasts a parrot, perched on a Turner prize rendition of the modern skyscraper: a heavily pecked trainer, three-quarters of a plastic ball and a dishevelled oven glove hang from different levels of a vertical frame. Like a recluse in his penthouse, the parrot is silent but occasionally comes down to inspect the lower orders.

Mary hangs her gilet on the back of a chair. Somehow one knows that the experiences which line her face are real achievements. 'You've cracked it,' she says, downing half of her bitter in a few gulps. At this rate Archie must be the designated driver. 'And I'm glad about that,' Mary continues, 'because BG scare the shit out of me.'

I say it feels like she has re-wired my acting brain – my whole brain, in fact.

Mary shrugs her shoulders. 'Re-wiring, re-plumbing, you do what you're qualified to do. 'The mystery is what they're going to ask *you* to do. However much I prod, all they will commit to is that you'll be on stage for less than an hour.'

'The profiles that have been coming through in the last few days? They've started to include some foreign prime ministers and presidents – France, Germany, that sort of thing. No sign of Trump as yet. Do you think I'm going to be signing a treaty? It seems the obvious thing I could do in less than an hour to change the course of the country. But there's nothing about any treaties in the media – we're not on speaking terms with that many countries at the moment.'

'There's no signing involved. Probably the second thing I asked them, where's the handwriting expert? You'd need to practise Bob's signature. But nothing doing on that front. So I'm as adrift as you.'

'Sack Annabel Wale? Close Shock News? Actually, that would probably need a signature.'

213

'Either would be a start. Fancy another?'

'My round,' I insist, though I'm only half-way through my first. I collect two more pints. Compared to London, the price is absurdly low. 'The other side of this, Mary, is I hope still to be an actor, doing normal stuff – plays and films. I've read up on your work and you know me really well. I'd really appreciate any tips.'

Mary guffaws. 'What, apart from don't go into the theatre?'

'Me specifically, or the world?'

'The world, Zack, not you. You can earn a living in drama. You made the best you could of an overly academic drama education. Guess what so many of us had? The same. One day each of us finds our way out of the pit. By chance you dug your way out of the pit by the seaside.'

'So, advice?'

Archie looks up. Mary's head hangs loose on the far side, her eyes closed. 'All right. Too many actors try to beat the audience over the head into believing that the play is the real world. That's violent and unnecessary. The audience know their own real world – the one in which hubby's having an affair, Johnny's fever's back again and the washing machine has broken down. All the histrionics in the world aren't going to wipe those things away. How scary would it be if they could?'

I agree.

'Don't act to create *the* real world, act to create *a* real world. Act for the people in the audience who have paid to come and live in *a* real world for an hour and a half, or two. Open the door. Make it believable. But let them walk through themselves. It's a poor man who only lives in one world.

'When it comes down to it, it will be the same with your show. Whatever door you walk through at curtain up, no-one will be expecting a brother they've never heard of. Open the door. Make it believable. But let them walk through themselves.'

37

London, Saturday 20 June 2020

Intranet post by Médecins sans Frontières:

Eight volunteer doctors wanted for 36-hour mission with refugees. Valid UK passport and strict confidentiality essential.

38

Totnes, Saturday 20 June 2020

Zack chose Totnes for the two of them for the weekend, about half an hour by minicab from Brixham. The minicab dropped him at the railway station. The bed in Brixham was too small ('back to our student days'), Zack didn't fancy the two of them becoming the manager's Monday hot video pick and Totnes had fast trains from London. The station was packed with midsummer holiday-makers spilling over into the car park. Kathy had to rise slightly on her toes to kiss Zack, who wore his Bob shoes all the time. He had also added some muscle.

'Nice wig,' she exclaimed. The appearance was much better than the emergency job, although the feel was no way like the real thing. Still, she liked having a bit of Zack back.

The racket made by towing their overnight cases over pebbles made talking an effort, but Kathy needed to share Alan's funeral. A pallbearer, she had gone in dress uniform, wondering if two travel packs of tissues was being silly. She wiped out most of the first pack while hints of the organ's reverberations washed down the west steps. She waited there in front of curious, snap-happy tourists with Alan's brother, the two eldest children from each marriage and former colleagues.

Once the coffin arrived, everyone could feel the tension on the steps despite the surrounding traffic. Inside the organ had fallen silent – two processions of City bigwigs and clerics followed by the Archbishop with his mitre, shepherd's staff and B took their places. It seemed an age before the six of them and the casket were lined up to the verger's satisfaction – he kept adjusting the B which sat on it, the one which Alan had made himself – but inside, with every seat taken, the feeling defied anything in Kathy's experience. They carried Alan in to the unaccompanied voices of the choir singing *I Was Glad*, a new arrangement which rendered the opening words in sharp tension to sombre music.

'Isn't that for coronations and royal weddings?' said Zack.

Kathy appeared to ignore his question. 'You know I don't do church, it was like angels were calling him home. I can't describe it. When they reached the words the Archbishop wanted – For there is the seat of judgement – the way the organ came in then, everything changed. That's what he preached on, you know: Alan's killers will be found and judged. There will be justice.'

'That's not what they reported on the news.'

'Well, what do you expect now? Even on the BBC. You can find what he said on YouTube, but you have to look harder than you used to.'

Zack caught her up on his progress with Mary. Kathy said it sounded like things were going really well. Back at the MOD even Patrick had gone a bit loopy, failing to imagine targets in Britain vulnerable to a handful of European paratroops. Maybe seizing the trophy during the Wimbledon final – the paratroops could land in helicopters on the outside courts?

Zack had booked a modernised room with a queen-size bed above a pub. Totnes's high street sloped steeply towards the town's pepper-pot castle, with the pub about half-way along. Suddenly they found themselves in the middle of vegetarian cafés and three butchers. For a few minutes they were entranced by the old-style displays of joints on hooks, chops and steaks and kidneys on trays, featherless poultry with heads and clawed feet, and not a scrap of plastic wrap in sight. One butcher in a white coat and straw hat intrigued them – a woman of their own generation with a B on her striped apron.

While Kathy unpacked, Zack borrowed the landlord's phone for a directory enquiries call for an Oxford number. He didn't want to use his mobile or Kathy's. Then they walked to the river where they found a different kind of drinking establishment, loud and large for twenty-somethings. The tide of liquid lunchers had gone out and a couple of hours would pass before diners followed by party-goers came back in. Zack ordered a gin and slim-line tonic, Kathy a Merlot. Staff wiped tables around them.

'No vaper?' Kathy asked.

'I'm trying to give up. Bob did five years ago, it seems. He has a bit of weed now and again, but that's it. I might as well be in character. I'm also trying to drink less.'

'We know nothing about your brother for years until he starts appearing on telly, and suddenly you know if he's got a pet hamster. It seems odd to me; it must feel weird to you.'

'You're right.' Zack grinned. 'He flosses. Can you believe that? Bob's teeth are great – end of. They put a camera behind the bathroom ventilator.'

For a few minutes they drank each other in. Then Kathy looked around and decided that the cacophony from hoovering was security enough. 'I think the crunch is going to be soon, Zack. The feeling in Whitehall is just horrible. Every day another horror. A week doesn't go by without the President of the European Commission looking for another way to needle him.'

'Christ knows why; he has enough populist movements on his own plate.'

'Ducros is on a do-or-die mission to avert Frexit. Making Britain look really stupid is the only thing that works in the

French polls, apparently.'

Zack switched to a low percentage beer and they sneaked in an extra round before dinner. The pub manager brought their drinks out himself. Kathy nodded skywards. 'Not too many drones in these parts,' she remarked.

'We climb up to the castle and shoot them down,' he replied with a grin.

Interesting, Kathy thought – so in some places there was a resistance. Maybe even a Resistance. In fact, she was part of it.

Dinner was modern Italian in a stunning upstairs find by Zack. They had the tasting menu and laughed a lot. At a certain point Kathy said, 'Before, we laughed more. I liked that better.'

They gnawed at that bone for a while – Kathy's responsibilities had increased (Cairstine as well as her career) and the world was going mental, but both of them sensed something else. Mortality? Hopefully it would be decades before Death tapped either of them on the shoulder, but maybe he had given their Facebook pages a glance out of curiosity.

It was Zack who came out with it. 'Don't let's pretend. My career isn't happening. You can't count this weird thing with my brother. When we were younger, everything was possible – we could be successes. You are. I'm not.'

'No, that's not it. Listen to me. Please.' She squeezed his right arm so tightly it almost fell off. 'Twenty years ago, we had no idea how much success would matter. It matters, certainly more than I realised. But what I want back from our twenties is how we felt about not having success. About being nobodies – no, not nobodies, ordinary – Alan's word. OK, back then everything was possible, but neither of us went to Eton. We grew up knowing that not being especially successful was by far our most likely fate. But we didn't let that throw us. We laughed, because we felt – yes it matters, but there's more to life.

'I'm so proud of you saving our country, but it's such a *heavy* job – so serious. Let's not lose us – us when we laughed more.'

After dinner they made love with the abandon of the wild horses Kathy remembered near Kings Bay, the crashing of their furniture masked by Saturday night music from the pub beneath. When the sounds died they lay quietly. Kathy's hands roamed over Zack's new muscles, on his chest, his belly and his thighs. 'You like?' he said.

'Promise me in Canada you won't have cosmetic surgery. Just re-grow your hair.'

Zack sat up and switched on the bedside light, his fingers pressing against his brow. 'What, no Richard Deshaye eyebrows?'

'I bought Tony Mortimer's and I'm sticking with them.'

39

Mid-Atlantic, Friday 26 June 2020

Vengeance turned twenty degrees to port, continuing her lethal pilgrimage which had begun five and a half weeks previously. At the depth she called home the Atlantic, like the far side of the moon, remained in permanent night, but on board the lighting changed from white (day) to night (red). The crew were ten days short of the traditional 'Sod's Opera' marking the mid-point of the patrol.

Although space on board had opened up, there were still stacked cases of 'train smash' (tinned tomatoes); there were still unwatched DVDs, including advance copies of summer trash due for release at the start of July. One hundred and thirty-seven bodies had adjusted to this environment. On land some would avoid driving for a few days, as eyes learned how to focus more than five or ten feet away. Some dreamed of air fresh off the highlands after three months of air-conditioning.

The closest land? The seabed two and a half miles beneath; the closest dry land was the Cabo Verde islands, five hundred miles away. Two hours previously *Vengeance* had adjusted course to avoid a geological survey ship. Twelve hours before that she had skirted a particularly raucous school of whales, in case something unexpected lay hidden behind their acoustic curtain. Earlier still, she had turned far out of the path of two Chinese submarines making their way to the Pole after showing the flag in Africa.

For five weeks *Vengeance* had sent no messages to anyone, nor would she do so for the rest of the patrol. Certainly *Vengeance* did not access the World Wide Web. Instead, occasional packets of information transmitted from the naval headquarters at Northwood dribbled in through a long wave antenna. A kilometre in length (six times as long as the submarine itself), the antenna was towed through the water. Terse announcements of general and sports news were posted weekly for the crew but, like gift parcels of condensed milk, these were mostly ignored except at times of crisis. Crew could receive short family messages once a week but not reply. Everyone knew the messages were filtered. If a family calamity threatened, someone might judge it best to sit on the news until twenty-four hours before the boat returned to port. Nothing was dreaded more than being called to see the commanding officer then.

In this artificial environment what blossomed was the British pub quiz, an art form laid low in its home environment by smartphones and the internet. *Vengeance*'s current crew – each boat had two crews that alternated – included two of the top quiz-masters in the Submarine Service.

Vengeance's weekly news summary for Friday 26 June was long on Wimbledon odds and British hopeful Tamsin Stewart. Wildfires were raging in California. French air traffic controllers had persuaded their high-speed train counterparts to join them in a twenty-four-hour midsummer strike. A summary prepared twenty-four hours later would have looked completely different.

40

Helensburgh, Saturday 27 June 2020

Like the tides in Morecambe Bay, the tears had welled up without warning. Kathy had spent the night alone in the room she had occupied as a child, something she had previously avoided. She had done it because this could be a last time: her warning to Zack the week before had been serious. Now there was no adult to comfort her. Cairstine was making things predictably worse.

None of it flustered Meghan, the mental health nurse. Her motto was the Australian version of 'Dinna fash yersel' – no worries. She was from far north Queensland. She had not worrying, dealing with poisonous snakes and cleaning up messes down pat.

'It's water off a duck's back, Kathy,' Meghan promised. She meant her 'adoption' by Cairstine as her missing daughter. 'Robert in Balloch thinks I'm his wife. He wants to know when we're going to share a bed again. I tell him I spend enough time touching his private parts as it is. With a towel, that is.'

'Meghan, if we didn't have you – well, Cairstine would be in a home, which would be such a shame. She hasn't had any falls for months.'

Meghan nodded. 'The kitchen was the only worry, but now we switch the hob off at the fuse box, it's right as rain.' The new fuse box had a two-handed closure which was beyond Cairstine.

223

'She's got the kettle and the microwave and she's laughing.'

An adviser had gone through the house and recommended new appliances. Kathy wanted the home as safe as possible before she went away. They had changed the microwave for a low power model with child's play controls and a safety on the timer. The new models included voice-recognition software. When the door opened, the microwave asked Cairstine what she was putting in or did she want to choose a time. When it finished it told her and reminded her of its contents.

The adviser had been so enthusiastic about 'the Internet of things' that Kathy had signed Cairstine up as a guinea pig. Come winter's gales, anyone with the right codes could see on their own phone what was on in the house and what was open. They could hover on icons to display for how long an appliance had been switched on, and double-click to switch it off. That included anyone in Canada. It embarrassed Kathy to admit that the blessing seemed mixed.

Meghan carried on with her unflustered update. 'Last week, Tuesday, she put apples in water on the stove to stew. Obviously the hob was off so they were still there on Thursday. What's that in the scheme of things? Nothing, really.'

In the scheme of things, nothing really. Cairstine had wandered into the garden, leaving the television on loud. Kathy went to turn the volume down.

'Leave it on, dear,' Cairstine called. 'Something nice might come on.'

Fat chance, thought Kathy, lowering the volume. Another discussion programme – Saturday morning filler. Once she had tried interesting Cairstine in CBeebies and been water-boarded on the spot.

Her mother came back with a handful of daisies. 'They're pretty,' Kathy said. 'Can you smell them? No? Maybe pick a few more, then? No, you won't find this interesting, it's politics.'

'Politics? I'd shoot the lot of them. I like that Bob, though. He speaks his mind.'

'It's not speaking of minds we need, mum; what we're short of is politicians with minds worth speaking.'

Cairstine turned and put one hand on Meghan's elbow. 'Did you say something, dear? No? I thought I heard something.' Cairstine turned her shoulders as far away from Kathy as they would go. 'Kathy's leaving me, you see,' she explained. 'But you won't leave me. I know that.'

'No-one's leaving you,' Meghan demurred.

'I am, for a while,' Kathy corrected. 'My work is taking me to Canada.'

'What did I tell you?' replied Cairstine triumphantly. 'I said so a long time ago. I speak my mind and she doesn't like it.'

On screen the discussion gave way to the news. To general consternation, Tamsin Stewart had come out as straight. After that excitable headline, the picture cut to the Folkestone end of the Channel Tunnel. Some refugees had taken advantage of the French train controllers' strike and got through. More than some – the camera pulled back to show perhaps four hundred motley figures – men, women and children – corralled behind makeshift barriers in a freight marshalling yard. Some more were still coming through, limping after the thirty-mile walk. A few were on stretchers. The picture switched to Zafir Khan, the Secretary of State for Transport. Kathy turns the volume up slightly. It was Hobson's choice: which could she bear least, Khan's words, the refugees' or Cairstine's?

Her phone chirped. Kathy removed herself into the garden. 'Yes!' she sighed, followed by an alert, 'I'm sorry, sir.' She closed the French windows. 'Yes, I just saw something.' After a pause, 'Oh shit, oh shit, oh shit. I've got a flight booked for tomorrow but I'll come right away – of course.'

She flew inside and upstairs to snatch her belongings, impetuously adding the koala with a missing ear which Cairstine had left on Kathy's window sill. The ideas of 'home' and 'goodbye' rang tinnily in her ears. Home – was that the small town in front of her, where she had grown up? Putney? The Navy? Perhaps Canada. She had no clue. That she no longer had time to think these thoughts was a relief, but of a sickening kind.

41

London, Sunday 28 June 2020

Annabel gets her arse round my way before we go into the Cabinet Office Briefing Room. There's something which the Vigilance need to sort *now* and she sorts it. What gets me through days like today: whatever doesn't kill you, makes you stronger.

What a crap room. Annabel has plans to jazz it up, but this Channel Tunnel disaster has happened too fast. So you find yourself a corner in a cramped box with crappy air-conditioning, a too-big walnut table which is six seats by four and a wall of out-of-date technology at one end. It's the kind of place I'd have expected a country with a naff football team to have used for reviewing tactical video in, maybe, 1993? If today feels like England 1993, I feel like Graham Taylor – do I not like that!

Annabel is opposite me, Patrick next to her, then Zaf, next to him one of his civil servants who looks like a hospital case. Looking around we've also got the Foreign Secretary, the Home Secretary, the Attorney General, Shima, Jennifer, one of the middle Bills, our chief spin doctor and the chief of the Kent police. The room's sweaty, but not half as sweaty as it's about to get. 'I've got one question and one question only,' I say. 'What the fucking Jesus happened?' I slam the table. *'Don't go pissing me about with how we're going to respond* – I've got the A team doing that. You shambles just tell me what happened, and how you were all so up your own arses you didn't spot it.'

Hospital case tries to speak but is too close to death. Zaf steps in. 'First thing to say Bob, right away – I know it's not good enough, but we're sorry. I'm sorry. All of us. We've let you down.'

All the heads nod – even Patrick's. I count them. I brush the apology to one side and gesture to Zaf to get to the sausage in the hot dog.

Which is a dog's dinner, right? The opening trick was the so-called French high speed train controllers' strike, which meant no trains – passenger or freight – through the Channel tunnel for twenty-four hours from 11pm Friday. Next the French authorities notify us they plan to take advantage of the strike to practise a bomb search of the service tunnel – all thirty miles of it. Diagrams flash up on the screens. The service tunnel is about fourteen feet in diameter and runs in between the two rail tunnels, with access every four hundred yards. Specially-built electric vehicles run in it. Of course we said fine. Third thing, we lost video of the service tunnel, but nobody fretted – the main tunnels were clear and empty, and everyone assumed it was part of the exercise.

The paratroops took charge. We've since searched the tunnel and found what they put in place. Talk about fucking Glyndebourne! Every six miles volunteer doctors, water, soft drinks, Portaloos and sandwiches. Fucking signs with LEDs showing the time and saying 'UK, so many kilometres, this way'! In the meantime, the refugees have been arriving at the French end – four thousand they trucked from around France, two thousand from the Calais jungle – there's always a new one. The paratroops search them for matches, lighters, knives, anything which could disturb the arrival of paradise. The refugees co-operate like mad, they're over the moon. Then they're shoved into the service tunnel like chop, chop.

Jesus wept. There's so many of the fuckers it takes until 4.30am, nearly dawn, to get them all shuffling through. The first ones start emerging in Folkestone soon after 9am on Saturday. The rest take half the day to come out. In the meantime, come dawn the engineers pour concrete to close up the French end of all three bores.

Zaf hands over to the police chief. About 5am our time the first rumours begin to circulate on social media; at 5.45am the 24/7 government news centre calls Kent police, who know nothing. The moment the lights go on for the police or the UK Border Force is 8.30am when half the Kent Red Cross turn out with blankets, tea and biscuits. Someone called them to come out for a train smash.

The French don't talk to us. We're embarrassing enough on our own – caught with our pants down, hung over, Saturday morning sluggish. Hundreds of refugees escape (the Vigilance are after them) although thousands are happy to be corralled with tea and biscuits behind road traffic cones. What a joke!

Eleven o'clock our time is the moment to read 'em and weep. President Le Pen and the President of the European Commission are on the spot in Calais. They declare the first operation of the European Defence Corps a complete success. The French President promises that there will never be a Calais Jungle again, since the Channel Tunnel is completely sealed. Hippolyte Ducros pats the fresh concrete plugs with affection and crows at scoring a killer blow against Frexit.

Thanks to swarms of media helicopters the world sees the contrast between the two portals: Beussinges is calm, tidy and diplomatically ordered; Castle Hill end is in chaos.

President Le Pen: 'This operation to safeguard Europe's borders has been conducted with total humanity as well as exemplary efficiency. Cleansing this festering sore opens a new chapter in relations between France and Europe.'

Ducros: 'I have to speak honestly about Brexit. It is desperately sad. It is as if Europe has had a miscarriage. But now we can move on. We have cut the umbilical cord.'

***

I throw my mobile at the screen and Ducros's face shatters. I tell the group that I've ordered the EU's ambassadors to attend a press conference at Number Ten on Tuesday morning. In the meantime, the Vigilance have been instructed to take certain steps.

Annabel nods. 'We have deployed thousands of drones to Kent, and we have hundreds of volunteers checking all the stations and trains up to London.'

'We've set up road blocks,' says the Kent policeman.

'Backed up with tanks,' says Jennifer. Too bloody right, General; we all read this morning's headlines: FIRST INVASION OF BRITAIN SINCE 1066.

'How the fuck did the MOD not see this coming?' I bellow.

Jennifer mumbles and starts unloading paper onto the table by the ream. I'm about to sack him on the spot when I remember we picked him *because* he was useless. I reckon we have forty-eight hours, if that, to show the EU this clever dick trick with the tunnel isn't a patch on what we can do – and for what I've got in mind I need Jennifer right where he is.

Patrick steps up. Shima doesn't, which catches my eye: she's always acting important and know-it-all, until suddenly she's not responsible for anything at all. Anyway, Patrick nails it. 'They fooled us with the paratroop battalion. Our scenarios were a waste of time. They outsmarted us.'

The only sound in the room is my breathing, which is as it

should be. Everyone else's breaths need permission.

'Bob – look,' says Zaf. 'If it's a question of someone resigning…'

I walk round and clap him on the shoulder. 'Zaf, there was never any question in my mind.' For a second he looks relieved – silly bugger. I continue, 'I told you, Annabel, this morning. I know Zaf – he'll do the right thing.'

Annabel nods. Zaf stands awkwardly. He whispers out of the side of his mouth, 'How do I resign?' but hospital case can't help himself, let alone his boss.

Patrick steps in once more. 'Go back to your office, they'll draft a letter for you.' Zaf nods gratefully.

I walk Zaf out towards the entrance at 70 Whitehall. Well before we see the doors we can hear the crowd chanting 'Britain's Great! End of!' with swelling anger. Inside the doors I shake Zaf's hand. On the steps is a member of the Vigilance in a scarlet cape with three chevrons. Zaf isn't bothered that his car isn't ready yet – he left the meeting unexpectedly – but the handcuffs which the Vigilance officer snaps on his wrists are a surprise. Then it's twelve paces in front of the baying crowd to the white prison van.

Like I said, what gets me through days like today is *what doesn't kill you makes you stronger*. The thing is, the same thing goes for your enemies, so it's best to catch them early. Like Tel, for example.

Roll on Tuesday – but first we need to buy some time with the Vigilance.

42

London, Monday 29 June 2020

Monday was the worst day of Kathy's life. Like the rest of Main Building she had worked sixteen hours on Sunday, but that was nothing. The first cancer was the news which unfolded all day long, so shocked watchers snatched every chance to be glued to TV screens inside the building. The second was an unpleasantness between colleagues, even friends, which she had never seen before. The third was her churning fear for Zack. She couldn't but think of him because she was covering Patrick's absence at critical moments, when he needed to be outside. He had secure equipment to talk to his fellow plotters, but using it inside the building was unthinkable. In one of those absences, she realised that if Zack's acting broke down, he might be shot on the spot. Why had she never thought of that? Fervently she prayed that it wouldn't.

Dominating Monday's news from breakfast were pictures of the Berlaymont, the fourteen-storey cruciform headquarters of the European Commission. Overnight someone had smashed gaping holes in three-quarters of the windows of the top two floors. The plush offices of Europe's richest bureaucrats now looked like the teeth of a smoker living his last years on the streets. Haze from fires scented Brussels with ash. From the wrecked nests fluttered white A4 birds, officially secret but now released to ride the wind – mostly to Etterbeek, Woluwe and the Free University.

The attack had started at three in the morning. Once the fire-fighters reached the top floors the source was in plain sight, although bulldozers had first to clear paths through a moat of broken glass surrounding the building. Inside the top floors lay more than a hundred triangular drones, buckled from smashing their way through shutters and windows and blown apart by detonating themselves or blackened by service as incendiaries. British social media seethed with back-slapping, high-fiving and video footage of the raid posted by youngsters in the Vigilance.

Downing Street made no comment beyond observing that any reasonable citizen would react to the extraordinarily provocative and highly publicised actions of the European Commission.

Across Britain exuberant crowds of all ages gathered. By lunchtime supermarkets had been emptied of beer. 'No-one likes us, we don't care' bounced off Victorian town halls, echoing from museums and mansions which had been produced by empire. The crowds showed no inclination to move. The government erected giant screens so that people could watch Tuesday's press conference together.

The euro and the pound plunged, the pound more so, breaking the buck to settle at eighty-nine American cents. Shock News' parent corporation took advantage of the turbulence to grab a fifty per cent stake in BBC World at a rock bottom price.

Back in the Ministry of Defence's three-slice toaster the atmosphere turned sepulchral, unrelieved by humour. The mood was blackest in PINDAR, the command centre in the building's bowels. PINDAR relayed to Northwood, for encryption and onward transmission to *Vengeance*, the details required to arm a Trident missile for a 50-kiloton burst at eight thousand feet above specified co-ordinates.

43

Camberley, Monday 29 June 2020

I arrive at the red brick Travelodge in Camberley about eleven-thirty. I'm relieved to be on the point of action, and am sick of picturesque trawlers. Camberley adjoins Sandhurst but the main point is it's only one junction up the M3 to reach London's circular belt, the M25. The plan was to deliver me there about four in the afternoon but I have some plans of my own so I kicked off. With curtains-up so close, they humour me. I can't work out why it's taken me so long to realise who has the power in my situation: no Zack, no show.

The call to move came on Sunday afternoon. By then we'd seen a day and a half of telly. The tunnel was like that advert in which more people keep climbing out of a Mini, except the six thousand people climb out of the Channel Tunnel. Mary drove in on Sunday evening to give me a hug. I was really chuffed about that.

There was nothing for me to pack. After going back many times to Nassia's pictures and voice on my tablet, last week I had left three phone messages at her college, all ignored. So by Sunday night I had written her off as well. Yet something must have happened, because on Monday morning I woke to three texts from her during the night (the last, soon after 6am, said 'Switch on the news!'). When I got through she said she had spent the night at Number Ten and could get to the Camberley Travelodge for one.

My minders went ape-shit but I told them to get over it. After 'taking instructions' they played ball, on condition they could wire me for the meeting. I'd have my wig on, obviously.

So out of an Alfa Romeo Spider climbs a stunning Oxford professor for lunch with me. On offer is Travelodge's culinary finest: a choice of three twelve-inch pizzas, quarter pounders or baguettes with tuna mayonnaise, BLT or cheese and tomato.

She doesn't seem bothered. The cameras in Number Ten haven't lied: she's hardly aged in thirteen years. No need for *Vogue* to cancel her contract, although when her dark glasses come off I can see that she's been crying.

'You've hardly changed,' I say.

'And we live in a society in which that is a compliment?'

Calm down, dear, I know you've upgraded from Eton to Oxford. While Christine tells us she will be our waitress today, Nassia scans me like one of the new-fangled machines at airports. We're sitting at an imitation café table on chairs with backs like musical staves. Nassia has a straw bag; I'm empty-handed, unless you count the wire under my shirt. Once Christine has gone I expose it briefly. 'I hope you don't mind if this conversation is recorded for quality and training purposes.'

Nassia frowns. 'I hope that means you are a player in this game, Zack. Because if you can do something, do it. I spent last night with Bob, and it was awful. He is not coping. You must know what that is like.'

She sips lukewarm tea. Mine's a Diet Coke.

'You told me you want to understand your brother better.'

I nod. 'Yes. If I get the chance to "do something", it will help if I understand him as much as possible. I used to think I understood him, but maybe I don't. What I do understand is the way things are going. The former banker who was murdered four weeks ago? He was our friend. Our neighbour.'

Nassia covers her mouth. 'I am so sorry. You know, it's not just Bob. There are those who will come after him. His ego stops him seeing that he's being used.'

I nod.

'I tried to tell him last night but it was pointless. Look, let's take our baguettes outside – I need a cigarette.'

I almost ask her for one as we dribble sticky mayonnaise onto the tarmac. It tastes synthetic. Maybe it started life as road marking paint.

'It's taken me years to get the measure of Bob. He's extremely bright, if that's what you wanted me to say. Close to genius level in some respects.'

'Just say what you see. When I look at him, I miss things. Or misunderstand them.'

'But he has a low attention span and extremely friable intellectual foundations. Owing to the inadequate education to which he was exposed.'

Friable foundations – too much egg and chips?

'His tactical intelligence is tops. Among the highest I have seen, including Oxford, the Sorbonne, *et cetera*. He also has some strength strategically, because he is neither afraid nor ashamed of what he wants. You might be surprised how common the latter weakness is.'

Too right; I'm afraid of getting what I wanted right now.

'What Bob cannot do is the middle game – long-term tactics. He gets bored too easily. And yet international relations is eighty per cent long-term tactics.'

'What did my brother want from you? Originally, I mean, when you were teaching at Eton.'

'He wanted to know how smart he was. I was a good measuring

stick: someone he could work with without too much pain, but also someone of the highest pedigree intellectually. I wondered whether you might want something similar, when I gave you my card. But you never called.'

'No-one's ever mistaken me for a genius,' I reply. Besides, I was a man at the beginning of a marriage, even if the moment with the card has never left me.

'How are you?' Nassia continues. 'You have a contract in the Middle East?'

Of course, Tad at work. I've been so busy being Bob that I'm forgetting to be Zack. I smile. 'Thank you. I can't say too much – agent problems – but yes, fingers crossed. Money, Shakespeare and air-conditioning – it could be worse.'

She studies me. 'Getting breaks has been less easy for you than for your brother.'

In a moment of clarity I realise that she has two jigsaw pieces which I want: what she thinks of my brother and what she thinks of me. For a month now I have been reconstructing my understanding of my brother; I've overlooked that the process involves reconstructing my understanding of me. Possibly in hours I will be on the other side of the world and an opportunity to put the pieces together will be gone forever.

I blurt words out awkwardly. 'If I had called you thirteen years ago, it would have been for the wrong reasons. Understandable but wrong. The wise reason would have been to get what you suggest, your assessment of me. So, you study the world. Leave Bob out of it: how do you see someone like me?'

Nassia's eyebrows rise. She lights a fresh cigarette. In four lungfuls almost all of it is gone before she replies.

'As a sociologist, my interest is in patterns, more so than individuals. Still, individuals can be interesting. You, I take it, aspire to the middle class. Politicians have long wanted precisely that. Now, the middle-class credo is education and meritocracy. Meritocracy with vast blind spots, naturally, especially around their own children. But still, the middle classes believe self-improvement on merit is possible and a duty. This used to be the religion of your grammar schools, now taken over by business schools and the professions.

'Such a credo could hardly work for the upper class. Their belief is that everyone – everyone who is in that class, I mean – is more or less guaranteed to survive. Effort is useful but not fundamentally necessary. If you do not understand this, then you are not a member of this class. What is fundamentally necessary in the upper class is to keep oiks out – to be the lid on the system, to keep one's finger in the dyke, to hold back the surging ocean of the aspirant middle class, and not to be distracted by the occasional storm wave which breaks overhead from the working class (your brother, for example). No matter if water keeps leaking through and you wade in ten centimetres of it, the dyke will hold. There is very little genetic about all this – the principles apply to élites of all stripes, the rulers in corporate boardrooms, your celebrities who are acclaimed even when they go to prison.'

I'm watching a lepidopterist lay out the board onto which she is going to pin me, but I have the feeling that it will feel more like a skewer than a pin.

'The upper class share something with the working class: an appreciation of the role of luck in life. This realisation would destroy the middle class, so they do not see it, even when – for example through house prices – luck accounts for more of their success and comfort than effort and talent put together.

'In addition to luck, the playing cards for the working class come in three other suits – toil, pleasure and survival. To these they add whatever jokers they can contrive to confer possibilities of dignity – respectability, God, family or gang. In this class there is no safety net. Their high watermark of success is the football club manager, well paid and famous for a time, but unceremoniously out on his ear after even a few bad matches. Not for them Teflon positions of leadership from which messages of failure can be returned to sender.

'So now I can say how you seem to me. What I see is that to the middle class, you are a failure. To the working class, you are a sponge and a traitor. To the upper class, you do not exist. I don't know, Zack, you tell me. Can you do something with that?'

44

Camberley, Tuesday 30 June 2020

Frank parks the bike in the back corner of the Travelodge, away from the street lamps. A summer shower has left the Kawasaki 1400GTR damp to the touch with steam rising from the engine intake. Is Frank police, special forces or something else? Enough that he is a cheery Geordie who is tickled pink to inform me, deadpan at four o'clock in the morning, that my date with destiny is scheduled for dawn at Heston motorway services. I don't waste time wondering whether to believe him: where he's taking me, I'm going.

He holds a torch as I struggle into black over-trousers with elasticated cuffs. The leather jacket is large across the shoulders. The black gloves have visibility flashes. I struggle to fit my head into the helmet's padding until I take the wig off. This prompts an up-and-down from the torch on my face.

'Nice job,' he says, surveying his imitation prime minister. 'You're better off without the wig anyway – they burn something horrid in a crash. Not that we'll have one of those. Here, let me.' He fishes out a crumpled Tesco shopping bag, wraps the curls and pops them in the pannier, before checking the helmet strap is snug and the visor two-thirds down. 'The best,' he opines, tapping the top of my skull through the helmet. 'Good airflow. But nudge the visor up a notch if you want more.'

He climbs on and eases the bike off its stand. I step onto a foot-peg and swing myself onto something which is more an indentation than a seat. We're hydraulically propped above four cylinders with more capacity than my car engine. The motor purrs into life and my hands grab the rail which cradles my bum. In less than two minutes we're London-bound on the M3 doing eighty miles an hour. I'd swear it was more but over Frank's shoulder the display is clear enough.

The bike's twin headlights angle through the darkness towards hesitant pink on the horizon. By the time we turn north onto the M25 and then east again onto the M4, a third of the celestial bowl is lighting up. Approaching aircraft hang in front of us, jewels on a necklace tethered to the heavens at one end and to runway 27R at the other.

I tuck in behind Frank and try to breathe slowly. This means ignoring the eighty-mile-an-hour wind, the tarmac inches from my feet and the traffic already clogging London's aorta. I still don't have a script, although some joker did send me a pictorial history of No 10. I've seen enough up-to-the-minute video footage to last several lifetimes. Surely to God they've not forgotten? I imagine a handful of double-spaced pages to be signed for on delivery, lost to the world inside a back room at Brixham post office.

To calm my nerves I've settled on a couple of mental drills. The one I'm practising as the bike flashes left, slows and turns into Heston services, is chairing a meeting of the Cabinet. I know the room; I know my chair – the one with armrests in front of the mantelpiece; I know the Bills and my Cabinet members and how I'll greet them; I know there will be other civil servants who I won't recognise. I've got something up my sleeve to tease Annabel Wale, who will be sitting on one side of me. Shima Patterson will be on the other side; I'll give her a pat on the back, which she hates but Bob does without fail. And then I punch the stop button in my head and rewind, because what the fuck happens next?

At Heston services we wait. I'm hoping for a Costa coffee or even – rash thought – a Krispy Kreme but Frank tells me to keep the helmet on to avoid identification. So we stand in the car park. After fifteen minutes of dawn I'm twitchy. After twenty-five the solar orb is bright. I'm tempted to chuck the helmet and ask Frank for a cigarette – I saw him have one at Camberley – but then a message comes through his ear-piece. He gestures me to follow. We head towards the lorry park and make for a ten-tonne DAF Aerobody painted 'Swansea Removals Abertawe', sitting next to a blacked-out people carrier.

I'm grabbing human contact where I can get it, so I take Frank's hand warmly and say thank you and good-bye.

'You're not shot of me yet. Now this truck – Britain may not be able to afford Air Force One but this is the next best thing – Wardrobe One.' He holds up the Tesco bag with my wig. 'All right if I keep this safe for you, for after?'

After whatever is about to happen.

The back of the truck opens up and a middle-aged man of Indian appearance leads me up the ramp into a dimly lit backstage interior. However once the back door closes, lights blaze – we're lit up as if in a mobile studio. This one comes complete with a shower and five racks of suits, shirts and casual clothes – a reproduction, I realise, of my brother's wardrobe. My guide has an assistant, perhaps his nephew.

I scrub myself down, have a shave and sit in a dressing gown for twenty minutes of make-up by the possible nephew, who hovers between me and a lap-top bulging with pictures of Bob. He uses very fine clippers to flatten my eyebrows. Then they dress me in a suit, something Italian in merino wool, very elegant in a shade between black and blue which I haven't seen before. I'm wearing a white shirt with gold BG cufflinks. I reach to tie a tie around my neck – also black and blue but with BG's red and white lion. The older man shakes his head, and I realise I haven't practised tying ties Bob's way. I've chosen my talisman, a torn sheet of paper; I slip it folded into my breast pocket.

A squeaking in their ear-pieces calls both men back to the screen for a hurried consultation, before the nephew returns with a tube of yellow acrylic paint. He gives me a smear below the third button of my shirt. 'Sir was a little careless at breakfast,' he explains, and gives me my first look at myself in a full-length mirror. Bob – end of.

The only person in the back of the blacked-out people carrier is Frank, now changed into sweatshirt and jeans. Next to my Tesco bag is a Heckler and Koch MP7 machine pistol with a suppressor. From recessed speakers Karen and Richard Carpenter sing 'We've Only Just Begun' at a low volume. I laugh – I assume it's Patrick's sense of humour. We join the motorway and drift at considerably less than eighty miles an hour towards central London. When I say to Frank, 'I don't suppose they gave you a script,' the answer is predictable.

We take the Hammersmith crawl-over and filter our way along the Cromwell Road and Earl's Court, cutting down through Edith Grove to the Chelsea riverfront. I count the bridges – Battersea, Albert, Chelsea and Vauxhall – before the Thames swings north, taking us with it. Passing Lambeth Bridge we cross over from the land of *London Spy* to that part of the capital where history is part of the day job – Lambeth Palace, the Houses of Parliament and Westminster Abbey. We go round Parliament Square, navigate a barrier and are admitted into a courtyard of the Foreign and Commonwealth Office. It's mid-renovation and looks like a builder's yard. We pull up ten yards behind another people carrier, stopped underneath improvised PVC sheeting with its tail lights glowing. The carrier is next to a doorway.

'How long?' I ask.

Frank shrugs.

There'll be no cosmetic surgery in Canada, I've decided. The hair's coming back, obviously, but the Tony Mortimer eyebrows are staying.

45

London, Tuesday 30 June 2020

At ten minutes to nine on Tuesday Kathy followed Patrick and Shima Patterson into the Pillared Room at 10 Downing Street where a firing squad of cameras had been set up. All the seats were taken. The assembled mass was like a cryogenically-sealed *crème brûlée*: in the first two rows the ambassadors of the European Union with expressions frozen with liquid nitrogen; behind that crust, a seething lava of media vultures.

Two rows of officials stood behind the lectern to the left. Kathy was in the second row behind Patrick, with Patrick next to Shima, and Shima next to the lectern. On the other side were Ministers, including Zaf's replacement. Annabel and Jennifer were deep beneath the MOD. Citing national security, Patrick had insisted they take their places in PINDAR, protected by a thick blanket of steel and concrete. It was now too risky to have all the nation's leadership in one place. Besides, the whole show was screening live.

Sixty seconds before the man they were all waiting for strode to the lectern, Kathy practically wet herself. Had she told Patrick that she and Bob had met once, at Bob's housewarming party? It was too late to do anything but stare at the floor. Bob passed in front of her without a flicker of recognition. The figure was the same height as the man she had kissed at Totnes station but the smell was unmistakably Bob. In addition to the scents of sweat and power, she thought she detected fear.

Bob's suit was charcoal with a blue steel wash, the colour of twenty minutes before nightfall on a mountain lake. The white shirt with gold BG cufflinks and a BG tie were let down by a smudge of egg yolk below the third button. He laid a single sheet of double-spaced A4 on the lectern.

Normally Bob had no use for speeches from paper or autocue, but today for a full minute his eyes were glued to his script and not to any of the cameras. Kathy's stomach wobbled briefly – could it be Zack, fluffing things? No, this was the real deal. For once the Bermondsey swagger had buckled.

Then a line arrived – 'No-one mocks Britain, our proud country, our decency and our generosity' – which brought a roar of support from the crowd half a mile away, gathered in Trafalgar Square since the evening before. The cheers were audible through Number Ten's open windows. Bob found his groove. His shoulders came back and forty camera lenses saw his eyes blaze.

'When the bedlam starts, stick to me like a leech,' Patrick had said on the walk over. 'When I disappear, stick with Shima.' So Kathy stuck to Patrick as the crust of normality shattered and lava erupted in every direction. Two Royal Marines stepped from behind pillars. Patrick had his hand on Bob's elbow, piloting him towards the door.

Shima took the lectern for a scant four seconds, shouting, 'The Prime Minister will answer the questions of the British people in Prime Minister's Questions tomorrow,' but the attempt was pointless so she plunged after Patrick. The French Ambassador foamed at the mouth, 'Anglo-Saxon madness – *force de frappe* – Birmingham in cinders – '

46

London, Tuesday 30 June 2020 (2)

You know I don't *read* statements but we're shooting for 'statesmanlike'. That's the first reason I struggle with the first few lines. The second is, I'm suddenly queasy – not like me at all. I go to the lectern head down, catching no-one's eye.

What's deserted me, like a lifelong buddy abruptly missing, is my innate belief in how it's going to turn out. Not the details, of course, but the big picture. The kind of confidence I took for granted when I packed in school, set up my business, or did the Millwall rally. It's as if, as I place this piece of paper on the lectern, some time ago my confidence bucket sprang a leak and I didn't notice. Shit timing, eh? Still, the bucket's not empty. And whatever doesn't kill me makes me stronger.

STATEMENT BY THE RT HON BOB GRANT MP, PRIME MINISTER, AT 09:00 ON TUESDAY 30 JUNE 2020 (CHECK AGAINST DELIVERY)

Fellow Britons:

On Saturday the European Commission and the Government of France treated six thousand immigrants as pawns in a game. The game's point was to make fun of Britain. The first thing for me to say is that all those individuals, whether they are migrants or refugees, are safely in our care. A big thank you to the Vigilance, the police and all the great people of Kent, for rising to that challenge. But the immigrants, and all of you, want to know – what's next?

No-one mocks Britain, our proud country, our decency and our generosity without paying big time. The British people already spoke on Sunday night. They punished the game-players with their own hands, but rightly they expect more.

The resignation of the President of the Commission? – let's save our breath. Where there's one cockroach, there are always more. It's the nest we have to deal with.

In our time the Berlaymont has become Nero's palace – an obscene statement of arrogance and decadence. Britain gives the Commission until 9am GMT this Friday, 3 July to vacate this space permanently. Having accommodated three thousand bureaucrats in style, the building will in time house more deserving occupants – six thousand homeless people from France.

If this demand is not accepted, the building will be pulverised at noon on Friday with an airburst of a nuclear warhead. The altitude of the burst will be sufficient to leave minimal radioactivity at ground level. Some surrounding buildings will also turn to rubble, but by Saturday the ground will be safe to walk on. In either case, the nest of cockroaches will have come to an end.

Britain's Great! End of!

Organising a couple of Marines to help me make a fast exit is good thinking on Patrick's part. The crowds outside are wild so I follow them into the damp tunnels which join Downing Street and Whitehall. We're going at a brisk jog. The more bedlam, the merrier: I'm thinking about the next move, about making sure Jennifer delivers pictures for the evening news of the refugees being embarked (very nicely) onto Naval auxiliary ships in Dover harbour. Of course, I need Annabel…

'Where's Annabel?' I ask Patrick. He's beside me. Shima's

following, with a junior naval officer.

You know times on the playing field when your blood is up – when everyone's blood is up – when it's a knife-edge game? Today's like that in spades. Some times like that you don't hear the ref's whistle. People swear he whistled, but you don't hear it.

So here's the first whistle I don't hear – the navy bird. She rings a bell but I've no time to figure it out. To be fair, it was just the once, thirteen years ago; she was out of her uniform and I was out of my tree.

Patrick's got his in-charge voice on. 'General Wale and CDS are in PINDAR already. I'm taking you to the Alternate National Command Headquarters. Standard procedure for the transition to war, Prime Minister – you have just threatened to nuke a NATO ally.'

We climb a flight of stone steps back to ground level. 'What Alternate Headquarters?' I say.

Patrick grins. 'We have to have something in our bag of goodies that we haven't shown Peter Hennessy. How embarrassing if we didn't! Shall I go first?'

There's the second whistle, right there. The grin reminds me that what punched a leak in my confidence bucket was ACERBIC. ACERBIC blew my mind! But what I miss about the grin, during the briefing and now, is that Patrick is far happier than he ought to be with what's going down.

The Marines stand on either side as Patrick opens a wooden door. A people carrier is waiting, door slid back. Two soldiers with automatic rifles, covered in black and green goo, sit facing the back seat, black taxi-style. That's the third whistle I don't hear. Another time, this could be my Birnam Wood moment: in command headquarters in Britain, even alternate ones, we're not big on jungle foliage. Instead my blood's up, the jog has got my adrenaline pumping, and by God those soldiers look like they're ready for war.

Patrick dives in. I follow. I don't see who slams the door, probably one of the Marines. I'm thrown against the back seat by the vehicle's acceleration and the soldier opposite me leaning towards my right shoulder.

'Seatbelt, sir?' he says. He thumps me on my right chest. I feel an electric shock and black out.

47

London, Tuesday 30 June 2020 (3)

Frank holds three fingers up and taps his watch. I flex my neck and start the breathing exercises I always do, counting down to on stage. With no opening line to focus on it's harder. He opens the door a couple of inches so I can see.

Patrick is first out of the entrance, followed by Bob: the silver fox leading Bob with the same assurance which brought me to where I am now. Shima Patterson and Kathy follow but remain on the pavement. Kathy sneaks a glance at our vehicle even though she can see nothing inside. She looks sombre in her blue dress jacket with gold sleeve lace and Navy tricorn. A Marine slams the vehicle's door shut. She salutes as Bob and Patrick accelerate away sharpish.

We pull forward and Kathy remains at the salute. Frank says, 'Break a leg,' and slides the door fully open. He waves the Tesco bag with my wig. 'I'll see this gets back to you.'

'Thanks,' I reply, climbing out.

Shima steps forward. When I pat her on the back she flinches, and then smiles. 'Welcome, Prime Minister. Don't smile, don't wave, don't crack jokes – you've just threatened to nuke Brussels.'

'What?!'

'Nuke Brussels. This Friday. If you didn't think this was deadly serious before, think it now. Follow me through Number Ten, out of the front door and into the car. Look like death and say nothing to anybody – literally anybody. Ready?'

What saves me is there's no time to think. I oscillate between a scowl and a frown, and settle for grim determination. Two Marines are in front, I follow Shima and Kathy follows behind me. We go down stone steps and stoop to enter an underground passage before surging upwards into a corridor at Number Ten, which I recognise from the videos. Everything is shouting and hysteria, like a Hallowe'en party at which several people have died. The volume is unbelievable. The Marines act as our ice-breaker.

Do the weeks of training pay off? I haven't a clue – I recognise faces but don't consciously exchange glances with any of them, even Aude. I doubt they notice – I've never seen so many frightened people in my life. After two long minutes of forced slow breaths I'm through the front door of Number Ten. The Jaguar and driver are waiting. Shima holds the rear door for me and steers Kathy towards the front passenger seat.

'Nuke Brussels,' I say as the Jaguar noses into Whitehall, followed by a police Land Rover. 'So where's my script? I was promised.'

'You don't need one,' Shima replies. From her jacket pocket she takes out a card on which someone has written Europe – falling £ – global warming. 'Here's what you discussed with the Prince Regent last week – as far as we can piece it together. What you tell him now is that you are tendering the resignation of the Cabinet. Please repeat that back to me.'

I do and follow it with, 'And when he says why?'

The Jaguar turns left half-way down Whitehall. Shima Patterson fixes me with brown eyes whose batteries have died. 'Because you talked to a mulberry bush. Because Ant and Dec appeared to you in a dream. Trust me, he won't be that interested. Ever since the election he's been itching to ask the Labour and Conservative parties to form a national coalition. If he asks, tell him that's a top-hole idea.' After showing a pass we drive through the arch and cross Horse Guards Parade.

'You OK, Zack?' breathes Kathy from the front seat.

Of all the manifold ludicrous replies, I settle for 'I'm fine'.

She turns to face me. 'You've got to stop him. He's going to kill us all.'

The car pauses at the north end of Horse Guards Road where it joins the Mall. As we wait to make the turn, the pulse of the crowd – one-two-three, one-two – one-two-three, one-two – courses through the conduits of Admiralty Arch like a torrent from a hydro-electric dam. Britain's Great, end of! One-two-three, one-two.

To our right drones dance to the beat high above Trafalgar Square. A giant screen shows us the action in the Square: the performer is the twenty-four-year-old white rapper Dizzy V in his reversed baseball cap and ripped jeans. A sub-machine gun is slung across his T-shirt. Celebrity gossip says the gun is fake but made of gun metal to hang right. The T-shirt is in Vigilance colours: a Great Britain, Great Artists gig no doubt. The *Guardian* commented on Annabel Wale's talent for crowds – give her even a hint of one and out of nothing she'll whip up a show to please.

Unnoticed, two devotees half his age slide up to the Jaguar on motorised skateboards. They spot me and excitedly hammer the three-two beat with their fists on the Jaguar's armoured glass. I give them a thumbs up and check my Rolex (heavy, the same model as Bob's).

The roaring torrent rolls down the Mall and I, the people's chief representative, follow. I try to remember to breathe. My blood flow must be pure adrenaline, of which there is no hint at our destination: stare as much as you like, Buckingham Palace gives off that it's seen it all before. Or tries to.

'You'll be on your own with His Royal Highness for the conversation,' says Shima, 'but Kathy and I will be just outside. You call him 'guv'nor', by the way – for some reason he seems to like it. If you get into trouble, ask about the vegetable garden.'

The car pulls into the Ambassadors' Courtyard on the Palace's south side. I wasn't shown any Palace footage in Brixham; clearly it was one of the places which defeated the ubiquitous cameras. But Mary's training pays off. There's no hesitation or repetition in the way I greet door-keepers, *aides de camp* and other flunkeys, one of whom leads the way. I can distinguish Shima's and Kathy's footsteps in the gaggle following me, but as prime minister and First Lord of the Treasury I don't look behind. We stride corridors with red carpet the length of an airport, guarded by pairs of marble pillars. Then three flights of back stairs take us to the first floor. The *aide de camp* abandons me to my fate in the White Drawing Room.

Someone has run a bath of gold paint above the ornately-carved four-tier ceiling and left the tap running. The ceiling includes two friezes of intricate sculpture and geometric patterns. Everything in the room from about twenty feet up reads like a four-stave orchestral score. Crotchets, minims and quavers interlock on each level and the whole thing is saturated in gold paint. Leaking from the bath above, the gilt dribbles down pairs of white pilasters and around mirrors and cabinets before finally staining the rest of the furniture – a roll-top marquetry table, the frames of settees and chairs and more red carpet. Restrained patches of white wall beneath the gold rush don't provide much relief. From a portrait at one end of the room, Queen Alexandra waits for my performance. I've played to an audience of one before, but whatever this production lacks in bums on seats, it makes up in the set.

A tall mirror and cabinet swing open together. The Prince Regent steps through the hidden door wearing a double-breasted pinstripe. 'Bob,' he says.

Bob is what I do, a quick nod rather than a bow. 'It's good of you to see me, guv'nor. I'm really sorry for the short notice.'

'Not at all. It's been rather a busy morning.' The Prince rests his left hand inside his jacket pocket. He makes no move towards the settees: we're going to stand. With my raised soles I have two inches over him.

'The telephone has been falling off the hook,' he continues. 'I've just been offering fraternal ministrations to brother Philippe, the vexed King of some rather vexed Belgians. Apparently the Pope, the President of France and the Secretary General of the United Nations are also hoping for a word with one.'

A possible nuclear coshing has handed the Prince a piece of the action. Well, the seventy-one-year-old has waited long enough for it, and so have I.

I begin to speak but his right hand halts me. 'Given the unprecedented circumstances I had a word this morning with Jennifer. On a precautionary basis.'

I'm blank. So far as I know the top of British public life is a Jennifer-free zone. A mistress, presumably? They form part and parcel of the royal job description, it seems.

'I expressed my wish to be consulted before the release of any nuclear codes.'

A mistress with the nuclear codes? Shit! The Prince's expression leaves no doubt that I'm expected to find all this makes sense, so I nod. The clock speed of my grey cells must have doubled.

'But you asked to see me. You have news?'

'I do, guv'nor. I am tendering the resignation of the Cabinet.'

This information proves cranially divisive. The Prince's left eyebrow starts breakdancing while the cheek beneath makes a mad lunge for the right side of the face. His pursed lips expel the words, 'I see,' while his eyes probe me every which way. Maybe a speech bubble will pop out of his side saying 'but' or 'only joking'? 'Will you remain the leader of your party?' the Prince asks.

'I suspect I'll be lying low, guv'nor. General Wale already does an outstanding job.'

'I agree. What she's done getting unemployed youth off the streets and into The Vigilance is quite remarkable. In fact, I'm hoping some of these youngsters will work here at the Palace. I'm sure the next government will want to keep The Vigilance. Certainly I'll encourage them to do so.'

For a minute or two his concentration is somewhere else, thinking (I imagine) which politician to call first in order to get as wide a coalition as possible. My instincts are telling me to end on a high and get out, but I'm struggling over how to end the conversation. My understanding of royalty is that they end conversations with you, not the other way around.

Unexpectedly from the Prince, 'Before you go, tell me what you think of my vegetable beds.'

I join him at the window. Buckingham Palace's manicured lawns, incongruously large in central London (also the city's largest no-drone zone), stretch in front of us, bordered with shrubs, flowers and a high wall. The wall removes the traffic coagulating around Victoria Station and Hyde Park to another planet. But today gardeners on mini-tractors are tearing gashes of brown in the green. 'Food needs not just to be organic, but grown at the shortest possible distance from the table. I'm putting in three vegetable beds. It's a shame you won't be in office to taste the results.'

The shapes of the vegetable beds have been pegged out. The

Prince explains that there will be a crescent, a cross and a star of David, making the Palace organic, locally sourced and multi-faith all at the same time.

I reach for a Bob response and find one to hand. 'If you ask me, guv'nor, that idea is a pile of shit.'

The Prince emits a sound perfected in the BBC's Radiophonic Workshops – canned laughter. 'I will say this for you, Bob – you never gave me guff.' He glances at a clock on a nearby mantelpiece. If it's true that the Palace has more than 300 working clocks, why are they so behind the times? 'Goodness, we both need to be getting on. But what about ACERBIC? You promised to spill the beans.'

'Acerbic, guv'nor?'

The Prince frowns. 'Absolutely. Our Super Secret Squirrel conversation. You suggested I ask mater whether any of her prime ministers had mentioned ACERBIC.'

'And?'

'She doesn't remember. Which, alas, doesn't mean –' He breaks off quietly.

Thank God a door opens. Shima and Kathy are waiting outside: it's time to get off stage. But I'm Bob, and Bob doesn't slink. I say with exaggerated firmness, 'I'm sure that should be a matter for my successor.'

'Of course. We should do the proper thing. And if an ageing monarch-in-waiting may be allowed to say so, I think that's exactly what you've done just now – the proper thing. Thank you. I believe Britain and history will thank you.'

I know what Bob would do. I've trained. I don't have to think about it, except in my mind to say yes. I clench my right fist for a fist bump. The Prince doesn't move. You can do fist bumps right-right or right-left. With my left hand I reach over and grab his unpocketed hand and apply a little pressure on the fingers.

They fold. We bump. 'Take care of yourself, guv'nor,' I call out, to Shima's and Kathy's amazement. 'See you around.'

I reckon he enjoys the brief flirtation with cool, but within a couple of seconds the regal gaze dismisses me in favour of another perusal of the organic, locally sourced, multi-faith vegetable beds. I exit. My hormones are like two tribes of football supporters getting steamed in a seaside town – one lot elated to have got out in one piece, the other crestfallen that showtime is over.

48

London, Tuesday 30 June 2020 (4)

In the Ambassadors' courtyard the Jaguar and the Land Rover are ready to go. Kathy is now in the back seat of the Jag with Frank next to the driver. He smiles and points at the Tesco shopping bag. Kathy and I kiss.

Shima taps me on the shoulder. Having bawled endlessly for a script, I've never been less happy to be given a page and a half of 14-point font.

'You were wonderful.' Not knowing how to gush, Shima extrudes unconvincing product from a sentiment factory. 'The moment you've been waiting for and then you're done. The steps of Number Ten – the famous door – the government has resigned, goodbye world. Our media team reckon about three hundred million people are watching live. You should reach over a billion in twenty-four hours.'

I skim two minutes of government-speak mixed with more product from the same factory. It's a funeral oration for a desk chair. When I say 'Who wrote this shit?', the bad-tempered slam of the car door tells me. There's something I meant to tell her, but the Cabinet Secretary has gone. She has a coalition to fix. Oh, that's it – the Prince has a mistress who has the nuclear codes.

The gates open and the car inches forward. 'I can't say this,' I say to Kathy as I show her the sheets of paper. 'In a million years Bob would never say anything like this.'

'Didn't your coach say you *would* come out with something strange, quite different from what Bob would say?'

Mary's black gilet and a fish-needs-bicycle T-shirt flash into my mind, along with a white horse on the moon. Focus – focus on the right problem. A white horse on the moon? No problem. But I need to rip the covers off it Bob's way.

We've started down the Mall. Bob wouldn't go to Number Ten and announce the government's resignation to the media – that was the old way. He'd announce it to the people (and, of course, the media). Like the Red Lion, stuffed full of cameras. But this is a whopper of an announcement – *I've just pitched BG out of power – even if less of a whopper than why don't we nuke Brussels?* So he would...

I lean forward to speak to Frank and the driver. Frank jabbers excitedly into his communication device.

The stage ramp erected in Trafalgar Square is guarded by the lions at the base of Nelson's Column. Armed police form a box around me as we access the ramp. Backstage Dizzy V is tearing into an assistant who has forgotten the right moisturiser. The fake sub-machine gun is slung over the back of a folding director's chair.

Dizzy high-fives me, I high-five back. 'Bob, great you came to catch the show.'

'Always a fan – hardcore. Look, Dizzy, any chance I could say a few words?' I gesture towards the stage. His T-shirt colours, the way he's looking at me, I see he's going to play ball. Duh! – of course he is – I'm his hero, for about four more minutes.

'No sweat. Look, do you want to use my hand-held or have the guys check for a lapel mike?'

Theatrical training to the rescue – if you're pumped and

haven't practised with a hand-held, most of your words get lost.

Dizzy calls to a bloke with headphones, wild hair and pebble glasses. A lanyard round his neck tells me his name is Arvind. He tells me that the sound feeds the broadcasters direct as well as the amps for the gig.

I bounce up the ramp onto the stage. In front of me is the re-named Gallery of National Art; the sculpture of the Queen on her favourite horse is on the fourth plinth. Between me and them dances a cauldron of centipedes splashed with Vigilance colours. Ten thousand uplifted arms clap three-two, three-two. When the crowd see me a gale of chanting re-starts, and the drones above us start their new 'firework' move – four or five form a circle, almost touching, and accelerate vertically upwards before cascading gently back towards the crowd like falling leaves. I smile and wave, sometimes with both hands, sometimes with a half-clenched fist. I point to individuals in the crowd, particularly in the Vigilance, and give them the mock-salute which Bob has taken up lately.

It takes two or three minutes before the crowd quietens down – enough time for the TV channels to start broadcasting live. I look at the faces near me and realise that the brother who trained to read audiences is me.

'It's great to see you all (*applause*), here in this place which celebrates our country's fantastic victories (*cheers*) over the French (*hysteria*). Britain's Great! End of! (*applause and chanting*) I love Dizzy's shows, a big hand for him please for letting me say a few words.'

I lead a round of applause to Dizzy V who is standing to the side.

'Let's not forget a great show this morning from our drone pilots (*cheers*). Thanks guys and gals. Could you calm it down for two or three minutes?'

There's a delay of thirty seconds and then the drones stop fireworking and slide off to hover next to Admiralty Arch.

'This morning I want to say some special words to those of you in BG. Do you remember when you joined BG? Because I do (*laughter*). We created Britain's Great because we were angry.

'Angry that people like you and me were not being listened to (*applause*).

'Angry that people like you and me were being treated as stupid, foul-mannered, selfish and generally full of shit (*whistles and applause*).

'Angry that whenever there was any good stuff to go around, we didn't get any of it (*cheers and applause*).

'Angry at a country brought low by contempt. Contempt for you and me – contempt for people never thought good enough to run Britain, but only to work for it, to play the Lottery, to pay taxes, waiting for housing which never came, waiting for healthcare which only came too late (*shouts of 'Tell them!'*). Meanwhile the doing-nicelys were too busy dialling Uber and telling the rest of us to jump' – I snap my fingers – 'to notice their boots pressed against our necks (*silence*).

'Bringing this country low was taking away the greatest thing many of us have.

'This needed to stop – and thanks to BG, and thanks to you – it has (*applause*). Thanks to you, British politics, whoever is in power, will never be the same again (*applause*). Britain is great, and will be greater, because we have stamped on this contempt. We have said no to the people who arrogantly assume they understand their neighbours' lives, their brothers' and sisters' lives, and know them to be worth less than their own (*prolonged cheers and applause*).'

On stage next to me, Dizzy V is clapping his hands together above his head. Okay, so much for the toboggan ride so far –

now comes the difficult bit.

'I knew what this contempt, this poison, had dmne to Britain. But only through the chance to become prime minister have I realised how much this same poison is screwing up our planet. As a country, we have neighbours, across the Channel and beyond. And on both sides of the Channel, there is too much poisonous conviction that we understand our neighbours' lives and know them to be worth less than our own (*silence*).

'The games from the President of the European Commission made all of us angry. Anger is pain. To ignore pain is to be a fool. But threatening to nuke Brussels was no medicine, it was an extra helping of pain.'

Dizzy stops mid-move, his arms and one leg at an angle, awkward, a dancer with an intuitive sense for any music other than this one.

'That threat was a step too far. Of course we had no intention to nuke anything, but the world didn't know that.'

The people in the Square are like fresh grounds of coffee brought to boiling point. Into their cup I'm pouring sour milk. The silence in the Square curdles. The first scraps of something unpleasant begin to surface. Dizzy moves to the side of the stage.

'Here's a great British rule: when you make a bad mistake, resign. Too many ignore it. BG won't. Threatening to kill innocent men, women and kids like you was a bad mistake. Evil, to be honest. So I've just come from Buckingham Palace, where I have tendered my government's resignation. No missiles will be fired on Friday.'

There are scattered cheers, more boos, but also a growling. The scum takes shape: black, triangular velociraptors move in my peripheral vision. From the front rows of the crowd two beer cans are thrown but fall short. Dizzy's gone but my police protection is on stage.

I look at the TV cameras. 'Thank you for your support – and because we're doing the right thing, I hope we will go on having it.'

An angry black triangle hits the lighting gantry and falls into the crowd. I see it but hear nothing – not the clash of metal against metal, not the crowd, not the police officer to my right who may be shouting. I'm not numb, I'm happy – happier than I've ever been in my life. I've nailed it, or come damned close. Who knows, maybe I've also saved some lives.

My left jawbone collides with the base of an amplifier rig. Frank has rugby tackled me from the right. From the opposite direction a second drone slices through the space I've vacated, kicking Dizzy's gun-metal artefact into the air before disintegrating, pouting, smoking and electric against the hindquarter of a Nelson lion.

I'm bundled into the people carrier – I assume the Jag is needed by Number Ten's new occupant. I hold my face in anticipation of the pain which will kick in shortly – for now everything is still adrenaline. Next to me Kathy's rib cage heaves twice, wheezing in protest against the world. As we shoot down onto the Embankment her fingers unclutch a Tesco carrier bag, and she starts to unfasten her lieutenant-commander's epaulettes. 'I resigned my commission. While we were in the Palace.'

'Who else has ever done that?'

'I don't know.'

'Maybe no-one. Ever.'

'I can't believe that.'

'Then believe this.' From my jacket pocket I slide the torn page which has spent the morning next to my heart, keeping me going. It's from a travel brochure. 'Admiralty Island. It's in south-east Alaska, north of Vancouver.'

'Admiralty Island – that's funny. You chose it for the name?'

'Yes. And it's amazing. It's one of the most concentrated brown bear habitats known to man. We'll be there next week.'

We've crossed onto the south side of the river and are heading west, I'm guessing for a switch underground in the land of *London Spy* – MI6's headquarters in Vauxhall.

PART FOUR

Chaos

49

London, Sunday 5 July 2020

Water. Pounding. Gasp. Water. Pounding – water – water…

I'm running the Grand National in Easter sleet, and not as a jockey. I've got a thirst from hell. Right now I'm waking up to disturb an autopsy – my own. 'Sorry love, didn't mean to startle you. Carry right on, I was sure I was a goner myself.' I must have ticked the box for black sheets at my autopsy – black sheets and curtains in spew-green velvet.

The curtains can't make up their mind whether to let the daylight through or not. The air is stuffy and warm with an undercoat of nicotine, but I'm shivering violently. The bedsheets have been tossed about by an Atlantic weather front.

I turn my head to the right. A black pillow has become a quad-biking park for snails. Either that or council road-painters have streaked it all over with lube. Two huge mirrors, tackily-framed stage props for a brothel, cover opposite walls. The mirrors reveal a receding line of bald white whales lying on black-sheeted double beds with 'Britain's Great. End of!' tattooed on their left buttocks. Turning left, an ash-tray has suffered an Aberfan event. I count four different brands of cigarette, about thirty butts and three kinds of lipstick.

I need water. Still naked, I stagger out of bed. Lying on the bedroom carpet is a stained vibrator which looks … forget it.

My stumbling shatters a third, free-standing mirror into a jigsaw puzzle. When I scream nothing answers – no rat at the skirting board, no air-blocked pipes, no fridge or washing machine. No computer, no music, no people.

I sniff the sheets before picking one to wrap around my waist. One calf cramps up. It's a dead slow and stop one-legged walk down the stairs, barefoot on planks with protruding nails and exposed carpet gripper. The kitchen is a shell with a stained sink and no hob, glasses, cups or plates. I knock back fistfuls of tap water and rub the sides and back of my head. About four days' stubble, maybe five.

Item, one three-bedroom semi with the master bedroom done up like a whorehouse. Item, a semblance of a living room – the cheapest possible net curtains, no settee, two Ikea armchairs and a Jack Vettriano poster. Item, every other goddam room completely bare. Because there's no hob, microwave, telephone or TV, so there's no clocks on these things either. No toilet seats or toilet paper, no clothes, no phone, no Rolex.

The lock has been smashed so the front door swings freely. Where is junk mail when you need it? I'm a half-naked prime minister wandering in the only house in London (is it London?) without a thick doormat of direct mail and special offer crap. A junk letter might have a date as well as an address. A leaflet might boast 'the thickest crust pizzas in …'.

I make it a full hour and maybe thirty more fistfuls from the tap before I hit the street. I'm a guru with no sandals. The black sheet covers my left shoulder and my midriff downwards. Come to me you who are heavily laden and I will nick your Nikes. And, while I'm about it, your Nurofen.

Well, at least I'm in England. Everything under the grey sky is hot and damp without the relief of rain. The tarmac is hotter than the pavement but less dog-fouled. Semi-detached houses stretch away on both sides of a long street. It could be this light at half past six in the morning in early July, but the street feels baked in afternoon heat. Is it early July?

Someone shouts in my ear, 'You've forgotten your pills, grandpa!' Two teenagers race past on a shared bicycle. Teenagers, so maybe it is the afternoon. The passenger has donated her earlobes to geometric science and is riding side-saddle. She whips out her phone for a pic. The pedaller is a peach-haired punk. They must be about fourteen.

I count house numbers from 86 down to single figures before hitting a minor junction and a street sign in the London borough of Brent. There are no shops or traffic, nor any clue to finding these things.

I cross two more residential streets and find a small park, its promenade lined with the mottled bark of plane trees. I look for drones but see none. I'm hungry now as well as thirsty. Two race-walkers pass me, all Lycra and slender muscle. They are too busy to give me a glance, wrapped in their own surround-sound worlds, pumping their fists like Victorian steam engines.

I stop beside a park bench and a recently tended bed of scarlet flowers. A bony seventy-year old turns and angles her body in slow motion watched by sculptures. A notice dedicates the sculptures to prisoners of war and concentration camps. Scrawled on the notice in red paint is 'BG! End of!'.

The woman's eyes watch me while her limbs revolve around her like a three-dimensional Dutch windmill. 'You should try it, Bob,' she says, recognising me. '*Tai chi*. For balanced strength and mental clarity.'

Yeah, grandma, gimme some of that.

Twenty minutes later we are exceeding the speed limit anti-clockwise from Neasden on the North Circular. We're looking to pick up the start of the M4 at Chiswick. Yvonne doesn't hold with speed limits, she thinks everyone should drive up to their age – in her case seventy-six. The phone pumping out Lynyrd Skynyrd's 'Sweet Home Alabama' is the same cantaloupe orange as the speakers in her two-door Fiat 500.

We did this deal: Yvonne gets me to my place in Eton with a homemade sarnie and a flask of sweet tea. In exchange she gets video on her phone of the bedroom and me coming out of the front door of no 86. She stands to make a few hundred quid on the footage. I draw the line at getting back into the bedroom.

On the ride Yvonne passes me one of yesterday's tabloids – yesterday being Saturday 4 July. I've underestimated her fee by a couple of zeros. 'BOB IN SHOCK ORGY HIDE AWAY' displays various butcher's cuts of my torso in configurations with two girls (twenty-two girls, if you look in the mirrors). The girls are fifteen years old – ha bloody ha. The good news: since I was comatose, there are no shots needing a porn star Equity card and only one shows my face, eyes blissfully closed in the embrace of a pair of boobs. The reporter states that my location remains a mystery.

Yvonne watches me as well as the road.

I say, 'Did you read all this shit? I'm surprised you picked me up.'

'I might fancy my chances. Sex in North London isn't all it's cracked up to be, except apparently at number 86.'

'Including number 86.'

'You don't remember anything about it?'

I shake my head.

'Ketamine?'

'Elephant anaesthetic, by the feel of it.'

'What will you do in Eton?'

I look back at her. 'Get some of my own clothes on me before I do a nuclear explosion of my own. Where the fuck was my police protection? How does the Prime Minister of Great Britain get abducted in full view of the world? Why haven't the Vigilance been into every single bedroom in the United Kingdom, let alone Willesden, looking for me? The four Bills – the Met – Jennifer – they'll all be bricking it when I show up.' I fold the paper and put it beside the hand-brake. 'But when I do, I don't fancy showing up looking like that twenty-four page spread.'

'You're not the Prime Minister, Bob. You threatened to toss Brussels onto a nuclear barbie and then resigned. It's a five-party national coalition now, two Labour, two Conservative and the SNP. And that youngster is running BG – Annabel something.'

The grey sky starts to come apart. Gobbets of rain, the first of many, spatter the windscreen.

For a moment I think the show isn't over: the streets were empty for a reason and Yvonne is a plant. Then I snatch the paper back and open it. Even in a titty tabloid, you can find out who the Prime Minister is, if you know where to look.

When we get to my driveway we both stand in the rain, Yvonne filming. The lights in the flagstones change colours while I throw a brick through the stained glass inset in the front door. Inside I step over an alpine range of junk mail and delivery leaflets and fetch Yvonne a card with Angela's number at Shock News. By the time the police come Yvonne is long gone. I'm in an Orlebar Brown poplin short-sleeve shirt and chinos. One and a half litres of Coke and a home-delivery pizza (thick crust with double meatballs and extra cheese) have appeared and disappeared again.

50

London, Sunday 5 July 2020 (2)

I debate whether to call Annabel but decide just to call Angela. She can get to me in two hours. I spend the time before she arrives surfing the web big time and thinking. Goddammit, bro, you really pulled it out this time – where did that come from? I never knew you had it in you to say boo to a goose.

I see the work he put in – the gestures, the creasing of the forehead, the walk – unbelievable. That speech in Trafalgar Square is hypnotic, I play it a dozen times: I want to believe some agency which charges several thou per hour wrote it, but somehow I know the words are Zack all the way down. I agree more than he or you might think.

Day five and the coalition is already in a mess. It seems the leaders of the two Tory and two Labour parties and the SNP take turns to decide which day of the week it is. The SNP's price signed up an independence referendum at a time of their choosing.

Straight off the bat on Wednesday Annabel did a blinding interview as Leader of the Opposition with the Beeb's political editor. Who lost Bob Grant? Where is he? Cover up, cover up, cover up. Then she's back laying out the new politics: student debt cancelled in return for five years of patriotic part-time service. Fifty thousand quid of debt gone in return for joining the Vigilance at weekends. She knows what she wants – power – and she'll have it soon enough.

When I banked £20 million and had no plan, Angela Deil showed up with the keys to Number Ten sticking out of her bra. That solved a whole bunch of wants, but it was also ten years ago. Getting the keys was cool but even a month on the buzz was fading – just too many fucking problems with your name written on them. So if I don't want that power back, what do I want?

A tanker load of revenge, obviously, anyone would want that. Patrick Smath needs that grin I failed to understand wiped off his face. And ACERBIC, I need to factor that in. Looking back, that's what knocked my mojo – discovering that twenty-six years ago a bunch of dull grey men dreamt up a shocker beyond anyone's wildest imagining. I want my mojo back, which means thinking equally big.

It takes about half an hour but gradually I get things clear. If I go for revenge for the coup, a couple of mandarins go to jail, maybe some military, I get quarter of a million for a book advance which I don't need and the ruling class get away with everything – as per usual. They hop about screaming, 'Shock! Horror!' and sometime after climate change gets fixed, a sixteen-volume inquiry report lands. By the way, my part in that story is a victim, a dupe – not a good look. But if I go for revenge for ACERBIC … well, that's a whole other ball of wax.

**

Angela shows up after three hours, not two; she went in to the office to cut the deal she wanted with Yvonne. Today she's in 1930s platinum coxcomb curls, a navy-blue jacket with padded shoulders and a strapless white top. We kiss, no tongue.

She helps herself to a vodka and tonic from the bar, hollow

cubes clinking into her glass from the ice-maker with a nude on the side – a memento. I show her where they hacked in: eight needle marks in my arms. She knows I didn't have any needle marks.

'You asked, so we've got grannie and her pics on hold for twenty-four hours if we need it.' Angela wriggles her behind into one of my armchairs. The armchair doesn't seem to mind. 'So what's your plan? And what happened? We've been wondering, to put it mildly.'

'"We" being?'

'Annabel and I, plus most of the world's sentient creatures. Hasn't Annabel done an amazing job, given that none of us had the foggiest what you were up to? Not just the Beeb interview but Prime Minister's Questions. Lab-Con went straight back to doing PMQs the old way, in Parliament, and she knocked the socks off them. They held her incommunicado in this bunker under the MOD until you had left the Square. Then they marched to her office to collect her stuff and threw her out, like they'd caught her with her hand in the till.'

Angela stops to think what else has happened. 'We lost twenty-eight of our MPs, they decided to start their own party – wankers. Anyway, give Annabel eighteen months and we'll be sorted. Lab-Con will have fallen apart and the country will be ready for her to be its saviour. Will you mind being forgotten? I'm sure Annabel would offer you a job in the House of Lords except you promised to abolish it.'

'How about we get Annabel into Downing Street in eighteen hours, not eighteen months?'

Angela eyes me sharply. 'Really?'

I nod. 'By tomorrow evening.'

'I'm all ears. But first, what did happen to you? Everyone's been told that you were coked up to the eyeballs when you threatened Brussels and then went to the Palace. They've pumped out a ton of non-attributable stuff about your getting dealers round to Number Ten, getting more and more out of it each week. Implication, because you couldn't hack it. To be honest, I'm surprised they didn't truss you in lead foil and shoot you out of a torpedo tube in the middle of the Atlantic.'

'I'm guessing my brother made them promise not to.'

'Your brother?'

'Jack Grant. Goes by the name of Zack Parris. You met him here, thirteen years ago.' I fire up the tablet on the coffee table and scroll to the speech in Trafalgar Square. I've bookmarked *'people who arrogantly assume they understand their neighbours' lives, their brothers' and sisters' lives'*. As he says the words, Jack looks at the camera.

I scroll back to Jack coming out of 10 Downing Street to head to the Palace. I point to the naval officer with him. 'That's Kathy, his wife. You also met her here. She was standing behind me when I told the EU where to get off.'

Now that's one for the album – the chief executive of Shock News shocked. What a rarity. Angela starts gabbling, 'We'll find them. Both of them. My God, my God, what a story…'

I hold up my hand. 'Sure. That'll make for some really good armchair TV when you find them somewhere in the world in six months' time. Tell me when you do because I'd like to see Jack again. Make that Zack – I reckon he's earned it. He really stepped to the plate and delivered.

'But that's not the story that will bring down this government in the next eighteen hours. For one thing, Patrick and co will have done a decent job. Zack will have an alibi for Tuesday – they'll be able to show he wasn't even in the country.'

'I'm onto Zack's Facebook now. Something about a Middle East assignment.'

'There you go. In three or four days Shock News will knock that alibi down, but that's still missing the main chance.' I quickstep Angela through the moves. No Labour or Conservative MPs cross the aisle to BG. Not their fault – civil servants to blame – one or two bad apples – the national unity coalition commands a majority in Parliament.

'Instead we can do a story which has half the Labour and Conservative MPs deserting to BG. Annabel as prime minister with a big majority by Monday evening, and the ruling class smashed forever. Just turn up here at six tomorrow morning, and deliver me Patrick Smath three hours earlier. You'll need the Vigilance to get him, I expect he's got protection. Can you do that? Get him here by three in the morning, and you come along for six.'

'I don't see a problem unless Patrick's out of the country. General Wale is still in charge of the Vigilance, I just need to tell her the story. So what is it?'

So I spill the beans about ACERBIC. When she's gone I open the French windows onto the patio, lawn and garden. Beyond the sycamores at the bottom are the playing fields of Eton. The air which rolls in is still clammy and tropical.

In the middle of the lawn lands an Indian peacock, resplendent in a royal blue ruff and a long, furled maharajah's train. I stand on the patio to watch. The fowl and I tease each other for a few minutes before he turns and elevates his display, fanning out a satellite dish made of jewelled silk. Thirty turquoise ocelli stare at me from the densely interwoven wicker fan.

That's some display, fella. Now catch mine.

51

London, Monday 22 June 2020

(two weeks earlier)

I catch the Tube from Temple to Embankment, one stop, and walk the rest, flanked by four Vigilance six-footers in scarlet capes. Ahead of me a BBC crew is reversing up Whitehall Place and there's a Shock News drone. I've just given a statement on the first day of the bank chief executives' trial. The trial proper won't start for eighteen months – lawyers will be next up against the wall if I get my way! – but finally they're in the dock. BG's popularity is sky high and my confidence bucket is brimming over.

And so to my ACERBIC briefing. Patrick greets me inside MOD Main Building, once I have stepped onto one of the weight-sensitive glass cylinders – very 'beam me up Scotty'. Inside there is a smattering of applause from younger staff; last week Annabel Wale signed the contract to build *Dreadnoughts* five and six. The way the maintenance cycle works, two extra submarines will near enough double our strategic punch – Britain's Great, end of!

We pass armed Marines and sink into the building's bowels. To my surprise Patrick doesn't head for the PINDAR blast-proof complex. Instead we trek miles of corridor, stopping eventually at a door marked B3G70. Patrick and the Marine escorting us produce separate keys for separate locks.

What a letdown – it's an empty broom cupboard with a walk-in safe on the far wall, layered in dust which makes me sneeze. Leaving the Marine outside Patrick locks the corridor door from the inside, before spinning the dial on the safe to and fro. I notice the safe door has an eye-piece. What lies inside isn't a safe but another broom cupboard with walls of buttermilk-coloured brick. One has a corkboard with curling Polaroid photographs. Two boot sale chairs bracket a scuffed wooden table. To my left is a wooden locker. Once I've stopped sneezing, Patrick bolts the safe door from the inside. Behind a small ceiling grille a cheap plastic fan starts up.

'Welcome, Prime Minister, to the ACERBIC briefing room. Do take a look at the photographs – it won't take more than a minute for me to set up.' Patrick takes out another key and bends down to the locker.

So, look at the photographs or count the flies waiting to be autopsied in the ceiling light? Each is a Polaroid head-shot pinned to the corkboard with a drawing pin. They're jumbled but there's some chronological sequence. Some pictures are faded and curled while the most recent, almost damp, is Jennifer's. Shima's portrait must be about two years ago, Patrick's slightly older. It makes sense – everyone is photographed soon after starting their job.

Right in the centre is a fresh-faced John Major. All the prime ministers since Major are here, pegged before too many wrinkles set in. Blair glows. I recognise the Cabinet Secretaries of the same period. I've now accounted for more than one-third of the faces. Add in the Chiefs of the Defence Staff, some suited, some in uniform, and all the Permanent Secretaries of the MOD, and that leaves perhaps half a dozen other individuals I can't guess, including a few youngsters. Shima and I will be the only ones showing a splash of brown in our skin colour. Four of the photographs have black dots stuck to one corner.

I realise all the photographs have been taken in this room. The wall on my right appears first in white, then fades and at some point turns buttermilk.

Patrick uses a handkerchief to wipe the lens of the boxy Polaroid 600 which he has removed from the locker. It looks like a museum piece. The locker contains cartridges and batteries.

'Please,' he says.

I move to the wall. The camera flashes and extrudes a moist picture after thirty seconds. Patrick peels the backing off and pins it to the corkboard.

'Welcome to ACERBIC. It may not be the cheeriest club in the world but it may well be the most exclusive. Everyone who has ever been party to this secret is pictured here. What you hear you will take to your grave, as four already have.'

'Ah,' I say. 'The black spot – *Treasure Island* with Polaroids.'

Two knocks, faint because of the thickness of the safe door, come from the other side. Someone has been admitted to the broom cupboard without our hearing. Shima Patterson steps inside – in a trouser suit, inevitably. One of her pin-stripe reliables.

'Prime Minister.' She looks at me and nods. 'Patrick. Please don't let me interrupt.'

Patrick eyeballs me with a brief grin. 'Point one. When the atomic bomb was born, the United States chose not to share its know-how with any other country. Congress legislated to ensure this. So the United Kingdom had to develop its own bombs and warheads which, after a few ups and downs, we did.

'Point two. British submarine deterrence dates from 1968. Since then we have paid for American missiles but designed, installed and serviced our own warheads. Built at Aldermaston, stored at Coulport, all that.'

'Point three. Trident missiles went into service in *Vanguard*-class Royal Navy submarines twenty-six years ago, in 1994. Trident was a different generation of technology from its predecessor, Polaris. Instead of one, two or three warheads per missile, Trident carried up to twelve. Multiple, independently-targeted warheads was the response to better anti-missile defences. Potential aggressors had to be convinced that however good their defences, sufficient warheads would get through to turn them into toast. Without that, we would have no deterrent against an anti-ballistic missile-equipped power: game over.

'In any case the Americans were upgrading their missiles. They would hardly keep a Polaris museum going just for us. Besides, we couldn't have afforded it.

'Pre-Trident our last effort on warheads was Chevaline. We dropped from three to two warheads on a Polaris missile to squeeze in a cluster of chaff – decoys. If that sounds gloriously British and unconvincing, that's because it was. The truth was, we'd invited ourselves into a poker game for boys and girls with much bigger pockets. Trident was bad news for us – a huge increase in the stakes.

'The middle week of September 1992 was not John Major's best. The pound dropped like a stone. But my predecessor Chris France had worse news for him. Our warhead programme had been going badly: now we chalked up an outright fail. The computational, scientific and engineering problems of fitting twelve independently-targetable warheads onto an American missile which we couldn't reconfigure had defeated us. Of course we could have succeeded if we had had the kind of money which the Americans threw at it. But we didn't: we were a medium-sized power trying for historical and sentimental reasons to play in the premier league.

'Need we discuss the history of excruciating British defence technology embarrassments? Taking just the ones we've owned up to, there's the Blue Streak missile, the Tigerfish torpedo, the Nimrod aircraft, the SA80 rifle, would you believe the Nimrod aircraft *again*, the type 45 destroyer – our eyes have always been bigger than our stomachs.'

It makes complete sense, but my chair rocks uneasily. How many times before has it done that? I realise I can count them on the wall.

Patrick continues, 'Major had been Chancellor of the Exchequer. He realised immediately that we could not match the American spend. Three options remained. First, to ask the Yanks for much, much more help than they were giving already. They would say no. American Presidents have never wavered: if Britain wants to play, it has to make its own warheads. To ask for help would disclose our vulnerability and ask them to breach their own law and international law. Besides, for what? A deterrent as British and "independent" as Hawaii?

'The second option was to tell the British public that at the end of Polaris, we would no longer maintain a strategic missile deterrent. But Trident had been announced by Thatcher as early as 1980. To fail to live up to her legacy in this respect would have been political suicide. The "bastard" wing of Major's party was after him anyway. New submarines, too large and slow for any other purpose, had been built. Billions had been spent because the Iron Lady had spoken. She couldn't unspeak.

'Which left the third option: ACERBIC.' Patrick leans back in his own flimsy chair and eyes me like a chef examining a squid.

***

Patrick's grin returns. Shima smiles too, which annoys the hell out of me: it's the humiliation of our country we're talking about.

'To bluff?' I venture. 'To build the submarines, pay the Americans for the missiles, maintain the patrols, spend a fucking fortune – knowing the warheads are duds?'

'Duds is a little harsh. They're complex miracles of British engineering, fissile material and all that, perfectly capable of causing a very nasty accident indeed. Or being detonated one at a time in a test. But as independently-targetable warheads riding on Trident missiles, yes, duds.

'But you're right, eureka: sorry about the pantomime with the last resort letters, but in truth the warheads were never going to be detonated anyway. Michael Quinlan, the permanent secretary before Chris France, conceptualised ACERBIC and thought it all through. He was the cleverest nuclear strategist this country has ever had. He retired with the slim hope that at the eleventh hour, the technology would come right and ACERBIC would stay locked in its safe. But it didn't.'

I look at the pictures of Major, Blair, Brown, Cameron and onwards. Liars all, but this? 'And the *Dreadnought* programme, which we've expanded to six boats? Ninety billion quid to carry blanks?'

Patrick coughs. 'The first time you hear it, it is a bit disorienting. But your mind will sort it all out soon enough.' He points at the pictures. 'Every one of us remembers our first time here, just as you will. And you'll come round to seeing why it's the right thing to do – as they did. The only thing to do.'

'But the waste!' I bang the table. Blood attempts to burst from a vein in my temple.

'You see, there is no waste. The programme is rigorously managed and very efficient. To date – BG's commitment to six submarines apart – Britain's hasn't spent a penny more than necessary to have a continuous, credible at-sea deterrent. Think about it: if the warhead clusters did work, our marginal costs would have been slightly higher. And we've got exactly what we've paid for: it's continuous, it's at sea and it deters. Everyone believes in it. A little odd to call it a lie, when for all practical purposes it's true. We're just punching above our weight, like we usually do.'

'It can't work,' I protest. 'There must be hundreds of scientists and engineers working on the warheads at Aldermaston. Their photos aren't here.'

'No need,' Patrick replies. 'Think Formula One. A car races off the track and into the pit. Highly trained technical hands swarm over it. Each engineer makes their own precise contribution. The car races out of the pit. It's the same at Aldermaston, but with need-to-know in spades. The worker ants don't have the big picture and don't expect to have it.

'At the big picture level, all we have to do is shift a decimal point in the computer simulations of how well the warhead clusters work, from a nine per cent chance of success to ninety per cent. In any case, Chevaline gave credibility to the idea of planned decoys – the idea that a proportion of our warheads are intentionally duds. We've popularised that a bit, especially as our younger generation scientists were less happy about potentially killing millions of people. It's a variation of the one blank bullet in a firing squad's rifles. If the order to fire will never come, all the bullets can be blanks.'

'This isn't even Suez or Dunkirk – it's worse.' I turn to Shima. 'And you're here to gloat?'

'Hardly, Prime Minister,' she says. 'I'm here to make sure you understand…' – she purses her lips – '*fully* understand, that our country's security hangs on ACERBIC's security. So none of us talk about the content of ACERBIC, write about it, or even *think* about it, except in this room. To do any of those things, come here. It's a fragile thread which keeps sixty-seven million people safe. Am I clear?'

I've been keelhauled. The room's floor and walls are moving. I stare at the pictures again, grasping at straws. 'There are no Defence Secretaries here.'

Patrick's grin is really under my skin. It's yet another of the ways he brags that the ruling class have been everywhere before – seen it, got the T-shirt and returned the garment under warranty with flaws identified. 'At the political level, only the Prime Minister is ACERBIC-indoctrinated. As you know, the Prime Minister and the Chief of the Defence Staff constitute the nuclear command authority.'

He scrapes his chair along the floor and fishes keys out of his jacket pocket, gesturing towards the unreal world from which we have come. 'Shall we?'

52

Eton, Monday 6 July 2020

Behind the naked buttocks a row of oak and birch, and a sycamore in a garden; behind the sycamore a house in shadow; behind the house exploding orchid petals of pink, with pistils of sunlight landing on Dutchman's playing fields. Dutchman's and Agar's Plough alone comprise more than twenty of Eton's playing fields. I shift on my collapsible golf stool and swig coffee from a flask. It's just gone five thirty in the morning.

The man is naked, shivering on mown grass, his head face down towards the west. As the planet's rotation propels him feet-first towards the sun, he sees between blades of grass the school he attended for six years. Rope from a ship's chandler tethers his wrists and ankles to pegs. On his left buttock 'Britain's Great! End of!' has been written in purple lipstick. The bleeding from his left earlobe, now augmented with a single *diamanté* ring, has stopped. An hour ago he writhed and pissed himself.

'I'm not sure who you bought your coup from, Patrick, but you might want to take it back,' I comment. 'Your after-action police protection was a shocker.' The police officers parked outside Patrick's house hadn't noticed a night-time drone skimming the tarmac to arrive underneath them, releasing a gas. 'Still, sevoflurane isn't the kind of vile shit you used on me. The binding and gagging had to be on the generous side but they'll be up and about stopping black teenagers again in no time.'

'Dawn. So what's going to happen?'

'Angela Deil, with a news camera.'

'Spinning some cock and bull story about how you were drugged and hypnotised will be a waste of time. You may not have noticed but your current reputation stinks.'

'Please think of your bodacious coup with Zack as the Yorkshire pudding in our meal: beside it is beef which has hung and matured in the dark for twenty-six years. Its incredible flavour is about to become a worldwide phenomenon. Don't bite your lip so hard, Patrick, you've bled enough already.'

A column of ants climbs up Patrick's right shoulder. A ping on my phone says Angela is maybe ten minutes away. A grasshopper tires of blades and lands on the curls of Patrick's hair. Most grasshoppers are vegetarian, but to this one the column of its insect kin looks like lunch on the go.

'So, the black dots in the ACERBIC room.' I slop water from a plastic bottle over Patrick's nose and lips. He sucks in what he can.

'What about them?'

'How young they were. I mean, some of the generals were well old when they were snapped, but they still haven't kicked the bucket. They do say being a senior officer is like living in Switzerland; it's particularly good for your health.'

'The adjutant I knew died of a particularly aggressive cancer.'

'Why did you have any youngsters in on the secret? Of course, to shift the decimal point – far too inky work for all the gold braid pinned to that wall. But then being young and junior and all that, they're not quite as trustworthy, are they, as the ruling class? No peerages or knighthoods to lose. Not quite enough skin in the game. They risk succumbing to the sweet smell of cash. So a risk, but one which you managed. You might call it cancer – I'll call it a life-shortening dose of being junior.'

'Bob, we have to keep ACERBIC safe to keep Britain safe.'

'I make you wrong on that.'

'Good God, you'll leave us defenceless!'

'Good God yourself! Conservatives, Labour, you lot – *you* left the country defenceless for twenty-six years! Instead you've lied and lied again to the man in the street about his own defence. We didn't count enough to be told the truth.'

'Everything was done in the man in the street's best interest.'

'Looking through your ruling class telescope, you knew it was OK to deceive our enemies. In that telescope the ordinary people were not so different from enemies.'

'That's a lie.'

'Not a word I'd use if I were you. And I have to put the world straight on Brussels, don't I? Brussels was never at risk.'

'You're going to claim that because of ACERBIC?'

'ACERBIC is a fact.'

'Which I'll deny, obviously. Your drug-addled brain has invented a delusional children's story.'

'Patrick, you can do so much better than that! And you will. Let's have a go together, shall we?' I fold my chin towards my chest and furrow my brow deeply.

I step back and fling my arms wide. 'Got it! There is a dark secret called ACERBIC, but it's not twenty-six years old; it's only about six weeks old. After the election all you had to do was find a disused broom cupboard, stick a few locks on doors and get the props department to mock up the pictures. You were confident I'd fall for it –after all, I'm a fool, aren't I? You needed to shock me, to throw me badly into doing something frightening so that the other parties would form a coalition. But what-ho, it's only a disused broom cupboard. Nothing to worry about, our submarines can still wipe out our enemies 24/7.' I squint at Patrick. 'How am I doing? I fancy putting fifty quid on it, don't you?'

***

Xenon headlights race towards us out of the west. Angela has abandoned Eton's winding lanes to drive straight towards my phone signal over the college's fields. Is this the field where Jules watched me play? Patrick will have played here many times.

Angela's Range Rover is a long wheelbase SV Autobiography in drake's-neck green, with ten-inch screens in the back and a chauffeur in the front. She steps out, covered in zips and something more expensive than white leather. When her boot touches the turf, it's one small step for Angela but one giant step from 1960s sci-fi. No kiss this time.

The chauffeur opens the boot to release a Shock News camera drone. When the drone has me in the foreground and Patrick behind, I spill everything – the little that I know of my whereabouts since Tuesday morning; who Patrick is; the switch; the coup; ACERBIC; Brussels. Patrick spits out denials like Gulliver tethered in a nefarious land. My fifty-pound bet pays off handsomely.

'Shall we get the back view?' says Angela. While the drone inspects Patrick's buttocks, Angela stands out of his eyeline unscrewing a one-litre carton from a supermarket. 'The idea that you invented ACERBIC just for Bob would be terribly clever, Patrick, but Jennifer got an ACERBIC briefing just like Bob's. He's as outraged as the rest of us.'

'He's just trying to save his own skin,' Patrick growls.

'Well, yes, and – oops! – you might want to do the same.' Petrol vapour rises as the contents of the carton splash across Patrick's buttocks and onto the grass. I step back. The fluid reaches Patrick's scrotum and he winces. Angela moves away from the petrol to stand by Patrick's head. She strikes a match.

'Besides, whether ACERBIC is actually true will become a moot point,' she continues. 'If conspiracy theorists think Britain doesn't have a deterrent, and enough of our enemies are conspiracy theorists, then we don't, even if we do.' She drops the match beside Patrick's face, where it flickers and dies.

'You're wantonly destroying £100 billion worth of national defences!'

Another match. 'Something was going to put Trident out of business one day, it's just not what you anticipated. But hasn't that always been the way? The Maginot Line, the fall of Singapore, and all that.'

'You media tarts spend so long fucking around with words, you think words can do anything. Let's see who's laughing when we detonate a warhead.'

'That's bottom of the class for you, Patrick,' I observe, while Angela strikes a third match. 'We've exploded single warheads since the 1950s. To blow ACERBIC out of the water you'd have to fire a missile and detonate, oh, at least six warheads? It's not going to happen.'

'Besides, who is the "we"?' Angela asks. 'The coalition won't last twelve hours after this story is out. By this evening Labour and Conservative MPs will be disowning their parties and streaming to BG. Tonight we'll have a new prime minister and a majority BG government.'

Patrick's hopes have flared and died like the smoking matches beside his face.

'Oh look!' Angela suddenly exclaims, kneeling beside Patrick's left buttock, moistening a Kleenex on her tongue. She wipes some existing words, fishes out her own lipstick and writes something new. 'Annabel is re-launching BG. She's putting young people first. Cancel debt. Subsidise starter homes. Tax second homes. Guarantee first jobs for apprentices and graduates. Votes after seventy-five to depend on GP assessment. Euthanasia free on demand – there's more than one way to deal with the crowding on these islands. And there's a brand refresh to go with it. She hopes you'll like it, Bob.'

The drone's pilot composes the desired shot of Patrick's arse which Angela wants. After 'Britain's Great!' it now says in the colour of vomited cherries, 'Start of!'

EPILOGUE

Hope

53

Helensburgh, Tuesday 6 July 2020

It's 9.15 in the morning. In twenty minutes the Clyde and the clear sky above it will succumb to slanting rain. HMS *Victorious* nudges out of Faslane and heads towards Rosneath Point. After a modification to her propulsion, it's time to verify her noise signature. For three days and nights she will play hide and seek with a frigate and two helicopters. When she returns, she will have four weeks to make ready to replace HMS *Vengeance* on a deterrent patrol. But ACERBIC has changed everything. In four weeks' time, ten of *Victorious*'s ratings will be in jail in Colchester for refusing to spend the next three months in a pointless tomb.

This morning the submarine's retinue of tugs and close protection vessels is led by a fireboat. Pecking repeatedly at the flotilla is a television crew and the Scottish First Minister in a motorboat. The BG government has scorned the coalition's promise of a second independence referendum, so the First Minister is announcing that Scotland will hold its own, with observers from the European Union. The skipper of the motorboat will get his bonus if he can get the First Minister hosed down on television by the fireboat.

'How confident are you of Scotland's future outside the UK?' asks the interviewer.

'Prosperous and brighter than ever,' the First Minister replies.

'Of that there can be no doubt.'

From a garden on the hillside a lady with partly combed, long grey hair looks down on the nautical gavotte. Since her daughter left her, her pompadour remains in her chest of drawers. A woman in her fifties in comfy trainers brings out shortbread and two cups of tea. 'Mind now Cairstine,' she says, 'the tea's hot.'

'My Kathy left in one of those,' Cairstine says, pointing at the submarine. 'I waved her goodbye. I knew she would leave me. She didn't believe me, but some things a mother knows.'

On the Clyde, fierce swords of spray erupt from the fireboat.

Cairstine turns to her companion. 'But you'll never leave me, will you?'

Meghan holds her client by the arm and gives the answer which she is paid to give.

54

Admiralty Island, Tuesday 6 July 2020

Kathy and Zack flew north from Vancouver to Alaska, landing in Juneau. The high summer was offset by high latitudes: it was cool enough for Zack to be comfy in his wig. They missed by hours the chance to bellow 'Four more years!' at a seventy-four-year-old with more hair even than Zack. Fresh from his unveiling at Mount Rushmore, the President announced a second wall – this one around the blue states, and the Democrats would pay. He was accompanied by Second Lady Sarah Palin. Paying no attention, Kathy and Zack grinned from ear to ear.

A float plane took them across fifteen miles of water. Their hike to the sanctuary's observation point was escorted by a ranger with a shot-gun. During July and August this visit was permitted to only twenty-four people each day. A pair of bald eagles kept watch.

Two mothers, one with one cub and the other with two, emerged from opposite sides of the creek. The single cub wanted to play. For a while his mother humoured him before turning, like the other mother, to the chores of food shopping. Lithe, lumbering and weighing one-third of a ton, the female brown bears padded out into the tidal flats. Within two or three minutes there was an abrupt jump of half a body length followed by a short scamper. In the paws of one mother flapped a salmon, silver, red and as large as an Alsatian. The skin made an *amuse-bouche* while the mother returned to her cub.

'Nature doesn't lie,' sighed Kathy. 'At least bears and salmon don't.'

'What about dogs and cats?'

'Never!' Kathy retorted.

'We might have infected them. Oh wow.' Playing in the water, one of the cubs had caught its own salmon.

'Do babies lie?'

'How would they?' mused Zack. 'By crying when they don't need anything, I suppose.'

'They cry when they need something, even if it's just attention.'

'If babies aren't born to lie, then it's us who teach them.'

Kathy thought about it. 'You mean when they are annoying and want sweets, and it's easier to say there aren't any more.'

'Oh, earlier than that!' Zack opined.

'Really?'

'It'll be like this. We'll hold our baby really close.' Zack cradled Kathy's waist. 'Then we'll bend low and whisper: listen – listen – listen – everything's going to be all right.'

55

Eton, Friday 10 July 2020

Nassia and I are sitting in a cake shop sandwiched between fluttering Union Jacks in Eton High Street (Slough Road to you and me). Around us Chinese and Japanese tourists are learning English tea ceremonies from Poles – so much for BG's immigration policies around these parts. Some tourists point, or take selfies with me in the background.

Summer is Eton's fallow time. Two weeks ago thirteen hundred adolescent males migrated to the four corners of the world. September will see new thirteen-year-old faces, mostly virginal and faintly stained with over-excitement. Which also describes the copy of *Copenhagen* on the table in front of us.

I've shown Nassia a few pictures of Zack and Kathy. They were snapped unawares through the glass front of a Vancouver coffee shop (witness protection is a bit crap if it's your government which wants to find you). The two of them look really happy and I'm happy for them.

Me? I fancy the Tokyo Olympics, following Fiji in the rugby sevens. Then August at Janine's in the Rockies, champagne round the campfire, helicopter access to keep the paparazzi away. Zack and Kathy wouldn't be so far away, I might even go see them. When I told Nassia that on the phone, she asked if I still had Zack's play.

Do I remember reading it? Sure. I tell Nassia again it was a waste of time. Two atomic scientists meet in the after-life (yeah, right) and tell again and again the story of one meeting during the war. Each version is never quite the same – 'another draft', the playwright calls it. How can it end and what's the point?

I tell Nassia, here's how I understand things. All of us play two chess games at the same time. The boards are next to each other but only one game counts: the game which happens outside your skin – fixing stuff, doing stuff, having stuff. The other game, what's going on inside your skin, is make-believe and ghosts – stuff you have to manage in order to concentrate on the first game. Zack was into make-believe and ghosts from the off. But when a bus hits you crossing the road while you're playing your inner game, the bus wins.

Outside my skin, I've made £20 million, become prime minister, maybe changed my country and become famous. So I've won, surely? Except now I'm looking at these photographs.

Nassia turns my chess story around. What if I always did stuff, and then had to do more exciting stuff, because I didn't know that the life inside my own skin was interesting? Maybe I sneer at the second game because I don't understand it.

'What's that got to do with the play?'

'The outside game in *Copenhagen* about an atom bomb. What's the inside game?'

'Who the hell knows.'

'Do you want to know?' she asks.

Damn, I can't believe it's happening again! I get myself sorted and then a smart sexy woman pops up with something which I didn't know I wanted, and maybe I don't want. Then I want it. Last time Angela waved the keys to Number Ten; this one is more of a mind-fuck.

I bite my lip hard. 'If the play's not stupid, then there's stuff which matters which I really don't get.'

'And who does?'

'You. And this is the shitty bit; my brother. But I'm not asking him, that's for sure.'

'You don't need to if you can be bothered to understand your own second game,' says Nassia. 'Two characters meet in the after-life to discuss one encounter. Two teenagers – you and Tel. Tell the story of what happened – you remember it like yesterday. Use your phone – record it. But then do Tel's story. He remembers it pretty well because it killed him. Why is he carrying a knife? Does he draw first, or do you do something? No, no you protest, but let him finish. Then okay, I forgot something, you say, but you got it wrong – it was more like this. Record again, play it back another day. Another go, another draft.'

What the fuck? I still don't see how it ends, or what's the point. How do I know what Tel thought? It's twenty-five years ago, I'll just be spouting make-believe. Look at me, I've done well for myself, I'm a super-confident guy, I know what's what. But then I look at Zack and Kathy's photos one more time.

END

Acknowledgements

This novel first stirred into life in December 2013. The main writing started in July 2015. Getting a finished product into your hands has been the work of a team pulled together by Dan Hiscocks at Lightning Books, notably Scott Pack, Ruth Killick, Hugh Brune and Katherine Stephen, supported by Andrew Samuelson. Each of them offered me years of expertise and warm enthusiasm. I am in debt to them for both – and to Dan for our longer journey together, including my first novel 'MBA'.

Tom Merrill allowed the use of part of a poem. He also read the whole manuscript and offered advice. So did Clare Ella and a third individual who prefers to remain, shall we say, submerged. Jonathan Morgan read multiple versions of this manuscript and, undeterred by having done the same on 'MBA', Peter and Rosemary Drew did the same. Peter and Rosemary: you are the *sine qua non* of this novelist. Guy Meredith and C M (Craig) Taylor taught me the writing skills which I brought to this project, and discussed early versions of the story with me. Kathy Jones, Rob Warwick and Alison Donaldson have been companions on broader writing journeys. Thanks to you all.

The Ministry of Defence will be happiest if you think that ACERBIC sprang out of Jonathan and I shooting an alcoholic breeze one evening. I can confirm that is the case. Then again, this is a post-truth novel.

Here in Bermondsey, Michael Hutton shared many experiences from his upbringing without knowing how they might turn out in the novel. Furkan Choudhury also helped. I thank them for their friendship and trust. Neither are responsible for characters or events created in my imagination.

I have lived in Britain since I was fifteen. Now I look back, class has run through my life like a live wire. Therefore thank yous for this book would be incomplete without some thank yous for my life. Trish, my wife, brought me to Bermondsey in 1987; I'd like to thank her, Ted, Pat and Jo-ann. From a different part of south London Jonathan also shared his experiences of class.

Many people in Bermondsey welcomed me or let me be myself among them. I hope they will understand if, rather than naming the many I know, I say thank you instead to Simone Wood.

Simone had a busy, commercial day job but worked a regular shift in the Wibbley Wobbley. The Wib was a much-loved, idiosyncratic pub in Bermondsey's Greenland Dock. Simone worked there because of the people. Around 2009 I would sit on my own of an evening, drinking beer and reading books for my doctorate. One day I returned from the gents having left the sociologist Pierre Bourdieu splayed open (so to speak) on the stained table. 'I've read books like that,' Simone announced. 'They don't frighten me. Come and talk.' She acted fearlessly from her belief that we all have more in common than divides us, for which I thank her greatly. Her own dream took her to a yacht and a scuba diving business in Mexico, where she died in Hurricane Odile in 2014.

Responsibility for any flaws in the book, or the life out of which it has grown, is of course mine.

December 2016

If you enjoyed this book, why not try Douglas Board's first novel, *MBA*? We are giving you 90% of it for free. Just visit https://douglasboard.com/novels/mba/html

MBA, A Novel
ISBN: 978-1785630057   £8.99

Why is so much of the world Managed By Arseholes? Were they born that way? Did they sweat to achieve it? Or did we send them to special schools to learn? Fired by an arsehole just as his career is taking off, 30-year-old MBA Ben Stillman finds his ideas about success have been turned upside down. No such confusion troubles William C Gyro, the American dean of Ben's alma mater: he is about to complete the transformation of Hampton Management College from a second-rate English business school into a world-class *madrassa* of capitalism.

When Ben agrees to spend 10 days helping Gyro, a vortex of events sucks in the world's fattest fat cats, banking-crisis culprits, the British Prime Minister and the only woman who can confront Ben with his own inner arsehole. Will any of them survive? Do any of them deserve to?

A contemporary farce with the pace of a thriller, *MBA* is also a piercing yet hopeful inquiry into success.

Here's what the reviews say:

"A must-read for anyone who enjoyed Franzen's *Freedom* or Eggers' *The Circle*."
Felicity Wood, *The Bookseller*

"Given their role in shaping and propagating the ideas that govern all our working lives, business schools have for the most part unjustly escaped the attentions of fiction writers. All the more refreshing, then, to read Douglas Board's wonderfully enjoyable dissection of the swirling currents of ambition, dissembling, power and fortune that are all too often rationalised away in textbook accounts of 'leadership'. Witty and deeply informed, Board's rich satire is nearer the bone of business than a lot of people would want you to think."
Simon Caulkin

"When the mindless, probably male, manager in your life puts you down, pick this up. Hilarious and spot on."
Sandra Burmeister, CEO Amrop Landelahni

"A virtuoso plot and unrelieved bass-note of suspense whisk the reader through *MBA* with no time to fasten a seat-belt. Iconoclastic and LOL hilarious, this story unpicks the fabric of leadership and interrogates the murky motives of the über-'successful'. Irresistibly funny and deliciously uncomfortable, *MBA* is a seductive cocktail of politics, human relating,

banking, feminism, the dangers of intelligent underwear and so many other unusual bed-fellows."
Rosemary Lain-Priestley, author of *Does My Soul Look Big In This?* and *Unwrapping The Sacred*

"By focussing his farce on the business schools he knows so well, Board updates the campus novel and takes a big swing at the insincerities inherent in the ideology of neo-liberalism."
CM Taylor, author of *Premiership Psycho* and *Cloven*

"This satirical novel is not just thought-provoking, it pokes your brain with a sharp pointed stick to get an explosive reaction. And the right reaction is laughter, constant chuckling coupled with a sheepish admission to self that MBAs are as full of bull as bureaucrats. Buy it, read it, then set a multiple answer exam on it. It's a hoot."
Peter Sullivan, former Group Editor-in-Chief of *Independent Newspapers*, South Africa

"Douglas Board has produced the next instalment of a great literary genre: the campus novel. Instead of following thwarted historians, faux-radical sociologists or cynical literary scholars, Board uncovers a cauldron of corporate claptrap, hubris and hard lessons which anyone who has been to business school will instantly recognize."
Professor André Spicer, Cass Business School, London

And here's a taster:

MONDAY 11 JUNE (EVENING)
London is being re-made. In 10 weeks the city's mop-topped mayor, a one-man Beatles revival with added bleach, will wave the

Olympic flag in Beijing's stadium. Back home, the construction of a 21st-century stadium and velodrome has already begun. But the city's re-making is much more than this.

The first re-making is up. Skyscrapers are sprouting on the city's face like a fungus. Southwark Towers – 24 floors of offices next to the southeast rail terminus – is being demolished. In four years' time the 87 floors of the Shard will take its place. If you're going places in London, you're going up.

Ben Stillman is going up. He's barely 30 and he's chief of staff to a billionaire.

The city is being remade back towards its centre. In places like Johannesburg, after the rich moved outwards they sent removal vans back in to take their jobs with them. But most of the jobs that matter in London are still in the centre, and the people with money have come back to hug those jobs more closely. In London, the centre is the place to be.

Where Ben's at in his career could not be more central. He is the hub of 26,000 people labouring worldwide in everything from chemicals and agriculture to re-insurance. Ben is Alex Bakhtin's right hand.

The third re-shaper of London is glass. All the new towers are glass from top to bottom. Welcome to a new kind of power, which sees all and displays all. It has no need to hide. Perhaps this power is modern and clean, democratic and accountable. But then a gust blows, a cable slips and a window cleaner's fingers get caught in the winching gear. As detergent and blood smear the glass, we glimpse something older. The cable that once suspended a human halfway between heaven and earth was the divine right of kings.

All-glass palaces: London's new way to tell passers-by that they count for shit. You're welcome to look in, because you're so lowly that what you see has no consequence.